SAVING

— *a novel* —

ABBY

Also by Steena Holmes

SAVING

a novel

ABBY

STEENA HOLMES

LAKE UNION
PUBLISHING

Text copyright © 2016 Steena Holmes

Published by Lake Union, Seattle

www.apub.com

Amazon, the Amazon logo, and Lake Union are trademarks of Amazon.com, Inc., or its affiliates.

ISBN-13: 9781503934160
ISBN-10: 1503934160

Cover design by Shasti O'Leary-Soudant

Printed in the United States of America

This book is for all the mothers who love their children more than life itself.
You are amazing.

CLAIRE TURNER'S BUCKET LIST
(AGE 13)

1. ~~Marry a man who loves me more than life itself and makes me laugh. And makes me cry, and then holds me as I'm crying and cries with me.~~
2. Learn to surf.
3. Speak Italian like a native.
4. Scuba dive the reefs of Australia.
5. ~~Learn to draw.~~
6. ~~Be an artist.~~
7. Go to Hawaii.
8. Be in a movie—even as an extra.
9. Meet someone famous and pretend it's no big deal.
10. See penguins in their natural habitat. *(But that would mean I'd have to go where it's cold—not sure I can do that.)*
11. Help build an orphanage in Africa.
12. Eat breakfast with Mickey and Minnie Mouse at Disney World, and take a graphic design lesson with a Disney illustrator. *(Wouldn't that be cool?)*
13. Be a mother.
14. ~~Travel.~~

15. Travel—everywhere. *(This can't ever be checked off. I'm sure there will always be places I want to explore.)*
16. ~~Learn to play the piano.~~
17. Skydive. *(I'm afraid of heights, but if my instructor were super cute, I could handle it.)*
18. See an actual fistfight or bar brawl as it happens. I always hear about it or read about it . . .
19. Tour Christmas markets in Germany and eat all the gingerbread I want without getting into trouble for it!

ONE

CLAIRE

Mediterranean Sea
First week of May

W ould you like to see my babies?"
Claire started at the question, making the wine in her wineglass slosh a little.

Did she want to see her babies? Who asked a question like that?

"They're really quite amazing. My staff created this photo album for me before I left home." Robyn, a woman in her late sixties, slid toward them in the booth seat and held the album out. They'd shared a table with her a few times during the evening dinners on their Mediterranean cruise, but they hadn't gotten to know much about her.

"I'd love to." Claire reluctantly reached for the book and forced herself to smile. "You don't see actual photo albums very often these days."

The private dining room reserved for suite guests on the cruise ship was full, and Claire and Josh sat in the back area, near bay windows overlooking the ocean. The sun was just setting over the water, casting a golden shimmer that danced along the waves. Claire's fingers ached from holding a pencil all day, and yet, she wished she'd brought her tools with her to dinner. To miss out on sketching this scene was frustrating.

"Robyn, how many children do you have?" Josh, Claire's husband, asked politely, while Claire steeled herself.

She could do this.

"Oh, about thirty-one right now. But that number will increase in the next few weeks. A few of my girls are due to have their own babies soon." Robyn sighed. "I really should be there, but I've had this cruise booked for ages."

Thirty-one babies? Unless this woman had donated her eggs, there was no way she could have that many children.

Catching the incredulous look on Claire's face, Robyn laughed. "Open the book, dearie. They are quite amazing."

Claire took a swig of wine and slowly opened to the first page. She swallowed just in time—the images in front of her got her chuckling.

"These are adorable." She held up the page for Josh to see, relief washing over her as she gazed at more photos of tigers.

"Tigers?" Josh said. "Your babies are tigers?"

The smile on Robyn's face couldn't grow any wider. "Well of course. What did you think I meant?"

"Not cats, that's for sure," Josh muttered, tearing off a chunk of bread from the baguette on their table and shoving it in his mouth.

As Claire browsed the album, Robyn looked on. "My husband and I couldn't have our own children, so when we had the opportunity to purchase a park in New Zealand and rescue these amazing creatures from being put down, well, the answer was quite obvious, don't you think?" Robyn turned the next page for Claire. It showed a lioness with a young cub.

With a tender expression Robyn said, "That's Isabelle. Her previous owners thought her to be barren and were going to have her destroyed. Can you believe it? All she needed was the right mate. She's had two litters now and five babies. That one"—her finger gently outlined a little cub—"was the runt of her last litter and almost didn't survive. I had to bottle-feed him myself."

"Do you find it hard to be away from them?" Claire could see on Robyn's face the passion for her animals. She truly loved them.

"Oh yes. They are my life now. But, my husband made me promise to come on this cruise, with or without him." She shrugged. "And I find, even with him gone, I still can't refuse him anything." A wistful smile graced her face as she fingered the napkin in her lap. "My Edwin. It was his strength that made each day possible for me. Now it's my turn to be strong." She swallowed hard.

Claire instinctively reached out and touched the older woman's arm.

"Excuse me for a moment, please." Robyn stood. "Keep looking at my little ones. Maybe it'll give you some inspiration." She winked, and then headed off in the direction of the restrooms.

Claire gritted her teeth, and the smile on her face tightened.

"She probably meant our stories," Josh said, reaching out to caress her hand.

"Right." So why did Claire have the feeling that wasn't at all what she'd been talking about?

Typically, when people learned they'd been married for seven years and were still childless, they chided the couple about the seven-year itch and gave Claire a look. *The* look. To remind her that she wasn't getting any younger.

As if she needed a complete stranger to remind her of that.

"I'm serious," Josh said. "She seemed pretty interested in our career last night. I don't think I've ever had someone ask so many questions about how we write one of our stories."

Josh wrote children's books and Claire illustrated them. For the past few months, they'd been traveling throughout Europe, researching book ideas. They had six new books contracted with their publisher, and thanks to this trip, they already had five books plotted out, along with illustrations in rough sketches.

All they were missing was the sixth book. Josh had suggested using this Mediterranean cruise as a setting for the story line, but so far, nothing they'd come up with worked. Instead, over the past four days at sea, they'd worked on fleshing out the scenes in the first five books.

The sixth book wasn't the only reason for this cruise, though. This was supposed to be their downtime, to unwind, relax, and refocus on them as a couple.

"Wouldn't it be great if our sixth book was set in Australia or New Zealand?" Claire asked as she flipped through the remaining pages, angling the book so Josh could also see.

"It would make for a great adventure," Josh said to her, as if reading her mind. "And we've always talked about heading Down Under."

She opened up the notes app on her phone and began to type out her idea. "Jack could be a parks keeper and help feed baby lions and tigers. Maybe one of them gets lost, and he helps find it—"

"Just as it's about to be attacked by some wild, ferocious beast," Josh finished for her.

Claire rolled her eyes. "And by ferocious beast, you mean a Tasmanian devil, right? Even though the real things don't resemble the cartoon in the slightest?"

Josh shrugged. "If we're going to be in Australia, you've got to let me have my Taz. That's not even up for debate." His eyes crinkled with glee, and Claire understood what Robyn meant when she said she was incapable of refusing her husband anything.

"How about we introduce a young friend called Taz? Jack meets Taz, who maybe has a whirlwind-type energy, and they set out together on a grand adventure in the outback?"

Josh's eyes lit up. "We should go—and do a few books while we're there."

Claire added the ideas to her notes.

"We really can't prolong this trip," Josh said. "But maybe we could fly there around Christmas?"

Claire sighed. She wasn't ready to head home, back to their life in small-town Ontario. Her mother accused her of running away from reality, and she was right. This trip was exactly that—a time for both her and Josh to run away and pretend the last three years of heartache and heartbreak had never happened.

"Why can't we?"

"Can't what?" Josh asked just before their waiter brought them their dinners of fresh cod and steak.

"Why can't we extend our trip? No, not Australia, but why can't we tour some more? How about Spain or southern France? We talked about looking into rentals in Positano, remember? Why don't we do that? We don't really need to head back, do we? Not yet, anyway." Claire kept her gaze on her plate, but without really seeing the fish in front of her.

When Josh didn't reply, Claire looked up and found him staring out the window.

"We have to go home sometime," he finally said, quietly.

"I know."

The trip had started just under three months ago with a children's literary conference, where Josh was the keynote speaker and she held workshops on illustrations and graphics. They'd intended to stay only three weeks, but each week she'd managed to convince her husband to stay, to visit another location, to play tourist just a little longer.

It'd been worth it. They made some great connections, she'd signed on a few new clients for their freelance work, and they'd been inspired to go a slightly different direction with Jack's Adventures, something their editor agreed with once they explained the change.

But still. It wasn't long enough. She didn't want to return to the real world.

Claire took a bite of her fish. The texture was grainy and dry, and it was nearly flavorless, but she forced herself to take another bite. And another. Then Robyn returned to the table.

"I know," Robyn said, almost as though she were aware of their private discussion. "You must come visit me in New Zealand. You can stay in my guesthouse and write a story about my park and babies. Come during our summer, yes?"

Josh gently nudged her leg beneath the table, and Claire forced a smile on her face.

"I think that's a wonderful idea," Claire said.

"Good." She reached into her purse and slid a card over. It was a cream parchment-like paper with embossed lettering spelling out Robyn's name and contact information. "I'll be expecting a call from you. Otherwise, I *will* hunt you down. Bring your little adventurer to my park, and let's introduce the children of the world to the beauty of my babies."

She must have caught the slight wince on Claire's face.

"I always wanted children of my own, and, my Edwin, he would have made a wonderful father. Sometimes life isn't fair and withholds gifts without reason. So I realized I had two choices." A soft smile appeared on Robyn's face. "I could give in and be miserable for the rest of my life, or I could forge my own path."

She reached across and grabbed hold of Claire's hand. "Anyone can tell you no, so it's up to you to stop listening." She stood up, gently dabbed the corners of her mouth with her napkin, and winked. "Wise words my Edwin once told me."

Claire nodded, trying to process why she was telling her this.

"Enjoy your evening."

Claire raised her hand in farewell and picked up her wineglass, swirling its contents before taking a sip.

"Did you tell her?" she asked Josh once Robyn had left.

Josh shook his head. "I figured you had."

And why would she do that? The whole point of this trip was to run away from the truth—not share it with random strangers, no matter how personable they were.

Not when she couldn't even face the truth herself.

Standing on their suite balcony, located at the stern of the ship, Claire wrapped her arms tight around her chest as she stared up into the black sky. The moon shone bright behind the clouds, and every so often, its light would escape and cast a glow upon the water. She imagined the fish below swimming up toward the light before plunging back into the depths of the sea.

For a moment, she thought of joining them.

Tomorrow their cruise ship would dock at their port in Italy, and they would take a shuttle to the airport in Rome. As much as she hated to admit it, their trip was almost over. They'd have to enter the real world again.

A world that involved family, friends, and the busyness of life.

"Do you want to head down to the bar? I think that jazz group is playing again. I'm sure Oskar would love to make you another one of his Italian crepes. The guy seems to have taken a liking to my Canadian beauty." Josh moved closer to her, and wrapping his arms around her, he placed a soft kiss at the base of her neck. She shivered and wasn't sure if it was from his touch or the brisk evening air.

"Can we stay in tonight?"

"I'd love that." Josh's hug tightened around her.

She leaned back, resting her head on his shoulder. "I'm not sure I'm ready to head home," she whispered quietly. She reached into her sweater pocket and pulled out the sheets of paper she'd carried. "I'm not ready to let this go."

Josh held on to the papers, not forcing them from her grip, but holding them along with her. "If you're not ready to say good-bye, to let it go, then don't. There's no pressure . . ." His voice trailed off with words he'd said a thousand times before.

No pressure to say good-bye. No pressure to end the grieving process. No pressure to let go of a dream, a hope, a future she'd always wanted.

A future she once had and let go because of poor decisions.

Josh didn't understand. As much as he tried, he just didn't understand.

Ever since she was a young girl, all Claire wanted was to be a mother. She wanted to have a house full of children she could love, a house full of laughter. All she wanted was to be Mom. To hold her child in her arms, to love and be loved back.

She'd been one, once. For an hour, she'd been a mother, holding her child in her arms before she gave him up to another family to be loved. She'd been a foolish child and too young to raise a baby. Her mother had held her tight as her little boy was taken out of her arms, and she promised her that one day, when she was older and ready, she'd have another baby.

For the past six years, she'd held on to that dream.

After three years of trying on their own and then three more years of infertility treatments, just a few months before they left for their European trip, they were given the news—their last treatment had failed.

There was no reason medically why Claire could not conceive, and yet, there it was. Her body had rejected her dreams. A betrayal she could never resolve because the betrayer and the betrayed were one and the same.

"The list has grown," Josh whispered as he turned the sheets over and saw items she'd added over the past few days.

This list in their hands was their bucket list as parents.

It was simply their dreams, their goals, their prayers, written down. She had many such lists.

For her own personal life—to travel, to try new things, and to become something more than she was today.

For their home—where they wanted to live, the type of home, and features they hoped for, like a white gated fence, beautiful rosebushes, a water fountain in the backyard, a walk-in closet, and a big pedestal bathtub in a large bathroom complete with heated floors and a Turkish sauna.

For her career—how many books they wrote, how many illustrations she created, the awards she wanted to win, the money they wanted to make and put away for a rainy day.

But the most important one was her parenting list.

> *To feel the first kick of her baby in her womb.*
> *To see the first smile, hear the first laugh, watch that*
> *first step.*
> *To teach her child how to draw.*
> *To read stories they'd written specifically for their child.*
> *To see the child's reaction the first time their feet touched*
> *sand.*
> *The first day of school. School photos. Report cards.*
> *Their first date. The wedding day.*
> *To travel the world and see all its amazing things through*
> *the eyes of their child.*
> *To share the magic of Christmas.*

They'd decided that on this trip, they would figure out a way to say good-bye to their dreams of having children. They'd lived the past three years focused exclusively on having a child. Now it was time to bring that period to a close. Josh came up with the idea of bringing with them the list they'd started years ago for their child and leaving it behind. Whether they buried it, burnt it, or tucked it away someplace special didn't matter, as long as they didn't bring it home and could never retrieve it.

Once they left Europe, Claire wasn't sure she could ever return. And if they did, she could never go back to the cities and towns they'd visited, because in each place, she'd found a way to say good-bye to her dream there.

"I wanted to make sure I didn't leave anything out," she said as he read the last few items she'd added.

"Watch baby turtles be born on a sandy beach. That one is new."

She nodded.

"Take a horse-and-carriage ride through the streets of Rome." He stopped reading and looked down at her. "But we did that." He looked away for a moment. "Is that what you thought about during our ride? What it would be like if we had a child with us?"

She swallowed past the lump in her throat.

"I thought that ride was for us. To check off something from our own travel list."

She heard the hurt in his voice but didn't have the words to soothe away the pain.

"Has any part of this trip been for us?"

She didn't say anything. She couldn't. He would never understand, and she didn't expect him to.

For him, this trip wasn't just about letting go, it was also about finding a way to carry on, to build happy memories, new dreams.

While she mourned the loss of having a child, he dreamed of a future in which they could do things they had never before imagined. He spoke about ways to advance their careers, and he told of hopes for the future that had nothing to do with raising a family and everything to do with experiencing life to its fullest. Together.

"Of course the trip has been about us." She turned in his arms so she faced him and stared into his warm green eyes. She breathed in deeply and thought about Robyn and the love she still felt for her husband, about the way that couple found something to replace their desire to have children in their lives.

A deep sense of belonging, of love, swept over her, and in that moment, seeing the love and acceptance in her husband's gaze, she knew she could do this—say good-bye to a dream and possibly make room in her heart for a new one.

"I couldn't have done this without you." She stood up on her tiptoes and lightly pressed her lips against his, while his arms pulled her close. "Without you, I'd be lost in my grief, lost to the death of a dream I've carried since I was a young girl. Without you . . . my world isn't complete."

She looked at the list in her hand.

"As hard as it is to admit this, letting this dream go, the dream of having our own child, of carrying our baby inside me, of seeing us in our son or daughter . . . it's easier to say good-bye to this than it would be to say good-bye to you." Tears gathered in her eyes. "You, Josh Turner, are my life. My heart. Don't ever let go of me, okay?" She leaned forward. As she rested her cheek against his chest, she listened to his heartbeat and took comfort in the feel of his arms as they held her close.

The tears slipped down her face and soaked through his shirt. She would say good-bye to the dream of having her own child because she had no choice.

"We can still have children, Claire. We can adopt, like we talked about before," Josh whispered.

She shook her head. "Not yet, though, okay? I can't replace one child with another one so soon, even if that child was only a dream."

She knew it sounded unreasonable. In their efforts over the past six year, she'd never even conceived a child, much less lost one. It was more the idea, the hope, of their own child.

One that looked like them . . . who maybe, like Josh, had sparkling green eyes and a dimple on his chin, or like her, had fine blond hair and delicate bone structure. Maybe their child would have shown a passion for storytelling like his or her father, or maybe the child's fingers would itch to draw as her own did.

Their child might have been a studious, serious little boy or a warm, giggling little girl.

But she would never know. Not anymore.

Any child they adopted would have its own characteristics inherited from the birth parents. His or her own history, nationality, quirks, and challenges.

"For now, let's focus on Jack and his adventures," Claire said. Their friends often commented that it seemed like Jack was their real son, the way they talked about him and kept his character in their thoughts no matter what they did. "And maybe . . ." She looked up at him as an idea formed. "Maybe it's time we add on to our fictional family and bring in a girl. Why does Jack get to have all the fun?"

Josh's eyebrows rose. "A girl, huh? That could be . . . interesting. We're contracted for more books with Jack, though. We'd have to talk to Julia about this." A slight smile appeared on his face. "Is this something you want to take on yourself? Can you?"

Claire shrugged. "It was only an idea." She turned around and braced her arms on the balcony railing. The sound of the waves soothed her heart, her soul.

She inhaled deeply and slowly let it out.

She could do this.

"Are we ready?" Josh asked, as if reading her mind.

She reached for the papers, her fingers lightly brushing against his.

They'd discussed burning the pages, burying them, or ripping them apart, but in the end, what they were about to do was perfect.

This cruise was meant to be a healing space for Claire. A time when there were no demands other than to relax. Yes, they would plot, write, sketch . . . but in a calm environment and on their own terms.

It was also the perfect place to say good-bye, to grieve for the death of a dream.

"I'm ready," she said.

They reached out as far as they could over the balcony and let go of the pages in their hands.

Claire watched as the papers separated and fluttered about in the wind, as if dancing along the air currents, before they dropped down, one by one, in the dark sea. Only one page landed in a moonlit shard of light upon the water, and as the boat continued on its journey, that page got smaller and smaller until it was gone forever.

Josh kissed the top of her head and pulled her close, tucking her tight to his chest.

"I love you, Claire Turner. This isn't the end. We'll figure out how to forge our own path now, that's all."

They remained there in silence for a few moments longer.

"Now, how about we go open that bottle of champagne we've been saving and cuddle while watching a movie. What do you say? End our cruise in style?" Josh turned her around in his arms and kissed her.

His easy smile and light heart was infectious, and Claire knew that no matter how hard each day would be, how difficult their journey may become, he would always support and help her, loving her as she was.

She wrapped her arms around his neck and laughed as he picked her up in his arms, carrying her through the open balcony door, careful to not whack her head as he had on their first night.

"Cuddle, huh?" she asked.

His eyes twinkled as he dropped her on the bed.

"At some point, I'm sure we will," he said.

Claire forced herself to keep her focus on her husband and look only into his eyes, which held promises of love and laughter. She restrained herself from gazing out the window into the dark night, where she wanted to lose herself in her grief.

TWO

CLAIRE

Present day

Twisting in her seat, Claire discreetly swallowed two extra-strength tablets and rubbed the back of her neck, trying hard not to groan as her fingers dug into her tight muscles. Maybe an hour on a massage table would help relieve the sudden influx of headaches she'd started experiencing since returning home from their cruise.

"Everything okay?" Josh leaned toward her in his chair and whispered.

Claire gave a slight nod and then forced another smile before she faced forward and greeted the next reader who stood at their table.

She glanced at the line and tried not to sigh. They had another two hours here before heading back to their hotel, where all Claire wanted to do was sleep.

"We come to see you every time you're here," the woman who stood there with her son at her side gushed. "It's because of Jack and his adventures that my Calvin here first started to read." She beamed down at her son, who stood, hands clasped behind his back, staring at Josh with admiration.

Josh was a natural storyteller. Each book signing he would sit down with the children and read through parts of the story, adjusting the reading to fit the time allotted and the number of listeners. Claire loved to pick one or two from the crowd of children and draw them, and when they came up to get their books signed, she would slide the drawing inside the book.

"Would you like to pick a picture? You can take it home." Claire leaned forward and pointed to a layout of images she'd had printed on postcards. On one side were images from the book, and on the other was a copy of the cover, a short blurb, and the words *Let's go exploring,* something Jack says in each book.

The little boy's eyes widened as he scanned the images. He slowly pointed to one. Claire pulled a postcard from her stash and added her signature. She slid it across to him with a warm smile before they went on their way, the latest book in the series tucked tight beneath the little boy's arm.

"I think we're going to sell out," Alice, the owner of Wonderland Tales, said. She knelt down at Claire's side and handed her a cup of coffee.

"You're an angel." Claire took the coffee and sipped it. "I can't believe how many people are still in line. This is probably our best signing yet."

"Jack just seems to grow in popularity with every book you guys write. It's fantastic, and I'm so thrilled to host your readings. You know it's always an open invitation." Alice beamed as she surveyed the packed store.

Wonderland Tales was a well-known bookstore in Toronto that catered primarily to children and teens. It was also Claire and Josh's favorite place to host a book signing or reading.

"A new Italian restaurant that I think you'll like opened up just down the street. I've got reservations if you're feeling up to it." Alice leaned across the table for a camera that a customer held out. She edged around the table to take a photo of Josh and Claire signing their book.

"Sure," Claire said after a pause. "Give me a few hours to rest, and I'll be as good as new." The last thing Claire wanted was to cancel dinner. Building this relationship with Alice had taken years, and now Claire considered her a friend.

Alice's brows rose. "A few hours?"

Claire nodded. "I think my body is still adjusting to being home. I can't seem to get caught up on my sleep, no matter how early I head to bed or how many energy drinks I sneak behind Josh's back."

"I heard that," Josh leaned over and whispered.

Claire winced.

Alice stood still for a moment before she leaned down. "You're not pregnant by chance?" she whispered.

Claire shook her head. "I wish. That'd be a dream come true."

She'd resigned herself to being motherless. Maybe one day they would adopt, but not right now.

"Have you let your doctor friend give you a checkup? You've been home for a while now. Your body should be readjusted."

Claire shrugged. Having a best friend who was a doctor had both advantages and disadvantages.

"Did someone say Italian?" Josh leaned back and smiled at Alice. "I'm starving."

"I think there are some cookies left over from the reading. Let me go grab you both a plate." Ever the hostess, Alice headed toward the back of her store, where they'd read from their latest book to a crowded circle of excited children.

"It's my birthday today." The voice caught Claire's attention. In front of their table stood a little girl. She couldn't have been more than seven years old, and she had the most adorable red cheeks, but it was her bald head that took Claire's breath away.

"It is? Well, happy birthday! Did you get a cupcake from earlier?" Claire leaned forward, her hands clasped in front.

"Chocolate. My mom made them for Ms. Alice." The little girl nodded.

"Your mom made them?" Claire glanced up and smiled at the woman who stood by the girl's side. "Did you know that they are Jack's favorite cupcakes?"

"That's what I told my mom." The little girl looked up at her mom with delight.

Claire reached down into a bag at her side and looked through some loose papers until she found the one she wanted. She held it on her lap, beneath the table, so the girl in front of her couldn't see it and quickly made some adjustments.

"How old are you today?" She asked as she looked up to find the girl staring at her intently.

"I'm nine." She must have caught sense of surprise in Claire's silence. "You thought I was seven, didn't you? It's the hair." She patted the top of her head. "I have cancer. I'm also basically blind, but I bet you couldn't tell."

She was so matter-of-fact about it that it caught Claire off guard. She'd guessed, from the lack of hair and bright red cheeks, but hearing her say it was another thing. And no, even after looking into her beautiful hazel eyes, she'd had no idea the little girl was blind.

"Jack should go visit some kids in a hospital. Did you know that we have all your books there? Ms. Alice donated them, and we all love Jack."

"That's a great idea." She'd have to ask Alice for more information about the hospital. "Maybe you could come join us when we go?"

The girl's eyes lit up. "I'd love to." She held out her hand. "I'm Samantha, but you can call me Sami."

"Sami, it's really nice to meet you. I'm Claire."

Claire added a little bit more to her drawing and then held it out. "Happy birthday, Sami."

Sami's mother took the paper and bent down. "She drew you something," she said softly.

Sami brought the paper up close to her face, and after taking her time to look it over thoroughly, she gave a little squeal.

"That's me." Sami's voice caught. "Right, Mom? That's me?" She held the paper out for her mother to look at.

"That certainly looks like you, Sami."

Earlier, Claire had noticed the little girl with the bald head and had drawn her portrait. The picture showed her and Jack sitting on a park bench, a stack of books and cupcakes between them. There was a little dog chasing its tail in the distance, and the sky was full of balloons floating in the air. She'd added the cupcakes after finding out it was Sami's birthday.

"Did you really draw me?" Sami asked.

"I did. I noticed you earlier, sitting right up at the front beside Josh. You were so focused on the story." She glanced over at Sami's mother. "I hope you don't mind?"

"Not at all," Sami's mother said. Turning to her daughter, she added, "We should get this framed and put it up on your wall, don't you think?"

"Sweet! This is the best birthday ever." Sami gave her mom a powerful hug before she let go and turned to Claire. "Can I hug you too?"

"Of course." Claire stood and walked around to the front of the table, where she bent down for Samantha's hug. She almost toppled backward from the intensity of it.

"You promise to come to the hospital?" Sami asked after she let go.

"Let me see if Ms. Alice can work her magic and get us in. Okay?"

By then, Alice had returned with a plate of cookies, which she set down beside Josh.

"Get in where?" she asked.

"Jack is going to come to the hospital!" Sami almost shouted. "Well"—she wrinkled her nose—"not Jack for real. But they'll come." She pointed to Claire and then to Josh. "And maybe read to everyone. It would be awesome. And my mom can make her cupcakes, and it'll be the bestest day ever."

Alice's eyebrows rose. "The bestest day ever, huh? I thought that was today when your mom brought you here to meet your favorite authors of all time."

"A girl can have more than one bestest day, you know."

Claire laughed. She loved this girl's spunk. After another hug from Sami, Claire sat back down and continued to sign books and hand out picture cards for the next hour. Little by little, her hand began to cramp and her energy waned, and once the last customer walked out of the store, Claire laid her head down in her arms and struggled to stay awake.

"All right, Sleeping Beauty, let's get you back to the hotel for a nap." Josh came over and placed his arms around her, giving her a hug. "Alice promised the best Italian food we've ever tasted, and considering we just came back from Italy, I'm looking forward to holding her to that."

"I'm not sure I can move," Claire said groggily. Another minute and she would have been fast asleep.

The next thing she knew, Josh had her in his arms with Alice laughing in the background.

"Our taxi is waiting for us," Josh said as he made his way through the aisles of the bookstore. Claire glanced over his shoulder to see Alice trailing behind, their bags in her hands.

"Guys, we can cancel dinner if Claire isn't feeling well." Alice held the door open with her foot as Josh walked though carrying Claire.

"I'll be fine." Claire yawned. "I just need a nap, and then I'll be good as new." She leaned her head against Josh's chest and listened to the thump of his heart.

"Are you sure?" Alice's voice was tinged with worry.

"Totally sure. Hey," she said as she reached out toward Alice. "Samantha—she's a sweetheart. Is she . . . okay?"

Alice's shoulders slumped. "She's pretty sick. Leukemia, but she's strong and refuses to let it get her down. She was out today on a day pass just for her birthday. You were her gift—all she wanted was to come and get her books signed. That picture you drew . . . it meant more to her than you can imagine." Alice looked off to the side, deep in thought. "I try to get in to SickKids in Toronto at least every other month and bring books for the kids. I can set something up for you if you'd like—I know they would love it."

"Let's do it. I was thinking about that earlier. We could do a reading, and then ask the kids to help us with a new adventure for Jack. I'm sure they'd have lots of ideas. It could be fun." Josh leaned down and helped Claire into the taxi. She scooted over while he handed her the bags Alice had carried for them. "Let's talk about it more tonight at dinner."

Claire leaned her head against the seat, trying hard to cover the large yawn she couldn't hold back and then snuggled up to her husband as their cab took them back to their hotel.

"On a scale of one to ten, how tired are you?" Josh lightly rubbed her arm.

"Twelve."

"I think it's time to go see Abby at the clinic. I've never seen you like this before." Josh leaned his head against hers. "I overheard you and Alice earlier. Do you think maybe you could be?"

"Could be what?" She wasn't following him.

"Pregnant. Do you think you could be? Were you . . . were you like this with your last pregnancy?" His fingers entwined with hers.

She slowly pushed herself upright and looked him in the eye.

"I was a teenager. I was more scared than anything else." That and angry. "And no, I'm not pregnant, Josh. I think I'd . . ." Her voice trailed off as she mentally counted back to when she had her last period.

"Just talk to Abby, okay? I don't like seeing you like this."

Claire nodded, unable to speak. She was late. Very late. But late enough to be pregnant? Could she be?

She was afraid to let herself hope.

Claire sat in her office, curled up in her large comfy chair, and struggled to read the draft Josh had handed her earlier in the morning. The words swam on the page no matter how hard she tried to focus.

"Why don't you go lie down?" Josh stood in the doorway, hip resting against the frame, and held his hand out to her.

"I'd love to, but I don't think I can get up." She smiled weakly at him.

"I'm sensing a theme here . . . you just like having me prove my brawny strength by carrying you to bed, don't you?" His eyes twinkled, but Claire noticed the look of concern.

"What did you think?" Josh gave a pointed look toward the papers in her hands as he pulled her up from the chair.

"I couldn't get past the tulips. Or were they daffodils? Sorry." She attempted to smother a yawn, but her arm wouldn't obey and remained listless at her side.

"Daffodils. I had a hard time with that scene."

"Maybe it shouldn't be in the story. Maybe that's just a memory for the two of us." She smiled at him, thinking back to that day in Bruges, remembering how they'd decided to ignore everything for one moment, one hour, one day, and just live. It was perfect. Almost heaven on earth. Almost.

"On a scale of one to ten, how tired are you?" Josh put his arm around her and walked with her along the hallway.

"You keep asking me."

"And you keep giving me numbers I don't like."

They lived in a two-story cottage in a little town called Heritage, located on Lake Huron. Their bedroom, with a large walk-in closet and master bath, and their office were upstairs, while the living room and kitchen were downstairs.

Her legs almost gave out as they were halfway down the hallway, and Josh picked her up in his arms and carried her the rest of the way.

"When do you go in and see Abby again? If you're not pregnant, then you might have caught a bug or something in Turkey. And isn't there some sort of virus that people get on a cruise ship?" Josh gently laid her down on the bed and pulled a hand-quilted blanket up, tucking it under her chin. "Don't tell me I'm overreacting either."

Claire yawned once more. "You're overreacting. Seriously." She could barely keep her eyes open. "I'll be fine, Josh. Honest. I just need to sleep." Her eyes drifted shut, and she knew from his sigh that he'd given in.

"Let's go to Germany for Christmas this year, okay?" She could almost taste the gingerbread cookies.

Josh laughed. "It's a little too early to be planning Christmas, don't you think? Besides, every trip we plan for the holidays always ends up getting canceled because you want to celebrate the holidays with your family." He placed a gentle kiss on her cheek. "How about we just throw a huge party this year, complete with sleigh rides and snowman building contests and cookie exchanges."

"We do that every year." She couldn't stop yawning.

"Exactly. I'll wake you up in a little bit, okay?" Josh pulled the curtains closed in their room, blanketing her in sweet, blissful darkness.

"Okay, love," Claire managed to whisper before she floated off into a dreamless sleep.

The smell of something both sweet and mouthwatering teased her awake, and when she rolled over, she saw a beautiful coconut cupcake sitting on her night table.

She inhaled its rich smell and reached over to it, letting her finger slide along the top edge until the tip of her finger was coated with icing.

"Kim stopped by and left that for you. She says there's a whole cake waiting for you tonight if you want to join the girls for the monthly get-together."

Claire groaned as she swung her legs over the side of the bed and let Josh help her sit up. "I forgot all about that."

"She figured, since you never responded to her e-mails or texts." Josh reached for the cupcake and bit into it, giving her a guilty smile as he did so.

"I thought that was mine. And you don't even like coconut." She grabbed the plate out of his hands and set it on her lap.

He dipped his finger in the icing and licked it. "It's not that I don't like coconut cake. It just doesn't compare to chocolate, that's all."

Claire thought about it. Would she go? She wanted to. She loved the nights out with the girls, and each outing was always something different. It might be a movie in the next town, dinner at someone's house, or a bonfire at the beach or in someone's backyard. Apparently, it was Kim's turn, and they were having dessert night at Sweet Bites Bakery.

That was always Josh's favorite because she often came home with goodies for him.

"What did you tell her?"

"Kim?" Josh asked. "That I'd drive you myself because you could use a night out."

"My personal chauffeur, huh?" She rubbed his arm before leaning her head on his shoulder.

"Anything for you." He kissed the top of her head before putting his arm around her. "I'm serious though. You need to get out. Maybe being with your girlfriends will help."

She looked up at him and saw the worry in his eyes.

"I'm not depressed, Josh." She knew he thought so, even though he hadn't said anything to her. She heard it in his voice.

"I didn't say you were."

"No? Then are you researching depression for a future book?" When she'd opened the iPad they shared, she'd seen the web pages he'd been browsing.

"I'm just . . . worried."

Claire sat up. "I know you are. I am too. This isn't normal, even for me. But I'm not depressed. Just really tired."

She would know if she were depressed, right?

"Tell you what. How about if I go for a few hours, and then we could go for a walk along the boardwalk? We haven't done that in a while." She forced a smile, hoping it also came through in her voice. She didn't like the idea of him doubting her, thinking she was depressed. She wasn't. She could handle this. Handle the life they'd been given. She could.

Josh reached for her hand and threaded his fingers through hers. "I'd like that."

Maybe this exhaustion and lack of hunger was her body's way of dealing with the loss. Maybe the emotional toil was starting to show physically.

Either way, it was unacceptable, and maybe . . . just maybe she needed to stop giving in.

"You know what would go great with this cupcake? A fresh pot of coffee. I can feel a headache coming on, and it's probably due to lack of caffeine. I'll need it, especially if you want me to look over that scene again too." The first step was to get back to work. She could do this. Sure, her body was exhausted, but that was no excuse. They had deadlines to deal with, and if this was a simple case of mind over matter, then it was time her body got the message.

"Coffee is made, and I made some changes to that chapter. Let's go sit outside, so we can go over it. But before we do that, how about you call and set up an appointment with Abigail for a thorough checkup." He leaned down and gave her a kiss. "I believe you when you say you're not depressed. But something is wrong, and don't tell me it's just jet lag, okay?"

She let him pull her up off the bed and stretched her back as she yawned. "I'm really not in the mood to be poked and prodded anymore."

Josh stared at her, unblinking, his face unreadable.

"I'm fine, but if it will ease your mind . . . then okay."

"Thank you." He smiled. "It does ease my mind. I'm here to take care of you, protect you . . . but this . . . I don't know what to do with you sleeping all day. Now"—he bent down and scooped her into his arms—"let's get you downstairs so we can get to work, otherwise . . . I may get some other ideas." He waggled his eyebrows the way he often did, and she laughed.

She leaned her head against his chest, held on to the plate with the cupcake so it wouldn't fall off, and let him carry her down the stairs.

She didn't know what to do about her lethargy either. Thanks to her mother, she was on a plethora of vitamins and herbs, and yet nothing seemed to work.

"I grabbed the mail while you were sleeping. One of the postcards we mailed finally arrived." Josh watched his steps as he carried her down to the main floor.

"Which one?" It was a tradition of theirs to send themselves a postcard from wherever they'd visited. It was something Claire's mom, Millie, had started on family vacations when she was young. Millie would mail a postcard home during a trip, writing to Claire about the adventures they'd had. On their trip, Josh and Claire had picked up so many postcards from every place they'd been—some they left behind, after discovering that was a tradition at the bed-and-breakfast where they'd stayed in London earlier in the year, and others they mailed to family and friends.

"The one from London." Josh set her down at the bottom of the stairs.

"Wow. That took quite a long time." Claire smiled. "It's been over four months since we mailed that."

"Do you remember what you wrote on the back?" Josh asked.

Claire had to think for a moment. "Wasn't it a recipe for those muffins Lolly made?" Lolly, the owner of the quaint bed-and-breakfast in London, had spoiled them with her homemade baking.

"I've got an idea," Josh said.

"Let me guess. We should make the muffins, and then send a note to Lolly telling her how much we miss them?" Claire liked the notion. "And by *we*, I mean you," she added.

His brows knit together.

"How about we give the recipe to your mom the next time she comes by instead. Since she loves to bake and all . . ." Josh trailed off midthought, as he expected Claire to agree with him.

"I promised to never share her recipe." Claire shook her head.

"Then don't tell her. Besides, you wrote it on the back of a postcard. I bet more than a dozen people read what was on the back just out of curiosity." There was a hopeful look on his face.

"Joshua Turner, don't you make me break a promise." Claire frowned at him.

Truth be told, between the two of them, Josh was the better baker, and her mother would probably try to make it a healthy snack and substitute disgusting ingredients for all the sweet stuff. No thank you.

"Never. Besides, your mom would turn Lolly's decadent treats into healthy muffins," Josh grumbled.

Claire laughed.

THREE

CLAIRE

A memory from London, England
March

Claire sank down on a plush chair in the library of Blossom Lane, a quaint bed-and-breakfast set in South Kensington. She groaned as she rubbed her sore feet.

"Why don't you let my dear Herbert drive you around tomorrow, love? He's got the day free and won't mind a bit." Lolly, the owner of the little home they were staying in, bustled into the room with a tray full of scones and hot tea.

"That would be lovely, if it's not too much of a bother." Claire raised her feet to rest them on an ottoman and took the offered cup of tea.

"You must have walked quite a bit today." Lolly sat down in the opposite chair. "Where is that dear husband of yours?"

"Out with Herbert looking at his gardens again." Claire smiled. Since their arrival three days ago, they'd discovered that Herbert loved to talk about his gardens and Lolly loved to chat over a hot pot of tea.

"Tell me, what did you see today?" Lolly settled back in her seat with all the appearance of genuinely caring about Claire and her day.

It was so refreshing to be here, more than Claire had imagined it would be. Their stop in London was quite long, close to three weeks, thanks to a conference they were both speaking at, and staying at a hotel would be expensive, so when their editor, Julia, suggested a cute bed-and-breakfast she knew of, they jumped at the chance. A simple English breakfast and a traditional afternoon tea were always served, and it didn't take long for Claire to realize both Lolly and Herbert lived for their teatime with guests and weren't quite able to hide their disappointment if they missed it.

"We followed Herbert's map today and walked to the Portobello Market in Notting Hill. It was lovely. I even found that bakery you mentioned." Claire reached for a triangle of cucumber sandwich. "Although, I will admit, I enjoyed your strawberry-vanilla muffin from yesterday over theirs."

Lolly preened at the compliment. "The Hummingbird is a fine bakery, but you can't beat homemade."

"We found that bookshop as well," Claire continued. "I bought a few books for our shelves back home."

"Oh, you did!" Lolly clapped her hands together. "George is amazing, isn't he? I just knew you'd like him. What books did you buy?"

"The Alice in Wonderland series. I couldn't resist. They were my favorite growing up."

Lolly nodded approvingly, and they continued on, talking about the vendors and the street food Josh and Claire had photographed.

"So is that one more thing to mark off your bucket list, then?" Lolly asked just as Claire leaned over the armrest to retrieve her book.

Every afternoon while having tea, Claire would pull out her notebook, which contained two sections. The front section was her set of list items, and the back section was a record of the places they'd visited and the things they'd seen.

"The market has always been something I've wanted to see, ever since reading about it in my Paddington Bear books." She loved checking off items on her bucket list, loved that sense of accomplishment and excitement.

"And did you find a postcard, as I suggested?" Lolly stood up and headed toward a cupboard.

"I did. We almost missed that little place with the old photos and postcards. I'm so glad you told us where to look. And you were right—it was hard to pick just one or two of my favorites. We ended up buying more than we'd intended."

"Good." In Lolly's hands was a box, and she set it down on the table between them. "We have a tradition here that my parents started when they first opened their home to guests. In this box you will find postcards from the last seventy years." She picked up a few and looked through them, a sweet smile gracing her face as she did so. "I used to love taking this box to my bedroom at night and going through the postcards. A few I even memorized." She handed them to Claire.

Some postcards were hand drawn, some were black-and-white photographs while others were in color, and many of them featured well-known London landmarks. As she started to read through the ones Lolly had handed her, she could see why they meant so much to her. They were like snapshots from the past, brimming with fond memories and wishes for future visits.

"I'd like for you and Josh to leave one here as well, if you wouldn't mind," Lolly said. "I remember my mother once explaining the idea to a guest. She said to think of it as a letter to your heart from your soul."

Claire held the postcards in her hands and thought about what it would mean to write one. She picked up the card she was looking at and read the back.

> *There is a peace here within the gardens that I haven't found elsewhere in a long, long time.*
> *My mind stops. The memories I'm running from disappear the moment I sit down and breathe in the sweet*

*scents of jasmine, of delicate roses, and hear nothing but
the sound of birds chirping.*

*My soul has finally found rest, and I'm not sure I
can leave.*

"That was written by a soldier after World War II. He went home
to create his own garden and was even buried there years later," Lolly
said quietly. "That's him there, standing beside my dad. His name was
David, and I used to watch him sit in our garden for hours on end."

"It's beautiful," Claire said.

"Feel free to look through the box, and then when you're ready, to
leave your own. Think about what you would like to say to yourself, to
your heart." She stood and patted Claire's hand before leaving the room.

Claire went through the postcards, tears welling in her eyes as she
read through them. Some were so beautiful, haunting even, with their
dreams for the future, their air of yearning, or their sense of loss from
the death or illness of a loved one.

What would she write?

MARRIAGE PROMISES

CLAIRE AND JOSH TURNER

1. Never go to bed angry with each other. *(No, Josh Turner, this does not mean you get to sleep on the couch if we're having a fight.)*
2. Never be away from one another longer than three days.
3. Learn to compromise. *(Claire . . . Don't get mad at me if I keep reminding you that it was your idea to add this to the list. Love you!)*
4. Have sex in every part of our house. *(Did you seriously need to add this, Josh?)*
5. We don't keep score of who's right and who's wrong.
6. Have hobbies of our own and a few we like to do together. *(So, does this mean you'll learn to golf with me, Claire?)*
7. Always be honest. But if it's going to hurt, offer wine first.
8. To make the decision to always be in love. Love isn't a feeling. It's a commitment. You can fall in and out of lust, but you have to decide to fall out of love.

9. Learn a foreign language together. *(Does learning the language of love count? 'Cause I'm sure we'll get an A+ in that!)*
10. To do one new thing every year.
11. Always part by saying "I love you." *(Should we add in a kiss too?) Sure* :)
12. Free hugs whenever the other needs one.
13. Nightly foot rubs *(Good try, Claire. How about weekly? Or biweekly?)*
14. Buy a vacation home right on the beach.

FOUR

JOSH

Present day

Josh crossed the street till he came to the tiny pub in their town called the Last Call. He was meeting Derek for their weekly wings-and-beer night, while Claire and Abby headed to the bakery for their monthly girls night out. Derek stood at the bar, speaking with Mike, a friend they'd gone to school with back in the day. Derek raised a glass in hello. Josh waved back.

"Well, look who's back! About time you showed your face in here." Fran, the owner of Last Call, blocked his path. "I was beginning to think you forgot about me."

"You? Never!" Josh held out a bag he had brought especially for Fran. "We love you so much, Claire kept buying you things on our trip." He leaned in close. "But don't tell anyone," he whispered.

She blushed. "This is why I consider you my second son." She peered into the bag, her eyes widening as she looked through all the lemon-scented products—from creams, to shampoos, to body wash, to all that other girl stuff Claire swore Fran would love.

"All lemon too. You tell that girl of yours to come in here for my special lemon drops."

"I'm not telling her that. Last time she was in here she thought she should go swimming off the dock at midnight—remember?"

Fran laughed. "Your girl can't really handle her liquor, can she?"

Josh chuckled. One glass of the right kind of wine and Claire was giggling like a schoolgirl. Three of Fran's lemon drops had her thinking she was Wonder Woman.

"I'm assuming she's over at the bakery with the girls." Fran yanked off the towel she had over her shoulder, grabbed a spray bottle she'd set down, and began to wipe a table Josh guessed was already clean.

Josh nodded. "The guys all here?"

"In the back." Fran nodded toward the back of the pub. "I always know when it's girls' night because my pub fills up with all the husbands."

"Then I'd better get back there before all the wings are gone."

"I've got a few more orders on the way for you guys, don't worry." Fran slapped him on the shoulder before she turned her focus to the customers who had just walked in.

Josh looked around for Mike, Fran's son, who was also a bartender and an old friend, but didn't see him behind the bar. Instead, Herb was there, pouring beer and frowning at everyone in the room.

"Hey, old man, I'll have whatever's on tap tonight." Josh leaned his forearms on the bar and waited for what he knew was coming.

"A tap? You want a tap?" Herb curled his hands into fists and held them up. "I've wanted to give you a tap since you were a teen dragging my son up onto our roof in the middle of the night to jump off down onto the trampoline—breaking his arm." Herb's eyes narrowed for a moment before his lips twisted into something that might be taken for a smile.

"That was all Mike's idea, and you know it." Josh shook his head. Every poor decision had always come from Mike. Josh just went along for the ride. The only reason he didn't break his own arm was because he'd been smart enough to climb off the roof as soon as he heard Mike's howl upon landing.

"My boy's an angel." Herb struggled to wink his right eye. A few years ago, Herb had suffered from a stroke, leaving the right half of his face partially paralyzed.

"He's an angel, all right. With black wings and a tarnished halo." Josh took the draft beer Herb offered him and headed toward Derek, who was sitting in the back with the other guys.

The evening went as it normally did—loud music, taking turns buying rounds of beer, and a lot of ribbing about childhood deeds. Josh could usually count on spending at least three hours at the pub, so he was surprised when he heard his phone's ringtone halfway through the night.

"Dude, you're seriously going to take that?" Derek tried to take the phone from him, but Josh stopped him.

"It's your wife," Josh said to him.

That set the other men laughing. Josh ducked out of the group and headed out toward the back deck, where it was a little quieter. If Abby was calling him, something was up.

"What's wrong?" he said as soon as he answered the phone. He glanced over at Derek, who had followed him.

"Your wife is fast asleep. I've tried waking her, but she's exhausted. I think you need to take her home."

"Seriously? She fell asleep?"

"You know what she's like when she's tired. She's getting crankier every time I try to wake her." Abby laughed, but Josh heard the tension behind her words.

"I'll be right there." Josh hung up and pulled out some money from his pocket. "This is for my share. I need to grab Claire and take her home."

"Everything all right?" Derek blocked him from leaving. "What did Abby say?"

Josh sighed.

"Claire fell asleep and doesn't want to wake up. I don't like this. She's become really lethargic, and it's not good."

"Talk to Abby. She'll know if Claire is okay or not."

Josh nodded and left through the back door that let out into the side alley. The bakery was just across the street. Abigail was at the door to let him in.

"She's okay, Josh. Don't worry," Abigail said quietly with a quick look over her shoulder to where Claire was resting against Kat, one of the owners of the bakery.

"You sure? Should I bring her to the clinic tomorrow?"

Abigail shook her head. "She's fine, and I leave tomorrow for the city for a few days. I'll be back after that, though. If she's still this bad or gets worse, then bring her in, okay? But maybe, for the next few days, just let her sleep. Her body might be fighting a virus or something, or maybe she's just not getting enough rest."

Josh snorted. "You're kidding me, right? She sleeps more than she's awake."

"I know. But there's no fever, no vomiting . . . so I'm not too worried. Not yet."

"What about her headaches?"

"How bad are they?"

"On a scale from one to ten, I'd say they're about a six." Josh frowned. Every couple of days they seemed to get worse.

"Okay, bring her in as soon as I'm back. I'm only gone a few days. But if it gets worse—if the headaches increase in frequency or intensity or anything else worsens, then take her in to see Dr. Will."

"Thanks, Abby." Josh made his way across the room to Claire. "Come on, Sleeping Beauty, time to get you home before the clock strikes midnight." He bent over to pick her up.

"Mixed up fairy tales again," Claire mumbled as she rested her head against his chest.

"Here. There's some treats in there for her to enjoy later." Kat put a bakery box on Claire, cradling it in the curved shape of her body as it lay draped over Josh's arms. "There might just be a little something in there for you as well," she said with a smile.

"You're like my very own fairy godmother." Josh winked at Kat before heading out with his sleepy wife.

Abigail held the door for him and then opened their car door as well. "I'll see you when I get back from my course, okay, Claire? Josh is going to bring you in to the clinic, and we'll see why you're so tired."

"No need to fuss over me. I just need a few hundred hours of uninterrupted sleep," Claire murmured.

Josh closed the door and turned to Abby.

"She'll be fine," Abigail said. She put her hand on his arm. "But keep an eye on her, okay?"

Josh's lips tightened. "I want to believe you, Abby, I really do. But I don't like this."

Abigail nodded. "Then take her in tomorrow to see Dr. Will. She's probably just anemic again." Abigail shook her head. "She has a habit of not taking her iron pills, in case you haven't noticed."

Josh frowned. It had to be more than anemia. He'd seen that in her before. "I hope that's all it is."

Through the duration of the car ride and Josh carrying her into the house and up the stairs, Claire slept. It wasn't until he laid her on the bed and started to undress her that she woke up and almost kicked him in the face.

"Whoa." Josh backed away, his hands held up. "I'm just helping you get into bed."

Claire pushed herself up on the bed and swerved as if drunk. "When did we get home?" she asked.

"Just now."

She winced and then rubbed the back of her head. "My head really hurts," she said.

Josh took a sudden interest in the carpet. "Yeah, I, uh, might have knocked your head against the wall coming up the stairs. Sorry."

Claire lay back down. "No, my head *really* hurts. It feels like it's going to explode." And then she groaned.

Josh reached for the bottle of pills Claire had been keeping by the bed and poured two into his palm. "Here, take these." He helped her sit up again and handed her a bottle of water.

"Don't make me move again, Josh. Please," Claire said, her voice gravelly with agony.

"Honey, you can't sleep like that on top of the bed. Let me get your pants off at least and get you under the covers, okay? And then you can go back to sleep. The headache will be gone soon." *Please, God, let it be gone soon.*

As she slept, Josh watched over her, his laptop open, unable to sleep. He watched Claire's face, the way her eyes would squeeze tighter, how her jaw would clench periodically. He waited, counting the minutes until the drugs finally kicked in. It took almost an hour.

Once Claire breathed a sigh of relief in her sleep, Josh relaxed, put away the laptop, and snuggled up to her, resting his forearm on her stomach, needing to be close, to feel her warmth beneath his hand.

The week dragged on. Claire continued to have daily headaches, but she refused to go in for a checkup until Abby was back from her course. Josh's frustration grew. He didn't understand her reluctance to be seen by a doctor.

He wanted to believe she was pregnant, that this fatigue was a result of early-stage pregnancy hormones. But nothing he'd read online confirmed that for him. If she were pregnant, she'd be nauseated, experiencing morning sickness, her skin would be sensitive, and she'd be craving salt. At least he thought it was salt. But she wasn't showing any of those signs.

And it wasn't just lethargy. She had lost her appetite and suffered a near-constant headache that seemed to get worse each day.

Claire thought her body was just taking its time readjusting to being in their home time zone. But this wasn't normal. Never, after any of their previous trips, had jet lag hit her as hard as this. Besides, her body would have adjusted by now.

The first few weeks back had been okay. She'd had a few extra naps and had been sleeping in past the alarm, but Claire had had no trouble running out for errands or a coffee with Abby. But the last two weeks—ever since their book signing, where she'd slept the entire three-hour drive to the city, had taken naps whenever she could, and had barely made it through dinner—she had gone downhill quickly.

Maybe the strain of trying and failing to get pregnant for the last few years was just too much. From the moment they'd met, they'd shared dreams of having a large family, of their house overflowing with the tears and joys of children. As the years progressed, those dreams changed for him. He still wanted children, but he began to envision the two of them adopting or being foster parents, of taking in children who needed their help and their love. It became less about having a child of their own and more about having a child to love.

But for her it was different. He knew the trip had been hard for her emotionally, and he'd done everything he could to help her with that, even to the point of extending their travel time to indulge her last-minute whims to visit more countries.

It didn't make sense. He hated seeing her so broken, and hated even more the feeling that there was nothing he could do to fix it.

He made his way downstairs to the kitchen, where he'd put on a fresh pot of coffee, and picked up the phone to call Derek, who worked as an accountant out of his home office.

"Is your wife working today?" Josh said.

"She just came home for lunch. What's up?"

"Do you think she could squeeze Claire in? Or maybe drop by after work?"

"There's an extra charge for home visits, you know," Derek teased. "But actually, is everything okay?"

"It's not an emergency, but I'm really worried," Josh said.

"Just a minute. Let me ask Abby."

Josh listened as Derek and Abby talked in the background. He heard Abby shout that he should go ahead and bring her in right away. Josh sighed. He wasn't even sure Claire would have the energy to get out of the house.

"You heard that?" Derek asked.

"Your wife is an angel. Claire is sleeping, so how about I bring her in an hour."

"Perfect. That gives her time to finish her lunch. Abs says not to worry."

"I can't help it." Josh hung up and looked at the clock. He'd give Claire time to sleep and wake her up just before they needed to leave.

Not worry? What was Abigail thinking? Of course, he was worried. He'd lost his mother because she had ignored the symptoms. He wasn't about to lose Claire.

FIVE

CLAIRE

Present day

"D o you want me to come in with you?" Josh held the clinic door open for Claire.

"No, I'll be fine." She yawned before rising on her tiptoes for a kiss while balancing a take-out tray of coffees. "I can't believe you did this. I would have called and made an appointment, you know."

"I know, but you were taking your time, and I'm worried." Josh gave her another kiss. "You sure you don't want me to stay with you?"

"All she's going to do is poke me with needles. Unless you're suddenly okay with the sight of blood, I'm sure you have better things to do than sit in the waiting room until I'm done."

Josh brushed a lock of her hair away from her face. "I'll be just across the street in the bookstore."

"I'll text you when I'm done." Claire would much rather browse in the bookstore with him than get jabbed with another needle.

Josh had woken her less than twenty minutes ago, saying he was taking her to see Abby. Getting dressed and being here was the last thing she wanted to do, today of all days.

Why couldn't he have just left her in bed?

Today would be *his* birthday, the birthday of the son she gave away, a day that was always hard for her. Josh knew that.

"Knock, knock," Claire said into the empty waiting area. The clinic was still officially closed for lunch.

Rebecca Elston, the medical receptionist, popped her head out of a door and smiled.

"Dr. Cox was just telling me you'd be coming in." Rebecca stepped into the room, buttoning up a light sweater as she did so.

"I brought some coffees as a thank-you." Claire held the tray out.

"Oh, perfect!"

"I brought one in for Dr. Shuman as well. I wasn't sure if he'd be in today or not." Claire reached for her own cup and held it between her hands, letting the warmth of the hot coffee permeate her cold fingers.

"Of course I'm here." Dr. Shuman's voice boomed in the small room. He stepped through the open door and came over to give her a hug. For an older man, he was quite handsome. In his mid-seventies, Will Shuman ran daily, worked out at the local gym, ran healthy-eating seminars in town, and didn't look a day over fifty-five, even with a full head of silver hair.

"Abigail was just telling me you need some blood work done. And I hear you haven't been taking your iron pills like she told you to." He shook his finger at her. "You always were stubborn, even when you were a child. It's because of you I still have strawberry lollipops in the cupboard, you know." He turned toward Rebecca. "She wouldn't have any other kind, just those." He shook his head. "Stubborn, just like her mother."

Claire's face flushed as she handed him his coffee. With a smile playing on his face, he walked her through to the back, where the treatment rooms and offices were. They found Abby sitting at her desk studying a file in front of her.

"Here she is, Abigail. She even brought coffee."

Abby jumped in her chair, dropping some papers she'd been holding.

"Will," she said, her hand pressed tight against her chest. "You've got to give me some warning." She shook her head. "You need to start whistling or wearing a bell or something." She smiled as she came to the door. "Your birthday is coming up, Dr. Will. Just you wait," she teased.

"She says that every year and then only gives me books." He shook his head before he sauntered back down the hall. "Rebecca, I think it's time we get this afternoon party started," he called, his voice ricocheting along the walls.

They both watched him until he disappeared through the waiting room doorway.

"He seems particularly chipper today," Claire said.

"He's getting ready to leave for a fishing trip." Abby smiled. "Have a good nap?"

Claire nodded. "I'm still really tired though."

Abigail narrowed her gaze. "You know Josh is worried, right? Frankly, I'm not liking what I'm seeing either. Let's see what your blood has to tell us."

Claire bit her lip.

"Honestly," Abigail said as she shook her head. "I've never seen a grown woman so on edge when it comes to needles. You should be used to them by now."

"I thought I'd be done with them, to be frank." She shrugged.

Abby led her into a small treatment room close to her office. It was the one Abby liked the most—she kept drawings that some of her younger patients had made for her on the walls to help brighten the sterile environment.

On the counter sat a tray with a needle, vials for blood, and a small container.

"What else did Josh tell you?"

"What do you mean?"

"He thinks I could be pregnant." Claire swallowed hard past the words. She would know if she were, and she wasn't.

Abby gently rubbed her arm. "It won't hurt to check."

Abby proceeded with her usual checkup—listening to Claire's heart and making her breathe in deeply, which forced her to yawn way too many times.

"Is it possible to be tired of being tired?" she asked after another big yawn. Claire watched as her friend inserted the needle with as much gentleness as possible, and then she turned her head away once the blood started filling the vials. That part always made her squeamish.

Abby chuckled, and Claire knew it was because of her reaction.

"Considering you're the one saying it, yes." She took one more vial of blood before easing the needle out and putting a bandage on Claire's skin. "But, don't worry. We'll get this figured out, and you'll be back to your normal energetic self again in no time." She handed her the cup. "Now, go pee."

The whole procedure of having to urinate in a tiny cup, being sure to catch it midstream, made her feel faintly ridiculous. When she was done, Claire headed back into the small treatment room, placed the cup on the waiting tray, and then made her way back to Abby's office, where she'd left her coffee.

"That wasn't so hard, was it?" Abby leaned against her desk and handed Claire's coffee to her. "Make yourself comfortable, and I'll be back in a minute or two."

Claire went to the window that overlooked the main street. She loved their town. There was a decided charm to it. The main street was vehicle-free during the summer months, and the roadway would end up colored in chalk drawings by the kids who attended summer camps in the town park.

It reminded her of the many European towns they'd visited, although without their Old World appeal.

Like Venice.

Just the thought of it had her longing to go back. There was something about the narrow streets, the open squares, and the canals that pulled at her heartstrings. They'd stayed less than a week, but she could have stayed longer.

Her husband stood in the window of the bookstore directly opposite and waved. She waved back. He held up something to show her, and while she had no clue what book it was, she could tell by the large grin on his face that he was excited. She gave him a thumbs-up and watched him walk toward the counter.

She checked her watch. Almost ten minutes had passed since Abby had left her. She walked over to the door and poked her head out to see if she could spot Abby anywhere in the hallway, but it was as quiet as a church.

Frowning, she checked her watch again and then sat down, swirling her coffee in the cup, suddenly uninterested in drinking the rest of it.

What was taking Abigail so long?

Dr. Shuman's voice boomed from somewhere in the building, but she couldn't make out the words. It almost sounded like a *booyah*. Something must have gotten him excited. Either that or he was seeing off one of his younger patients.

The minutes dragged on and various scenarios of doom played out in Claire's head, something no doubt everyone did when they were waiting for results to come back.

"Hey." Abby poked her head into the office. "Sorry for the delay." She sounded a bit out of breath, as if she'd just jogged there. "Um, where is Josh?"

Claire half turned in her seat. "Over at the bookstore. Why?"

"Just wondering." She shrugged. "He's coming to pick you up, though, right?"

Claire could hear the forced nonchalance in Abby's voice, as if she were trying hard to remain calm.

"What's going on? And yes, he should be here any minute." She attempted to give her friend the look—the one that said *Don't mess with me* and *Tell me what's wrong* all in one—but it didn't seem to work.

"Great." She popped her head out and then back in. "I'll be back in a minute. Promise."

She closed the door behind her before Claire could say another word.

What was going on?

She pulled out her phone and sent Josh a text message.

Can you come now? Abby is acting weird, and I think something is wrong.

She crossed her leg and bounced her foot up and down while waiting for his reply, suddenly very nervous.

Here now. One sec.

Claire pushed herself up from the chair and went to open the door. She stood there, arms crossed, fingers tapping against her ribs, while she waited for Abby to return with her husband in tow.

The moment they rounded the corner, Claire's heart stopped.

There was a look of panic on Josh's face. If it weren't for Abby's hand on his arm, it looked like he would have bolted toward her.

Abby on the other hand—her eyes danced with light and there was a contained smile on her face.

Dr. Shuman followed behind and rubbed his hands together as he stared at her. Claire couldn't tell if he was smiling or worrying.

"What's wrong?" Claire forced the words past the lump in her throat.

"Nothing, absolutely nothing." Abby reached out to squeeze her hand before pushing past her to step into her office.

Claire sat back down on her chair with Josh beside her, and they held hands. Josh's grip was firm, as if knowing she needed the grounding while they waited for Abby to get comfortable.

Dr. Shuman stood at Abby's side.

"What is going on?" Claire asked again.

There was a palpable tension in the air and goose bumps materialized all over Claire. Something was wrong. Something horrible. And Abby needed Dr. Shuman for support.

She was dying. Or . . . something equally terrible. There was no other explanation.

"Claire, honey, I don't know how to say this." Abigail cleared her throat. She stared down at her desk, at a sheet of paper she held in her hands. "We're going to wait on the blood work to come back for confirmation, but I ran some tests with your urine sample." She looked up and gave a weak smile. "A few tests, actually. And then made Will come and do more tests to make sure I wasn't imagining things."

Dr. Shuman placed his hand on Abby's shoulder and squeezed.

"Cut the crap, Abby. What is going on?" Josh leaned forward.

Tears sprang to Abby's eyes as she looked from Josh to Claire.

"We're going to wait on the blood work—" Abby repeated before her phone rang and Rebecca's voice came through the speaker.

"Dr. Shuman, you're needed at reception."

"Oh, bloody hell." The older doctor pursed his lips together as he headed to the door. "You come see me before you leave, you hear?" He left before they could say anything.

"Abby . . ." Claire's chest was tight, and it was getting difficult to breathe.

Josh put his arm around her and made her lean into him, which she did willingly. She needed his strength right now because she had a feeling whatever her friend was about to say would have her collapsing on the floor.

"Okay. I know I told you that if you were ever to get pregnant, that it would be a miracle, because that was the only option left. Well," she said. "Honey, I would say God just gave you a miracle." A wide smile spread across her face as she leaned forward, her hands reaching out to take theirs.

Claire just sat there, not understanding what Abby had just said. She looked to Josh, who sat there equally confused.

"What are you saying?" Josh asked, his voice raspy.

"I'm saying you're having a baby." By now, Abby's face was flushed, and she pressed her hands over her heart. Tears welled up, and for a moment, a brief moment, time stood still for Claire.

You're having a baby.

You're having a baby.

I'm having a baby!

Claire thought those words over and over to herself. Did Abby just tell her she was pregnant? How was that possible?

"How?" she whispered.

"You're asking *me* that?" Abby threw her hands in the air. "Maybe that cruise was exactly what you needed. A time to relax, unwind, and stop trying so hard. I've heard of this happening, but I've never witnessed it directly. Couples try for years to have a baby, they get extremely stressed, and then when they finally give up or make the decision to adopt . . . it's like they're free, and it gives their body permission to do whatever it needs to."

Claire shook her head. "There must be a mistake. The blood work will come back and tell you differently."

Josh's grip around her shoulders tightened.

"I don't think so," Abby said.

Claire didn't want to believe it. "What about the high protein in my urine?"

"This time, there was none. The urinalysis did confirm that you're anemic, which we already knew." Abby leaned back in her chair, folding her hands together with a satisfied look on her face. "Claire, honey, you're going to have a baby."

All the blood drained from Claire's face and the world around her tilted. She leaned forward and heard Abby tell Josh to put her head down by her knees. Things started to go black. A sound like waves crashing against the shore filled her ears, and it was all she could do not to be sick.

"Breathe, honey, just breathe." Josh's voice finally pushed through those deafening waves, and she could feel his hand rubbing her back.

After a few minutes, she finally sat up, feeling weak and depleted.

She let Abigail's words sink in. Words she'd always wanted to hear. Words she never thought would be said to her.

"We're going to have a baby," she whispered, gazing at Josh.

His eyes were bright with tears as he leaned in and gently kissed her.

"We're going to have a baby," he said.

Claire closed her eyes as his words washed over her. Miracles did happen. Dreams do come true.

Her heart felt ready to burst with something far greater than happiness or joy.

SIX

CLAIRE

A memory from Paris
Last week of March

The bells of Notre Dame rang as they stood watching a scene Claire itched to draw. Her fingers pushed together as if gripping a pencil while she studied a man in the church gardens. He walked in lazy circles, feeding the pigeons that followed him as he scattered seed on the ground. Every so often, he'd raise his arm, and a bird would fly up to perch there, as though stopping to chat with him before flying away.

Were they thanking him for the meal? Was he telling them when to come back for another visit? He was old, his back stooped, and his long coat tattered, but the smile on his face . . . it mesmerized her.

"Are you ready?" Josh tugged her arm, anxious to head to the Shakespeare and Company bookstore, something that had been on their bucket list from the day they'd met.

"Do you think we could go speak to him?" She couldn't tear her eyes away, as much as she knew she had to.

"And scare his friends away? I got a few shots of him for you to use later." He held up their Canon camera.

Claire wasn't ready to lose this feeling yet. "How about after the bookstore we sit at the café, so I can draw for a bit?" Just across the road stood a quaint Parisian café with an outdoor terrace.

"Sure. But do we get a coffee or a cappuccino? I always feel like I'm ordering the wrong thing."

"Espresso, Josh. That's all you need to remember."

They'd been in the City of Love for three days now, and he still struggled with something as simple as ordering coffee. The first day there, he'd asked for a café au lait in the midafternoon, and the look he received from the server had him hastily changing his order.

They headed to the famous bookstore, where a violinist played a soulful serenade outside the entrance. While Josh headed inside, Claire browsed the used book carts out front, finding an assortment of both French and English books. She was browsing leisurely and enjoying the music, when Josh popped his head out the door.

"You've got to see this place!"

His excitement drew her in, but once inside, she stopped dead in her tracks. A desk sat square in the middle, and it was surrounded, literally surrounded, by stacks of books, bookshelves, and chairs with books piled on top of them. On either side of the desk were narrow doorways outlined by more bookshelves.

Josh was bouncing in place as he waited for her to take it all in.

"Couldn't you see Jack in here? Itching to climb the shelves, taking down books and looking through them, even sitting in that chair, his legs swinging while he's waiting for his mom?" He brought the camera up for a shot, but before he could take a photo, the bookseller stopped him.

"No photos, monsieur." She pointed to a sign directly in front of them that held an image of a camera with a large *X* through it.

Like a kid denied his candy, Josh slowly lowered the camera to his chest.

"You'd better give it to me, and I'll put it in my bag," Claire said. The bookseller eyed her husband in a way that told Claire she didn't trust him to obey the rules.

They wandered the hallways, agog at all the books, before heading up the stairs, where photographs of the great minds of literature covered the walls.

"To think Hemingway sat here, in this room . . ." Josh gazed about him, fingering the spines of books, leafing through pages, and sighed with pure contentment.

Claire hated to break the spell.

"Actually, Hemingway never visited this location. He held readings at the original store. It closed during the war and never reopened."

The disappointment on her husband's face made Claire wish she'd never said anything.

"Are you sure?" he asked.

Claire held up a brochure she'd picked up and handed it to him.

"Opened in the fifties, huh?" Josh looked around him and shrugged. "There's still magic here. You can feel it. The creative energy . . . it's enriching. Let's each pick out a book—to say that we did."

Claire pointed to a book with old illustrations that she'd found. "I already did. How about I meet you over at the café? You can spend your time in here browsing, and I'll grab a table and start drawing."

Almost an hour later, Josh joined her. She'd completed the drawing of the man beside the church, surrounded by pigeons, and she was now enjoying her second cup of coffee.

Josh carried a brown bag with the store's logo on it and pulled out a box. "I think this will look nice in our office, don't you?" He opened the box, revealing a book inside.

She pointed to a similar box on the table. She'd bought an old book that she liked, but truth be told, she mainly wanted the box so she could set it on a shelf. The box was brown with the store's logo in gold. "Great minds think alike," she said.

He smiled as he looked at her drawing. "Wow. That's incredible, Claire." He helped himself to a sip of Claire's coffee, and then, setting it down hastily, he checked his watch. "We should probably go if we want to make the walking tour."

The walking tour turned out to be an enchanting excursion with a little epiphany at the end. Stumbling along one of the only original cobblestone streets in Paris, they delighted in the architecture and savored decadent hot chocolate. After the tour, they retraced their steps for another round of hot chocolate from their favorite stop. It was there, at Un Dimanche à Paris, that Josh was hit with a new idea for Jack.

Near the well-known chocolate shop was an old pub. Sitting in front of the pub was a puppy, brown with one large white spot on its forehead. Josh caught sight of him, and the puppy ran up to him, jumped up to put his paws on him, and then trotted off down the street. He would stop every few yards and look back, whimpering in invitation, to persuade Josh to follow him. But from out of nowhere, a little boy with a ball appeared. The boy chased after the puppy, laughing while the pup barked, happy to have someone to play with.

Claire could see it in Josh's eyes, the way he watched the two romping down the street. It was for Josh what the old man feeding birds by the church had been for her—inspiration.

She wound her arm through his. "Time to head back to the hotel?"

"I should have brought my notebook."

"Our hotel isn't too far away. You won't forget it. And I promise to enjoy my wine in silence while you scribble during dinner."

He leaned over and kissed her, his lips lingering over hers. "We make a great team, don't we, Mrs. Turner?"

"Yes indeed, Mr. Turner. We certainly do."

SEVEN

CLAIRE

Present day

Claire stood in the empty bedroom they had long ago set aside for their child and reflected on the wonder of her life.

She rubbed her belly gently.

Josh wrapped his arms around her and placed a kiss on her neck. "Are you thinking about decorating?"

Claire looked around her. The walls were a soft yellow, almost like a buttercream, and on them hung a few posters with inspirational messages—about believing in one's dreams, of fairy tales coming true, about the heart of a child containing a whole world of magic.

There were also drawings Claire had done over the years of small black sheep. She'd fallen in love with black sheep when as a teen she'd visited Scotland with her mom.

A rocker they'd found years ago, one she'd been immediately smitten by, filled the far corner. They'd had no room in the house to put it but here—its perfect place. But there was no crib, no changing table, nothing to welcome a baby home.

Their baby.

"I'm just letting it sink in. It hardly seems real." She turned in her husband's arms. "It's a dream come true, Josh. Especially after . . ."

"After letting go of our dream on the cruise."

He understood, and Claire loved him all the more for that.

"So we make new dreams with this little one. New dreams for a new baby." His kiss was soft, sweet, and full of hope.

"Guess I need to buy a notebook for all my future lists." Claire smiled at the thought.

"Well . . . look at that." Josh glanced meaningfully at the rocking chair.

She turned and noticed a yellow cloth journal sitting on its seat. She beamed. "When did you get that?"

"I picked it up at the store while you were with Abby." A sheepish grin appeared on his face. "I meant it as a little gift, because of what today is. But"—he shrugged—"it kind of fits."

"It's perfect." With tears in her eyes, she opened it to the first page.

To the wife of my life, the mate of my heart, the keeper of my secrets . . . I will always love you. Today will always be worth remembering.

She melted at his words. In each journal he bought for her, he wrote something personal. She loved the custom and treasured the sentiments. One day she planned on creating a word collage of the things he'd written to her.

She struggled to articulate her feelings, to say something that would adequately express her love.

"Speechless?" he asked. The way his eyes twinkled with laughter, as if he knew he'd caught her off guard, made her smile.

"Keeper of your secrets, huh?" She tilted her head. "I didn't think you had any secrets, thought you were an open book."

"Well, you're the only one who knows I wear tighty-whities and that I'm scared of spiders."

"My superhero, you."

Josh puffed out his chest and anchored his hands on his hips. "I'm here to serve."

"I thought you liked Iron Man?"

"I'm Clark Kent in disguise."

"Don't you mean Tony Stark?"

Josh looked taken back. "Tony Stark is Iron Man, honey. I think you've got your superheroes mixed up." He shook his head in mock dismay.

"*Me?* I think——" She stopped when she realized he was teasing her. "How about you be my Clark Kent by day and Tony Stark by night. I hear Tony has a way with the ladies . . ." She gently swatted him on the chest.

"As you wish." He winked.

She laughed, and let him get away with adding yet another hero to the mix.

"What do you think about adding a little sister or brother to Jack's stories?" Josh said as he stepped back and fiddled with his hands.

She could tell, just by that one gesture, that he was not only serious in his question but also nervous about her reaction.

"Are you sure you want to tackle that much in this series? How many adventures could he go on with a pregnant mother? Or are you thinking of jumping ahead a few years so that the sibling can join him?" Adding a sibling might be complicating matters too much for Jack's Adventures.

"Well, I . . . I guess I really didn't think it through." He stared down at the floor, but Claire caught the way he struggled to hide his emotions. She stepped toward him and then paused.

"Let's think about it. We can talk to Julia about it and see how she feels," she suggested.

"Julia's our editor, not the final arbiter." His lips tightened.

Claire knew she'd have to tread carefully here.

"I know. But it's still new, so let's think on it a bit. Besides," she said, linking her arm through his and walking him out of the baby's room to avoid discussing work in there. "Remember how I mentioned starting a new series, but with a little girl?"

Josh's eyes lit up. "Zoe, right?"

She nodded. "Or Hope. Or Sarah or even . . . what's Tony Stark's girlfriend's name?"

"Piper?" His eyes twinkled as if he knew her thoughts on the name.

"Oh . . ." Her voice dropped. For some reason she thought it was Charlie. "Well, we can keep thinking."

"So you're still planning to try your hand at writing it?" Her husband turned his face away, and Claire wondered if the idea bothered him.

Jack was his baby. She drew the illustrations and helped with some plot ideas, but the words, emotions, and excitement that charmed their readers . . . that was all him. When he'd decided on a name, there'd been no hesitation or second thoughts. He knew right away he wanted to name the boy in their book after the son she'd given up.

If she'd ever had any doubts about how Josh felt about her giving up a child for adoption, all her fears and worries were eased that day.

"You wouldn't mind? I'd need your help editing it and making sure it was okay, but I think I'd like to try." She patted his arm. "Who knows? It may end up being a horrible mistake, and then you'll have two projects to write."

They walked into the kitchen, where Claire got herself a glass of water flavored with sliced lemon.

"Do you hear yourself right now? You don't make horrible mistakes. It's because of you Jack became such a hit—I would never have believed in myself enough to submit it. Plus, you're the one with connections in the industry. You," he said as he stepped toward her and grabbed her hands, "Mrs. Turner, are our magic maker. And our proof isn't just Jack, but this little one as well." He rubbed her flat stomach.

"You did have a hand in it."

Josh straightened, his shoulders pulled back with pride. "I know. I'm pretty awesome too." The look on his face at these moments always won her over. No matter what, her husband always knew how to make her smile.

"Together we make an amazing team, if I do say so myself," he said.

"Yes." She stood on her tiptoes and kissed him on the lips. "We do." They stood that way for a few moments, their lips locked, until her stomach growled.

"Why don't you go on outside? I have your pencils and notebook out there, and I'll cut up some fruit?" Josh suggested. "You know, we need to celebrate this and tell everyone. How about inviting your mother over for dinner tonight?"

"Whoa. Slow down there, proud papa. Let's hold off on telling the world for a bit, okay?" Claire grabbed her water and headed out to the patio. Josh had indeed set everything up for her, even placing the umbrella at the right angle so the sun wouldn't beat down on her colored crayons.

Since they'd arrived home, she hadn't been able to work on the illustrations for their books as much as she'd hoped. She practically slept her days away, but now she knew why.

She was having a baby.

All she wanted to do was sit back and let it sink in. Her heart swelled with joy at the thought. She was having a baby. There were butterflies in her stomach as she contemplated this utterly unexpected gift. She still couldn't believe it. Ever since the end of the trip, she'd worked hard to be okay with the idea of being infertile, and she'd concentrated on moving forward with their lives. Even when Josh asked if she could be pregnant, she hadn't dared to consider it.

But he'd been right.

Yes, they needed to celebrate.

"I do need to tell my mom, though. She's going to be over the moon." Claire raised her voice so Josh could hear.

"What if you surprise her with it? Tell her over dessert? Don't tell her over the phone . . . I want to see her face when she finds out."

A glow of happiness spread from Claire's heart. She couldn't wait to tell her mother. Millie was going to be ecstatic.

She wasn't sure if she could keep the excitement out of her voice, so she sent her mother a text instead.

Josh set a plate of cut fruit on the table, and then not so discreetly pushed the pages he'd been working on toward her.

Claire smiled. She got the hint.

Josh's gift was creating unforgettable characters in the simplest of situations and having readers beg for more stories. Her passion was bringing those characters and situations to life through her illustrations. Before their Jack's Adventures series, she'd been a sought-after illustrator, but now she took on only a few select clients.

Her favorite project, hands down, was when she was working on Jack's story.

"So where are we today?" She looked through the pages and smiled.

Paris. Jack was racing after what he thought was a lost puppy, tearing through the winding streets of Saint-Germain while his mother was on a walking tour of chocolate shops.

She remembered that day so clearly, how Josh came up with the idea when they'd spotted a puppy after their own walking tour—a tour that entailed *two* stops at their favorite chocolatier.

"Of all the cities we visited, Paris is the one I felt we didn't have enough time in," Claire said before hiding a yawn with her hand.

"Then we'll have to go back. Do you need to lie down again, or do you think you can manage to stay up until dinner?" There was a teasing tone in Josh's voice, and Claire knew he was greatly relieved to finally know the reason for her exhaustion.

"Let me work on this a little, and then I'll go lie in the hammock for a bit."

"Are you sure you're okay?"

For the first time in a long time, she felt more than okay.

"I'm perfect."

EIGHT

CLAIRE

Present day

Claire couldn't have stifled her yawn if she'd tried. Just when she was about to relax in the hammock, her mother appeared around the corner of the house.

"Have one of the cookies I brought, love. David has a whole new selection of tea and biscuits this season to try. He said to say hi. I noticed a box with your name on it in the corner of his booth space at the market today."

David was an older gentleman Claire had known almost her whole life. He was also someone she swore her mother had a crush on.

"You should ask him out on a date, Millie," Josh called out through the kitchen window where he hovered.

"I'll do no such thing. If the man wants to let this"—she pointed to herself—"get away, then that's his loss."

"I think he's too scared you'll turn him down, Mother." Claire yawned again. Her whole body was tired now, and it was getting harder to lift her arms or to move her head.

"Every man needs a little encouragement now and then, Millie." Josh opened the door to the back patio and brought out a vase of fresh-cut flowers. He gave Claire's cheek a peck and gently rubbed her shoulders.

"Why don't you go lie down? Millie can tell you a story before you fall asleep." He blew a kiss in Millie's direction.

"Josh, love, Claire and I need some mother-daughter time." The pointed look Millie shot Josh's way had Claire chuckling.

He let out an exaggerated sigh. "In other words, you're telling me to get lost?"

Millie smiled. "Exactly."

Claire watched their interaction with amusement. "Would you mind, hon? Maybe run to the store and get some vegetables for dinner tonight?"

"Anything in particular you're wanting?" There was a hopeful tone in Josh's voice. Along with the exhaustion, she'd also had no appetite.

Claire thought for a moment. "Maybe some olives and . . . bananas."

"Bananas? What happened to your absolute disgust for the mushy fruit?"

She shrugged. "I don't know. But I was dreaming of making an orange and banana smoothie, and now I really want one."

"Okay then. How about I make you a strawberry and banana smoothie in the meantime? I think we have some frozen bananas in the freezer."

Millie prattled on about the market, the new vendor booths, and the people who ran them. Heritage was a small tourist town located on the shores of Lake Huron, and it held a daily market in the town square, open a few hours a day during the spring months and then open for longer hours during the summer.

Years ago, Millie had run a booth of fresh baked goods, like breads, buns, muffins, and tarts, and she still felt a connection to the people there, going daily to say hello and purchase something, anything, to help them out.

"Why didn't you pick up the box and bring it here?" Claire asked, interrupting her mom's monologue.

"Box? What box?"

"The one David had in his booth."

Millie leaned forward and took another cookie from the tray. "Well, I did offer, but he said he misses you."

Claire nodded. "I know. I need to go see him."

"Did I ever tell you about when I first found out I was pregnant with you?" Millie asked.

Claire caught her breath at her mother's words.

Millie stared out to the yard, oblivious to Claire's reaction. "Most women, when they first get pregnant are sick. It's usually the first symptom. That and swollen breasts."

"I don't remember that." She kept her voice steady. She wanted to stop her mom, to tell her that she was going to have a baby, but the memory of her first pregnancy was like a knife being thrust into her heart. She didn't quite remember how she felt—she'd never been sick, that much she recalled, but she had been scared of her body's changes and was angry at her parents.

"There's something I need to tell you." Claire cleared her throat.

Millie didn't seem to hear her.

"I always heard that morning sickness was a living hell, and I used to pray that I would never be that sick if I ever got pregnant. I watched enough friends rush to the bathroom at the slightest smell, and I never wanted that. I loved food too much." She patted her stomach as a wry smile flashed across her face.

Claire rolled her eyes. Her mother was tiny yet ate like a horse. There was never a time she wasn't snacking. Whether it was nuts she kept in her purse or a fresh piece of fruit she grabbed off a counter, she was always nibbling on something.

"Mom—"

"But with you, things were different." Millie cut her off. "I was the envy of all my friends. Did you know that? From the moment I found out I was pregnant with you to the moment you were born, you were easy. No morning sickness. No false labor pains. No prolonged labor either. A few pushes and you came out into the world—"

"With a wail to announce my arrival that the queen herself could hear." Claire finished for her. "You've told me this before."

Millie looked at her. "But I don't think you've really heard what I've said."

Confused, Claire rubbed her face. "What am I missing then?"

"I was never sick, but I was tired. Exhausted even. Which was very unusual for me, even then. I had to take time off work, and all I did was sleep. Your poor father had to cook his own meals, and more times than not, my friends would bring over a casserole to save him from his burnt creations. In fact, I only craved one thing. Bananas. It's probably why you hated them so much. I swear," Millie said with a giggle, "everything I ate had to have bananas. From eating them raw, to cooking with them . . ." She sighed. "It took me years to eat a banana after you were born."

Claire smiled.

"Dad never could cook. Even macaroni and cheese was a challenge." Claire leaned her head back in the chair and stared up into the blue sky. Obviously, Millie had something she needed to get off her chest. Once she was done, then Claire would share the news.

Who knew it would be so hard to get a word in?

"Yes, he was a lost cause when it came to making his own dinner. Thankfully, Josh isn't like that. He'll fend for himself just fine." There was a satisfied tone in Millie's voice, and Claire looked over at her.

"Josh is pretty amazing." So amazing that he actually suspected she could be pregnant before she did. Since when did a man know first?

Millie's head cocked to the side and she reached across the table to hold Claire's hand.

"Isn't it funny how our bodies work?" Millie said. "No matter how hard we try or how much we want something, until our body is ready, there's really nothing we can do about it."

Claire wouldn't quite let herself believe she was pregnant. Not completely. After everything that had happened in her life, Claire had the nagging feeling that maybe she didn't deserve to have all her dreams come true.

All because of one decision, one mistake that she would always regret.

"So now you want to be a grandmother?" The words just came out, unbidden and unprovoked.

At the look of horror on her mother's face, Claire stopped herself from going further down that road. "I'm sorry. That didn't come out right."

"Oh, honey, I . . ."

In that moment, before a veil descended over Millie's eyes, Claire became hopeful. Maybe, for the first time in years, they'd actually talk about what happened.

But Claire should have known better.

"It's easy to look back and realize the mistakes we made and wish we could do things differently. I regret a lot of things, but there isn't much I would change, other than that time in your life. But then, you know that already. This isn't news to you." There was a sadness to Millie's voice, the regret so obvious.

Claire put on a bright and cheery smile, pushing everything she wanted to say back into the tiny little box full of memories that her mother never wanted to deal with. "I know." She closed her eyes and let the soft breeze dance over her skin. This was not turning out the way she thought it would. She expected Millie to be ecstatic, over the moon . . . but this . . . this didn't feel right.

"Mom, I—" Claire decided to try again.

"I think I might go work in your garden a little." Millie interrupted her. "Those roses need some pruning."

Before Claire could say another word, Millie walked away. But not before Claire noticed her mother wiping away tears.

The guilt that remained whenever she tried to talk about what happened to her as a teenager was right there. It was always right there, as if waiting for the perfect moment to crash into her life and destroy anything worth holding on to.

Today was supposed to be about this miracle inside of her, but instead, Claire had made it about her past.

Why couldn't she let go and move on? Why?

If she could turn back the clock and have a do-over, she would do it in a heartbeat.

She would never have sneaked out of the house after being grounded by her father, or hitchhiked into town to hang out with friends at the beach for the first bonfire of the season.

She would never have stayed by the campfire after all her girlfriends had gone home, or continued to drink beer with guys from school. She would never have let herself get drunk.

There were a lot of things she would never do again, but if she could go back to that day and stay in her room, like the good girl she was supposed to have been . . . she couldn't even imagine how different her life might have turned out.

Her mother had been the one to realize she was pregnant. Claire had assumed she missed her period due to final exams and the pressure from her father to get perfect scores. But Millie knew better.

Her father had been furious when he found out. He refused to be the father with the pregnant teenager. Did she not realize what that would do to his career? He was supposed to be a respected council member and businessman.

He'd demanded Claire get an abortion, but in a rare instance of holding her ground, Millie had stood up to him and told him it was Claire's body, Claire's choice.

Except she really didn't have a choice.

If she kept the baby, she wouldn't be allowed to live at home. Those were the rules according to her father.

But if she got rid of the baby, he would pay for her college tuition, take care of her housing, and even provide a monthly living allowance so she could focus on school and not worry about finding a job.

After a lot of begging and pleading, Millie convinced him to let her and Claire live in their summer cottage until the baby was born, so Claire could give it up for adoption. She did her lessons at home, something her father arranged for her so that she wouldn't get behind in school. With the two of them at the cottage, he could tell everyone Claire and her mom were traveling as they'd always wanted to do.

He'd agreed, and the decision had been made. He even offered to send her on a trip to Europe after the baby was born.

She was supposed to be grateful for his understanding. Grateful. But not once had her parents asked her what she wanted to do. She'd had a desperate need to keep her baby. She knew she was young, but she loved children and dreamed of having a large family one day. Being an only child was lonely, and this baby meant she wouldn't be alone. She was willing to do whatever it took to be a mother, even if it meant finding a job and working for minimum wage.

Millie and Claire stayed at the cottage for the first month after she'd given birth. Millie called it her month of healing, but Claire cried every day.

Her father finally came to pick them up, handing her plane tickets the moment he walked in the door. They were all going on a holiday, a little road trip through the states. They had a timeshare in Florida, and her father thought they all deserved a vacation. From there, Claire and Millie would fly to the UK, where they would tour England and

Scotland before coming home in time for Claire to start school in the fall.

For the first few months, Claire managed to contain her anger toward her father and tried to be a good girl. She lived in a fog, her emotions shut off from everything and everyone. She kept her mouth shut as she traveled with her mom, toured the museums, and went on guided excursions of all the sights.

They arrived back home just in time to get her ready to move to Toronto to attend college. She hardly spoke to her father after her return, but when he handed her the keys to an apartment he'd found, completely furnished, and told her she'd made the right decision, everything inside of her exploded.

She could still remember the anger and the hatred behind the words she'd said to him.

"I can't believe I'm saying this, but I honestly hate you. You took away my decision, and now you're trying to buy me off."

She'd watched as his face softened for one split second and her words hit his heart. "I love you, Claire Bear. I'm just trying to do my best by you. That's all. When you're a parent, you'll understand," he whispered.

She refused to apologize.

"I was a parent. For one hour while I held my son, I was his mother." Tears gathered in her eyes, and she wiped them away angrily. "They asked me in the hospital if I was sure. I could have changed my mind, but I decided not to. Do you know why?" She spat the words out, loathing pouring out of her heart as her father just stood there.

"Because the people who adopted him, who would be a part of his life forever, they wanted him." She choked on the words. "He deserved to be wanted, and they could give him a better life than I could. That was why. Not because of you, not because of your demands and your threats."

For the next four years while she took a creative arts program, she also worked part-time to help pay for her basic needs. Other than what covered her schooling and apartment, she didn't take a penny from her father. Every month when he'd put the money into her account, she would write a check for a group home that helped pregnant teens.

For the first few years, Claire would attempt to talk to her mom about the baby she gave up, but her words always fell on deaf ears. Millie wasn't one to dwell on the past, and that became abundantly clear to Claire on the day of her son's first birthday.

Millie had come by her apartment to take her out for dinner, something she did frequently, and found Claire sitting on her couch, wrapping presents she'd bought for the son she didn't know. She had no idea what was appropriate for a one-year-old boy, so she'd picked up a few outfits, some toys, and books.

"Why would you do this?" Millie took the remaining unwrapped items and set them on the floor. "Why do this to yourself?"

"It's Jack's birthday, Mom. I needed to do something to celebrate it." Claire held a book in her hand and stared at the image on the cover, a little boy surrounded by toys.

"Jack? That's what you named him? I thought—" Millie shook her head as she took the book from Claire's hands. "I thought you understood that his family would pick his name?"

"I did. I do. But I still . . . he was still my little boy, Mom. I needed to give him a name from me."

Millie nodded as she processed that. "Jack, huh? I've always liked that name. It's strong. But honey, you can't be doing this. It's not healthy. Let it go and move on, remember?"

Let it go and move on. Her mother's favorite mantra when it came to anything unpleasant. Let it go and move on. Except, how could you let it go and move on if you've never dealt with it in the first place?

"We all have our own ways of dealing with things, Mom. You like to pretend it never happened. But I need to face it."

Millie sighed. "I don't pretend, Claire. I just choose not to dwell on what happened. And you shouldn't either. Come on. Let's go get dinner. I made reservations at a new Italian restaurant that's getting rave reviews. Why don't you hop in the shower and get ready, and I'll tidy up a little." Millie gathered the plate and cup she'd left on the coffee table and headed to the kitchen.

"Can we make a stop first?" Claire glanced at the wrapped gifts. "There's a group home nearby I'd like to drop these off at, if you don't mind."

Millie stopped but didn't turn around. "What kind of group home?"

From the way she asked, it sounded as if she already knew what Claire would say, but that wasn't possible, was it? Did her mother know about her monthly donations?

"For pregnant teenagers who have been kicked out of their homes, like I was."

"You weren't kicked out, Claire. Stop being so melodramatic." Millie sighed and walked away.

Claire fumed. She was being melodramatic, was she? As far as she was concerned, the moment her pregnant belly could no longer be concealed, she'd been forced to move into their summer cottage, away from family and friends, to live in seclusion. She'd stayed behind when her mother ran errands, drove three hours to a city hospital so she wouldn't be recognized, and then had given up her child.

She wondered if her mother still felt she was being melodramatic even after all these years.

She opened her eyes and watched her mother putter in the garden, tending to flowers that were doing fine on their own. When Millie turned, Claire gave her a little wave.

"It's a bit warm out here." Millie shielded her eyes from the sun. "How about I put the kettle on and make us a nice pitcher of home-made iced tea." She stood.

"You know his birthday is coming up," Claire said quietly. "Each year gets a little bit easier, but it's still like a knife in the heart." Claire sat up in her chair and leaned forward. "Do you ever think of him?"

"The things you ask some days." Millie shook her head. She squeezed Claire's shoulder. "Of course I do, Claire. He'd almost be the age you were when you had him. I'm sure he's had a very full life with his family."

"And there's that knife twisting," she mumbled as her mother walked away.

"Oh Claire. You're your own worst enemy," Millie said with a hint of sadness as she walked into the house, the screen door closing behind her with a loud bang.

NINE

MILLIE

Present day

M illie didn't know what was going on with her daughter, but she wasn't leaving here tonight until she found out.

For days, weeks even, she'd listened to Josh worry and fret over Claire's health, keeping her up-to-date on any little thing, like how much she slept or how little she ate. But today . . . nothing. Josh seemed calm about everything, and Claire seemed quite chipper and not as exhausted.

If she didn't know any better, she'd say Claire was pregnant.

No. She immediately dismissed the thought. Claire would have told her by now, especially after she had reminisced about the time when she was pregnant with Claire. That would have been the perfect time to tell her.

So if she wasn't pregnant, what was it? Did they get a new book deal? Were they going to go ahead with adopting a baby?

Little flutters of hope had Millie clasping her hands together. Maybe that was it. Maybe Claire decided she didn't want to wait after all.

When Josh walked through the front door, arms laden with bags of groceries, Millie was there to help him.

"Welcome home." She beamed at him.

"Um, thanks." Josh gave her a quizzical look, which she ignored.

The moment she'd met Josh, she'd sized him up and known immediately he was the right man for her daughter. He was a partner in life, not a dictator. He worshiped the ground Claire walked on, and that was fine by her.

"Why don't you let me take care of dinner tonight? You go out and relax with my daughter. I know you're working hard on your deadlines"—she patted him on the cheek—"and could use some good homemade food."

"We don't eat out every night." Josh followed her into the kitchen and set the bags on the counter. "I do burgers on the grill too you know."

"Of course you do." She rummaged in the bags, looking through the food he'd bought. Lots of vegetables, some chicken, and a squash.

"I thought I'd grill the chicken and vegetables." Josh started to unload the bags before Millie swatted his hands away.

"I've a better idea."

"Okay then. I'll leave it all in your awesome hands." Josh leaned in and gave her a peck on the cheek. "There's some mint tea chilling in the fridge." He eyed the kettle she had put on the stove.

"Mint tea sounds perfect right about now."

While Millie sorted the vegetables and finalized her plan for dinner, Josh headed out to the patio and gave Claire a hug. Millie couldn't hear what they said, but she caught the way Claire shook her head and Josh glanced back toward her.

Her ears should be burning, but she decided to ignore whatever was going on. If she were right—and let's admit it, she often was—hopefully she could get it out of them tonight. Over dessert.

Which reminded her . . . finding out you were going to be a grandmother, again, merited a celebratory cake.

"Mom?"

Millie turned at the sound of Claire's voice. She saw her daughter pop her head up from the hammock she was resting in.

"Are you cooking dinner?" Claire swung her legs over the side and yawned. "Let me help." She gave her head a small shake, wiped her eyes, and yawned again.

"Don't you even bother yourself. Stay in that hammock and just relax."

"We invited you over for dinner, not to cook it." Millie joined Claire in the hammock, and they swung together in silence.

"Honestly, what can I do to help?" Claire said.

"Nothing. I've got it all prepped. I was just about to make dessert, and no, you can't help me."

Her daughter groaned.

"What's wrong?" Millie squeezed her daughter's hand.

"I just got hit with a killer headache." Claire massaged her temple. "I've never had so many headaches as I have these past two months."

Millie didn't like the sound of that. "Have you talked to Abby about it?"

"No. They're just headaches. Maybe it's time for a good massage and a visit to the chiropractor."

"Sweetheart, you've never been one for headaches. Ever. You get that from me. If you're getting a lot of them, you need to tell Abby. You might need more than just an adjustment and a massage."

"Oh, but have you seen the new massage therapist at the clinic? I seriously think I need a massage." Claire's eyes twinkled.

"I heard that," Josh yelled out the kitchen window.

Claire blushed while Millie laughed.

"Keep him on his toes, girl. It does a marriage good." The moment Millie said it she winced. Who was she to give her daughter marriage advice?

"So," she said to break the awkwardness. "I'd better get busy."

"Seriously, let me help. I'm not an invalid," Claire said as she hopped out of the hammock and then held her hand out for Millie.

Millie ignored the help and stood up, letting the hammock drop from beneath her. "I never said you were. But you're exhausted. Don't bother denying that. While we both know Josh is more than capable of making dinner, you're probably ready for something other than barbecued beef, right?"

"I heard that too," Josh yelled.

"That boy had better not be messing with that food," Millie muttered.

"Oh, you have no idea. I was going to say we should go to the Wandering Table if he suggested another burger."

The Wandering Table was a cute diner owned by one of Claire's old friends from school. Gloria used only fresh, local ingredients. Millie approved of that restaurant, unlike the greasy spoon at the edge of town where everything was fried.

"Gloria would probably offer to make you anything you craved."

Claire laughed. "She would. She thinks I'm too thin as it is."

"But you're eating, right?"

Claire shook her head. "Not really. Josh makes me eat at least one meal, which is usually either lunch or dinner, and then the rest are protein drinks. I'm just not hungry, Mom."

Millie patted the hand resting on Claire's stomach. "It's okay. As long as you're getting something into your body, you're fine." She almost said *baby* but caught herself.

"What's for dinner?" Claire asked.

"Chicken Alfredo, but instead of pasta, I'm using spaghetti squash. And cake." She sat up. "Which reminds me. I'm making it from scratch, so I better get started."

"What kind of cake?"

"Oh, I don't know. Maybe coconut cream?" She tipped her head toward her daughter, knowing it was her favorite.

"I love you, Mom." Claire covered her mouth as she yawned again. "You're the bestest, you know that, right?"

"Oh honey, I know. Now, come with me, and we'll get you something to help with that headache." She recalled the mint tea in the fridge. That would help. She'd also talk to David, and see if he recommended anything else.

With the cake cooling on the rack, Millie prepared the chicken all the while keeping an eye on her daughter. Claire had to be sleeping again. She hadn't stirred for the past half hour in the hammock.

Josh stopped in the kitchen doorway as he caught the aroma of freshly baked cake. "Something smells delicious." Dropping his notebook on the counter, he said, "That's not chocolate." He crossed his arms and frowned.

"No, it's not." Millie smiled to herself as she shook her head at him. *Most men are like little kids when it came to their expectations. If they don't get their way, they pout.*

"When you said cake, I assumed you meant chocolate." His gaze narrowed as he scrutinized the kitchen, and then he went over to peer into the oven.

"No, Josh, there isn't another cake in there." Millie chuckled. "The last cake I made was chocolate. Don't you think it's Claire's turn this time?"

His nose scrunched up. "Coconut cream?"

She nodded.

He sighed. "Next time you'll make a cake I like, right? Please?"

"Go on with you." Millie swatted his arm. "I make you plenty of desserts your wife doesn't eat. How about those chocolate peanut butter cupcakes I brought over last week? Or the key lime pie I made to welcome you home from your trip?"

"True." He sighed again, drooping his shoulders melodramatically. "Fine. Let my darling wife have her cake. She deserves it." The moment he said the words, his eyes lit up.

For a moment, Millie's heart stopped. He almost said something. She could feel it.

"On that note—I have something for my girl to read, so I'd better make sure she's awake," he said as he headed for the patio.

Millie loved to watch the two together. Their love for one another was always sparkling between them, so alive. Seeing them—how good they were together, how in love even after everything they'd been through—gave Millie hope. Not hope for herself, she didn't need that, but for her daughter. That she would always be loved and treasured.

If anyone deserved it, it was Claire.

Millie moved closer to the open kitchen window. She wasn't one to consider eavesdropping beneath her, not when there was something for her to learn.

"Hey, beautiful. I've got some pages for you to read." Josh leaned over and gave Claire a lingering kiss.

Her daughter murmured something before Josh pulled up a chair and raised his legs so his feet rested in the hammock.

"What do you think of Alethea? We could call her Thea," he said. Millie leaned closer.

"We can add it to the list at least. Or Zane for a boy." Josh pulled out a little notepad he had in his back pocket and wrote in it.

Hmmm. Name hunting could mean one of two things. They were searching for names for a new character, something they normally let their followers on Facebook help with, or they were thinking of names for a baby.

She prayed it was for a baby.

After dinner and while they lingered over the coconut cream cake, Millie watched her daughter intently, catching the little hand movements toward her belly, the glances between Claire and Josh. They had a secret.

She hated not knowing secrets.

"Did you hear that Matt and Melissa are having another baby?" Millie leaned back in her chair and sipped at the coffee Josh had made.

Claire's hand stilled as she was about to take a bit of cake. "They are?"

"This will be baby number four. I wonder what they'll call this one." She smiled at the thought. Matt and Melissa owned the local bookstore in town called Something Different. They tended to name their babies after famous authors.

"I remember Matt telling me he always wanted to name a son Tennyson." Josh winked at Claire before he smiled at Millie.

Millie smiled back. "Who knows, maybe they'll actually have a boy this time. Tennyson is a nice name." She took another bite of her cake, keeping her gaze locked on the dessert plate in front of her. "I always thought Elliot would make a nice name for a boy or Avery for a girl."

"Avery"—Claire hesitated for only a second but one that felt like forever—"is a nice name. Maybe we can add it to our list, Josh?"

Millie almost choked.

"Avery is good. We could use it for either too." There was hint of laughter in her son-in-law's voice.

Millie looked up, struggling very hard to keep the smile off her face. "Is there something you're not telling me?" she asked.

"Mom . . ."

"Yes, Claire?"

"There's something we want to share with you." Claire reached over and grabbed Josh's hand. "I meant to tell you earlier, but . . ."

"It's okay, honey." Her daughter didn't need to apologize for need-ing to bring up the past. No doubt it was very much present in her life right now.

"Mom, I'm pregnant." Claire laughed as she made her announcement.

Millie shrieked, jumped up, and hugged her own baby, unable to contain her excitement any longer.

"I knew it!" She danced on the spot. "I'm so happy for you, for you both." She reached for Josh's hand and then realized that wasn't enough. She skipped her way over to him, squeezing tight as she wrapped her arms around his waist.

"So you're okay with being a grandma?" Josh asked, laughing at her.

He could laugh all he wanted. She didn't care. This was a dream come true.

"Well, I'm not sure about the whole *Grandma* part. We'll need to come up with a name that doesn't make me feel old. But having a baby to love, absolutely."

She went over to hug her daughter again. "I'm so happy for you, honey. You will be an amazing mom, full of love and laughter. This little one is a gift. One that will always be cherished. Always."

"You knew, didn't you?" Claire asked, her face beaming.

Millie nodded. "A mother always knows, sweetheart."

"What about Xavier?" Josh tossed the name out of nowhere.

"As in X-Men Xavier, the one who could read minds?" Millie asked. She knew her son-in-law was a comic book junkie, but wasn't that pushing it too far?

"What's wrong with naming our child after a man with superpow-ers?" Josh sat down and leaned back, entwining his hands behind his neck and looking content.

"You're not adding that one to the list," Claire said.

Josh's brows rose as his arms slowly came down, and he pulled out a notebook from his back pocket.

"Wanna bet? We made the deal that any name could go on the list. No name was a bad name. Remember?"

"Xavier is a bad name." Claire shook her head.

"Is not."

"Is too."

Millie laughed.

"Have you told anyone yet?" Millie asked. She was ready to announce it to the world, but knowing her daughter, Claire would likely prefer to keep it close for a little while longer.

"Just Abby. And Dr. Shuman since he was there too." Claire wiped tears from her eyes. "I kind of want to keep it quiet, just for a little bit. We've waited so long for this . . ."

"Well, if I had my way, I'd be throwing you a big party." She watched for her daughter's reaction, but all she did was smile. "Can I?" She clapped her hands together in excitement. There was nothing she liked better than celebrating something, and what better reason than a grandchild?

"No, Mom. You can't. I want to let it soak in first. Okay? They say the first trimester—"

"You just stop it right there." Millie cut her daughter off. "Nothing is going to happen to this baby, do you hear me? Nothing."

TEN

CLAIRE

Present day

Claire sent Abby a quick text to see if she had a free moment. *Bring me a cupcake and I'm all yours. Come to the back,* Abby had replied. So, armed with a cupcake from the Sweet Bites Bakery, Claire met Abby at the back door of the clinic. They meandered over to a picnic table in the grassy area behind the building.

"You are my hero." Abby sat down at the table and swept her finger through the icing of the cupcake. "This is so much better than the ham and Swiss I packed for my lunch."

"Don't ever lecture me on healthy eating again," Claire said with a laugh. The look of pure ecstasy on Abby's face almost made Claire wish she'd bought herself a cupcake. But then, the thought of actually eating it made her stomach a little queasy.

"Where's that too-good-to-be-true hubby of yours?" Abby wiped the crumbs from the corner of her mouth, having inhaled more than half the cupcake.

"Over at the bookstore. And he's not 'too good to be true.' What's up with that?" Abby had made a couple of comments along that line about Josh, and she didn't like it.

"I don't think I've ever heard you two fight. Like, actually fight—you know, yell and scream at one another. That's not normal. You know that, right?"

"I didn't realize yelling and screaming at one another was a requirement for marriage."

"No need to get snarky. I was just making a comment." Abby held her hands up in surrender. "Sorry, I obviously hit a nerve."

"There's no nerve." Claire shook her head, and then said, "Other than something's going on between you and Derek, and you're pushing it onto me. What gives?"

Abby turned on the bench. She splayed her arms across the top of the table and kicked her legs out beneath it. "My husband is a jerk, that's all. Sorry. You're right. Josh is amazing, and I'm just letting my jealousy show."

Claire moved to sit beside her. "All men can be jerks at one time or another."

Abby snorted. "Give me an example of Josh being a jerk in the past week or so. I bet you can't."

Claire took a moment to think about that and realized Abby was right. She couldn't. He might be overbearing and a little too concerned about her health, but that wasn't jerkish behavior—that was just Josh being Josh.

"You can't, can you? I think the last time you really complained about him to me was when you argued over a plot line in one of your books."

Claire winced. "No marriage is perfect, Abby. Not even ours." And yet, she really had nothing to complain about. Right now, they were in sync with one another, and it was amazing. Josh was the perfect partner for her. Did they yell and fight often? No. But they certainly disagreed, and things did get heated.

"Sometimes I wonder." Abby smiled sadly. "I look at you and Josh, and I wish I had a marriage like yours. With someone who was a partner, a real partner. All Derek and I seem to do lately is fight, and it's over stupid things. I'm just so . . . tired of arguing with him, you know?" She shook her head before giving Claire a forced smile.

"What's going on? Really going on?" Claire pressed. This wasn't the first time her friend had alluded to deeper issues in her marriage.

"No one ever really prepares you for what marriage is like. Not really. They don't tell you about the compromises you need to make, or the things you have to deal with. Sometimes," Abby said with a sigh. "Sometimes, I wonder if things wouldn't be easier being single."

"You don't believe that."

"Again, not everyone has the type of relationship you and Josh have. I hate to repeat myself, but . . ." Abby leaned her head back and stared up at the sky. "I love you, Claire, I really do. But sometimes I hate how easy things are for you."

"You've got to be kidding me." *She did not just say that.*

"I'm serious. I know, I know. You've had your own stuff to deal with, but look at you now? You're thriving in a career you love, you've got a husband who would do anything for you, and now you're having that baby you've always dreamed of."

Claire stifled a snort with a deep frown. "So you don't have a career you love? You don't have a husband who loves you? You're not following your dreams? Come on, Abby. What is actually going on here?"

"I don't know. Maybe I'm looking for something that isn't there. Things just . . . don't seem right, you know?" Abby turned sideways on the bench and rested her elbows on her knees.

"Should you go back to that marriage counselor? It helped last time, right?" Claire massaged the back of her neck, kneading deep into the muscle.

"Is that where you normally get your headaches?"

"Josh thinks I should get a massage, that it might help." Claire slowly rolled her neck, stretching to relieve some of the tightness.

"It might. That man loves you—it's so obvious."

"Derek loves you too, Abigail. I think you're just going through a rough patch right now. We all have those." Claire really didn't know what to say. While it wasn't the first time Abigail had mentioned issues with Derek, she'd never gotten a sense of what was beneath the vague complaints her friend made.

"We'll be fine. It is what it is." She checked her watch. "I need to get back inside. Thanks for the cupcake. It was exactly what I needed."

"How about you and Derek come join us for a barbecue soon?" Claire said as she lightly rubbed her belly. "We can celebrate you being the godparents of our little one." She dropped the news and watched for Abby's reaction.

"Sure. We can do that." She turned to walk away. "Wait—did you just say what I thought you said?"

Claire grinned and nodded, too excited for words.

Abby rushed toward her with her arms out for a hug. "Godparents? Really?" The elation in her voice was so apparent there was no mistaking how much this meant to her.

"I couldn't think of anyone else I would want in my child's life more than you. Derek just gets to come along for the ride." Claire felt her heart filling with joy, and laughter bubbled out of her.

"You just made my day. My month. My year. Oh my goodness, Claire. Yes. Yes, of course, I'll be in your child's life." Abby let out a little squeal and jumped up and down.

"Good, because I wasn't asking." Clair tried to smile but winced instead. Keeping her head still as the ache intensified, she closed her eyes and willed herself to ignore the pain, to breathe through it.

"Come inside for a moment. I have something that will help get rid of the pain," Abby said.

Claire grimaced. She wasn't sure anything would get rid of the pain.

ELEVEN

JOSH

Present day

For the umpteenth time, Josh glanced at the bedroom window and frowned. He'd kept the window open in hopes that the sound of the lawn mower as he cut the grass in the backyard would wake Claire up, but so far, nothing. Normally after her nap, she would come to wherever he was, in search of a hug. So he could only take that to mean she hadn't woken up, which was odd.

He'd cut the grass, cleaned up the yard, and decided to call Derek.

"Come over for an early dinner. I'll get the steaks out. You bring the beer," Josh said once Derek answered the call.

"Deal. I thought we were coming over anyways. The girls set this up before you left for Toronto."

Interesting. Claire must have forgotten to mention it.

"Good to know. Well then . . . come early anyways and bring your beautiful wife with you."

"Like I'd come alone." Derek laughed. "Is everything okay with Claire? Give me a heads up, man, 'cause you know Abby is going to want to know how Claire is feeling."

Josh poured fresh coffee into his mug and took a sip.

"I'm not sure. She's sleeping again. She's gotten worse since we came back from visiting Sami. Constant headaches, increased exhaustion." He rubbed his face. "I had to carry her down the stairs today because she was so tired she couldn't walk." He hated seeing her so weak. He wanted to be able to help her, to protect her.

"That can't be good. I'll mention it to Abby. See you later this afternoon then. I'll bring the beer. Abby will bring the wine. Just try not to burn the steaks this time."

"Ooh, ouch." Josh shook his head at the memory of their last barbecue. "Hey, at least my steaks aren't still kicking and mooing once I've cooked them." After delivering his parting shot, he rang off. He was still chuckling to himself as he headed outside to the patio, where he had been working earlier.

He had enjoyed the trip to Europe, but he'd missed his backyard. He liked to sit on the patio to work. Claire, on the other hand, liked to work on her illustrations upstairs, staring out the large bay window into their yard, where their garden beds flourished thanks to Claire's mom's faithful tending and where deer liked to nibble on the long, sweet grasses at their back fence.

Claire had sketches of those deer all over her desk.

He picked up the last page he'd been working on and thought about Claire's comments about them . . . something to do with the daffodils. He'd been struggling with the scene, which is why he'd asked Claire to read it over.

Jack was in Bruges, Belgium, not Amsterdam where the fields of tulips thrived. Maybe that was his problem.

Josh looked over his notes and Claire's chicken scratches in the margins and reread her ideas. Chocolate shops, water canals, convent grounds full of flowers. She'd seen a dog limping down a narrow street one day. In the notes, she had written the words *wounded dog* and underlined them three times.

A scene played out in Josh's mind: Jack, their little boy with an overactive imagination, let go of his mother's hand in the crowded square to follow a dog he'd noticed limping alongside the street. He could hear Jack's mom sighing as she followed her son, never wanting to hold him back, always giving in to his adventures, and always ensuring he was okay.

Except, he'd already planned a scene like that for Paris. He needed something else in Bruges.

Their goal with the stories was to teach children to explore, to discover, to let their imaginations run wild. Claire was the one who insisted Jack's mother always be there in the background, watching over her son. After all, what mother in her right mind would let her child wander off in a strange country?

He turned the page of his notes and saw another scribble from his wife. *Chocolate shops = my scene.*

It wasn't often Claire requested her own scenes with the stories. Normally she left those to him, offering suggestions if they occurred to her during her read-throughs, but keeping her focus on the illustrations. So when she asked to have her own scenes, he generally gave in.

Maybe he'd work on the London story instead. There were a few scenes he could flesh out, and he knew Claire was almost finished with the illustrations. If things went well, they could have that story in before month's end.

He opened up the folder and flipped to the section for London. He preferred to write everything longhand before keying it into the computer. He felt more connected to the story that way. He found a section he'd wanted to work on and let the story play like a movie in his head. Then he began to write.

There were funny men, all dressed up in red costumes, telling stories to tourists at the Tower of London. Jack's mom tried to drag him toward a large group to hear the story, but he wanted to explore.

Exploring was Jack's specialty. His gift. What he was meant to do.

While his mom listened to a funny man tell a story about a king, Jack looked around him. To one side was a green park space, right in the middle of the courtyard. It wasn't the green grass he was interested in. No, you can find grass anywhere.

What he found interesting were the large black crows that walked around the grass, as if they owned the place.

Jack slowly backed away from his mom, careful to keep his footsteps light as he approached the crows. Why didn't they fly away? What would it be like to be a crow, inside a palace, being stared at by people just like him?

Josh knew this scene was flat, that it needed more . . . but all he could think about was Claire.

He thought back to the day when they visited the Tower of London. It had been a cloudy day, and the grounds were somewhat empty. Beefeaters, the guards in the red uniforms, walked around the grounds and led the tours. Claire and Josh marveled at the history and the amusing stories the beefeater told of bygone kings and guests from years long past.

The grounds were full of bronze statues of animals, reminders of the zoo that was once housed inside for the sole pleasure of the king.

But it was the living crows that had caught Josh's eye. They weren't regular crows like the ones they had here at home. These crows were large and cheeky, coming right up to people as if questioning just what they were doing there. In fact, one followed Claire around and even tried to snag a thread trailing from her scarf before a guard came by and stood between Claire and the bird.

There was an old legend that if the crows disappeared from the Tower of London, then London would fall to its enemies, and so, they kept these crows here on the grounds, their wings clipped, to ensure that prophecy never came true. He wanted to use that somehow in Jack's London adventure.

He worked on the scenery, describing it in vivid detail so that, through his words and Claire's illustrations, the children reading it could picture themselves there, in the middle of the tower grounds. He'd let Claire sleep for a little bit longer before he woke her up.

"All right, where's the lazy bum?" Derek called out as Josh opened the door. Abby followed close behind, her arms heavy with grocery bags.

"She's out in the hammock. I thought you were just bringing some beer?" Josh grabbed the bags from Abby and led the way into the kitchen.

"Josh, we all know you cook a mean steak, but when it comes to the rest of the meal . . ." Abby put her hand over her mouth, pretending to stop herself from going too far. "With Claire being so tired, I figured if we wanted to eat something other than meat, I'd better take care of it myself."

"Hey!" Josh said in mock outrage. "I bought corn, I'll have you know. And it's currently in the pot waiting to be boiled."

He watched Abby unloading the grocery bags she'd brought, and his mouth began to water at the homemade potato salad and veggie kebabs she unwrapped.

"But I won't look a gift horse in the mouth either," he said.

Derek set the case of beer he'd brought on the counter. A superfluous case of beer, since Josh still had half a case left over from the last barbecue they'd held. Neither of the guys were big drinkers—they'd have a beer or two with the meal, and that was it.

"Why don't I just add these to our collection?" Josh grinned as he opened the fridge door and indicated the bottom shelf, where there were at least a dozen bottles already.

"At the rate we're going, we'll be able to throw another huge block party, and be the heroes with all the free alcohol." Derek rubbed the back of his neck then punched Josh in the arm.

The moment Abby left the kitchen to check on Claire, Josh turned to Derek, a serious look on his face.

"I'm really worried, man." He pushed back his shoulders, cracking his spine. "She can hardly stay awake, and it's getting worse by the day."

Derek pulled out a chair from the table and straddled it. "Dude, she's pregnant."

"I think it's more than that though." Josh frowned as he stared outside and watched Abby wake up his wife.

She was already so delicate. This pregnancy made her more so.

Derek's fist thumped on the chair with a dull thud. "I wouldn't worry so much. Besides, she has my wife taking care of her. She's in good hands. Now . . . I've been drooling over the idea of a steak all day."

Josh balled up a napkin from the counter and tossed it toward his friend. "Wipe off the drool, buddy. They need another half hour to marinate."

Derek popped up from his chair and went to the counter where Josh had set out a covered dish he'd grabbed from the fridge. Derek leaned in for a peek, putting his hand on the lid.

Josh slapped his hand. "Hands off. You don't mess with perfection."

"Fine, fine." Derek backed away. "Hey, by the way, I think you're missing some receipts from your trip. There's a whole two weeks missing from April."

Josh grabbed his phone and scrolled through his calendar. "That's when we were in Venice and then traveled to Rome." All throughout their trip, Josh had kept all their receipts neatly recorded in a file folder system. The receipts should all have been in there for Derek, their accountant, to manage. "Are you sure?"

"Dude, I got nothing for either of those places." He held up his hand and counted on his fingers. "I've got Istanbul, Bruges, London, Paris, your cruise, and . . ." His brows furrowed. Finally, he said, "And some other place. But no Rome and no Venice."

"I'll check my computer bag, see if they're in there, and get back to you."

"Great." Derek nodded. "You know, just as an FYI, you're already over budget without those two cities."

Josh nodded and stared out the window again. "Kind of hard to say no to Claire, you know? She needed more time, and I wasn't going to force her to come home."

Derek clasped Josh's arm. "I know. It's not like you couldn't afford it, and I get it. If Abby . . . I wouldn't have said no either." Derek leaned back against the counter. "How's Jack, anyways?"

Josh smiled. He got a kick out of how his friends referred to his fictional character as if he were a real boy.

"Jack is good. Jack has at least another six stories in him, and I may have found a way to get him to Australia." His eyes brightened at the idea. He'd mentioned it to Julia, their editor, a few days ago, and she was all for it.

"Good on ya, mate!" Derek forced an exaggerated Australian accent into his voice. "Abby and I will join you for sure if you go."

They'd talked for the past few years of doing a trip Down Under, but the timing had never worked out.

"I'm thinking a cruise. Cheaper than a flight and a lot more fun," Josh suggested. He had been so excited about the trip that he had already looked into the costs of a flight versus another cruise. Of course, once they found out that Claire was pregnant, all thoughts of another trip had gone right out the window.

He'd enjoyed cruising with Claire. Despite doing a little bit of work, they'd also relaxed, and for a few days, Josh had seen a difference in his wife. A glow on her face, more ease in her walk, less tension in her shoulders. He had no doubt he could convince her to do another cruise. What would it be like with a baby, though? Could it still be relaxing? He wondered whether Claire would suggest waiting a few years.

"Earth to Josh: you've got a baby on the way. Do you really think now is the time to be planning your next vacation? Dude, even I know that's not a smart move. Unless . . . we do it before the little tyke arrives."

"Something to think about at least. Let's mention it to the girls. For all I know, they've already got it planned, and we're the ones needing to catch up." Josh stared out the window again and noticed Abby struggling to help Claire out of the hammock. Even from this distance, he could tell she was pale. Paler than she'd been an hour ago.

TWELVE

CLAIRE

Present day

"Claire honey, you need to wake up."

The weights holding down her eyelids wouldn't lift.

"I can't." Her voice came through a fog, heavy and thick.

"Sure you can. Just open your eyes."

Claire felt the soft brush of Abby's hand on her forehead and then a hand on her shoulder. She tried her best to comply with her best friend's request. Abby and Derek were here for dinner, and she needed to get up. Josh had promised to wake her up in time.

"I'm sorry," Claire murmured, although she wasn't sure if she was apologizing for not being able to wake up or for being asleep when Abby arrived.

It probably didn't matter.

"Honestly? I thought we broke you of this habit years ago," Abby complained as she gripped both of Claire's hands and attempted to pull her into a seated position.

Claire tried to help, she really did, but her body had turned to lead, and there was no way she could move.

"Wow, you weren't kidding when you said you were lethargic, huh?" She heard Abby let out a long sigh before she released her hands.

"She's being stubborn, eh?" Her husband's voice was close by, and despite the teasing tone, she heard the concern beneath it.

"If I'd known this was a slumber party, I would have worn the new pajamas Derek bought me while you were traveling. You'd like them, Claire. Wonder Woman bottoms and tank top."

"All she needs is that golden lasso, and I'm in wet-dream heaven," Derek's voice called out.

"That's enough out of you," Abby admonished him.

"I've got a fresh pot of coffee on. I think you might need to drink it tonight. All of it." Josh placed a kiss on her forehead before he lifted her out of the hammock.

"Claire, have you been taking the prenatal supplements I prescribed?" Abby asked once Josh had set her down in the lounger. He tucked a wool throw around her feet, knowing that her toes were cold without her having to say it.

"She has," Josh answered for her. "I make her take them every morning."

Claire caught the look of worry on Abby's face and turned her gaze toward her backyard.

"Claire?"

Claire shrugged. "They make me feel sick."

Abby threw up her hands.

"You've got to work with me, Claire. One pill, three times a day, with meals." She shook her head in disgust. "How many meals is she eating, Josh?"

"I'm right here you know. I can speak for myself." Claire knew her voice was weak, but she hated being treated like a child, even if she deserved it.

"Well then?" Abby asked, her arms folded over her chest.

"Calm down," Derek said.

Abby turned toward him, and Claire could see the fire in her gaze.

"Look at her, Derek. I can't help her if she won't help herself." She turned toward Claire and waited a few moments. An angry Abby was never a good thing.

"Take the pills, Claire. Please?"

Claire nodded.

"Are you still nauseous? Or has that passed?"

Claire shrugged. "If I said yes, would you lay off?"

"No." Abby was stern. "You still need to eat. You've got a little one to take care of now. Your first job as a mother is to do everything you can to ensure a healthy start for this baby, and you can't do that if you aren't taking care of yourself." She glared at Claire. "That means you have to eat." Her voice was stern, her gaze sharp, but then it softened. "Are you at least drinking the protein shakes I brought over?"

"You do realize they're disgusting, right?" There was only one powder she really liked so far—Creamsicle flavored. She had it for breakfast every morning . . . or at least she tried to have it for breakfast every morning.

"I don't care if they taste like chalk. You need them. Seriously, how do you expect your body to function if you're not giving it enough fuel? Take the pills. Eat or drink your calories. You want to get better? That's my medical advice."

Claire looked to Josh for support, but he shook his head. He was probably happy to have Abby play the heavy, repeating everything Josh had been saying for weeks now.

"Fine." She might as well argue with a rock.

"Great." Derek rubbed his hands together. "Can we please start the grill for those steaks?"

The tension broke, as always, thanks to Derek. Abby visibly relaxed in her chair. Claire reached out and skimmed her friend's knee with her fingers.

"How are you doing?" It was a loaded question that sounded inno-cent enough, but with the boys out of earshot, it was the perfect time to ask. "Things don't seem to be getting better."

Abby rolled her eyes. "Let's not ruin the day with talk of my mar-riage, okay?"

"Okay." Claire covered her mouth as she yawned. "You seem tense. What gives?"

Abby sighed. "The anniversary of Mark's death is tomorrow." Her body slumped forward as she rested her elbows on the patio table. "It's been two years, but it still doesn't seem real. Sometimes when the phone rings, I think it's him telling me his tour is over and he's on his way home."

"How is your mom handling it?"

Abby's head drooped, and she sighed with resignation. "We always knew there were risks with Mark being in the military, but my mom never thought anything would actually happen. And she didn't get a chance to say good-bye."

"She didn't, but you did," Claire said softly.

Abby nodded. "Every so often she'll ask me about our last Skype chat, as if she can't live without hearing his last message to her again. It breaks my heart every time I have to retell it."

"She should get the words printed and framed. That way your mom can hang it on the wall and stop calling every time the sports recap is on," Derek grumbled halfheartedly as he walked back into the room.

Claire arched an eyebrow. "That might not be such a bad idea, Derek." She readjusted herself in the lounger so she was sitting more upright, a sudden burst of energy hitting her.

"What do you mean?"

"Mark's message to your mom is short but heartfelt. I can sketch something out, maybe paint a watercolor scene for it, and get it framed. It's a nice idea."

Abby closed her eyes for one brief moment before she smiled at Claire, leaning over and giving her a slightly awkward hug.

"You'd do that?"

"Of course." She'd actually love doing it. "Didn't Mark send her a bouquet of flowers for Mother's Day too?"

Abby winced. Mark had arranged for flowers to be delivered, never realizing she would receive them on the same day the news of his death arrived. And, he'd preordered for the following year as well, thinking he'd still be overseas.

Claire remembered how destroyed Liz had been when those flowers arrived.

"If you by chance have a photo of him, could you send it to me? I'll add those as well." An idea formed in her mind of what she would create. It had to be beautiful and touching—something Elizabeth could look at for the rest of her life, a way for her to find some semblance of peace around the death of her son.

"Claire Turner, you are an amazing human being. You know that, don't you?" Derek had leaned forward and grabbed hold of his wife's free hand.

Claire blushed before she turned her gaze. She wasn't amazing. Far from it. But she loved Abby and her mother, and if her gift could help them, then it was the least she could do.

"Ready for coffee, love?" Josh joined them on the patio, carrying the coffeepot in one hand and the platter of steaks in the other.

"Claire, have you thought about maybe switching to decaf?" Abby said.

Claire eyed the mugs and shook her head.

"With the amount you guys drink, it might not be the best thing for the baby. Drink more tea instead."

Derek jumped up from his seat to grab the steaks. He carried them to the grill, and carefully arranged them, one by one, on the hot grate.

"I've got firsties on whatever portion of steak Claire doesn't eat tonight," he called out over his shoulder.

"*Firsties?* Is that even a word?" Abby asked.

Derek shrugged. "If the hobbits get elevenses, then I get firsties."

Josh poured fresh coffee into a mug for Claire, filling it halfway.

Claire rolled her eyes. "Can I please have a *whole* cup, Josh?"

With a hint of hesitation, he topped off the mug. Then he went over to Derek and mock pushed him away from the barbecue.

"First off, the only person who eats my wife's steak is me. That was in our marriage contract." He winked at Claire. "And second, you don't touch another man's barbecue. That is in the man code, paragraph three, section two." He grabbed the spatula, and pointing it toward Derek said, "Don't make me burn your steak, buddy. 'Cause you know I'll do it."

Derek shuddered before backing off with his hands up. "Whatever you say, man. Whatever you say."

Claire laughed. Inviting their friends for dinner had been a good idea. She was still exhausted, but she could see that having them over was helping Josh. The worry that had descended on him was starting to let up. There was a lightness in his stance and demeanor now, as though he no longer felt alone in carrying the burden of anxiety, the sense that something was wrong with her.

As if reading her thoughts, Abby leaned over.

"I expect you to eat as much steak as you can, I hope you realize. Doctor's orders and all that. The protein will be good for you."

Claire lifted her arm slightly in a weak attempt at a salute. "Yes, ma'am. Whatever you say, ma'am."

"On that note," Abby said, raising her voice. "I expect to see you in my office first thing in the morning, for some more blood work."

Josh turned and flashed Abby a smile. "She'll be there."

Claire leaned her head back and stared up at the sky. "I hate getting poked. You know that."

"Guess you should have been taking those pills." There was a satisfied gloat in Abby's voice for a moment. "Only a couple of jabs, I promise. You're probably just anemic. Besides, you've got a baby to take care of now, so pull up your big-girl panties." Abby said.

"I'd like to wear my sexy-girl panties for as long as I can, thank-you-very-much. Which reminds me . . . Will you come shopping with me for maternity wear? I'd rather you than my mother."

"Can we please stop talking about underwear and your mother in the same sentence?" Josh asked.

THIRTEEN

MILLIE

Present day

Millie rang the doorbell to her best friend's home and then let herself in.

Liz was in the kitchen, wrapping an apron around her waist.

"I need your help," Millie said as she walked in.

"Did you bring the apples?" Liz looked at Millie's empty hands, and her eyebrows rose to heights only Liz could accomplish.

"Don't give me that look. They're in the car. I think. Or maybe I left them at the booth at the market." She bit her lip. "I can't remember, but that's not important. I need your *help*." She wrung her hands and could hardly believe the way her stomach felt. Forget butterflies in your stomach, what she had was a swarm of bees, stinging her over and over with fear and doubt, and excitement, all at the same time.

What had she done?

"Unless this has something to do with helping me make an apple pie, it can wait." Liz's lips tightened into a thin white line.

"Don't you be like that with me, Elizabeth Dorn. I think I made a mistake—the worst one yet. And I really need your help. Your apples can wait."

"Millie . . ." Liz shook her head, looked at the ball of piecrust still wrapped in plastic and sighed.

Millie sat down at the table and waited for her friend to put the dough back in the fridge and join her. Her knee bounced rapidly.

"Claire might kill me," she blurted out the moment Liz sat down.

Liz leaned back in her seat. "I doubt that. She loves you."

Millie shook her head. "No, I'm serious."

"What did you do, Millie?" Liz sighed. "Does this have anything to do with her having a baby?"

Millie bit her lip. "I should go get those apples for you." She couldn't admit what she'd done, not even to her best friend. She knew it'd been a mistake. She didn't need Liz's frowning face to confirm it.

"Yes, you're going to go get my apples. But not until you spill the beans."

Millie rubbed her face and then, putting her head in her hands, sat still. "I contacted Marie." She closed her eyes at this confession. Silence filled the room.

Marie was the woman who had adopted Claire's baby sixteen years ago. Unbeknownst to Claire, Marie and Millie had kept in touch throughout the early years. Millie had an envelope full of photos of her grandchild hidden away in a desk drawer.

She'd promised Liz years ago to end contact with Marie. She realized maintaining a relationship with Marie wasn't worth the risk of losing her daughter.

Finally, Millie opened her eyes and saw her friend staring at her with a look of exasperation.

"Stupid move, right?" Millie said.

"I'd say." Liz got up from the table, shaking her head as she did so.

"We'll talk about how you got the idiotic idea that that would be even remotely acceptable after you go get my apples." Liz grabbed hold of Millie's hand, pulled her to standing, and walked her to the front door.

"I'm sure they're in my car." She distinctly remembered buying them this morning.

"No, they're not. You left them with David. He called to see if I wanted him to drop them off."

Millie blushed. "I left them with him, huh?"

"I think you did it on purpose." Liz frowned. "Just don't flirt too much, okay? Keep in mind I'm here waiting for you."

Millie stiffened and straightened her shoulders, in a show of taking no notice of all the other emotions flooding through her right now. "I do not flirt." She walked past her friend, a serious look on her face. But once she was at her car, she looked back and smiled. "Well, maybe just a little." She needed to see a smile on her friend's face, to know that while she'd made a really stupid mistake, it was still a forgivable one.

"Then maybe stop holding back. Hurry up now."

Stop holding back? This little flirtation between her and David had gone on for years. She liked the man, liked the attention he gave her and the way he made her heart beat a little bit faster, but she didn't need him in her life. She enjoyed her independence, the feeling that she was free to do what she wanted, when she wanted, and with whomever she wanted.

When her husband passed away ten years ago, she had promised herself that she would never need a man again. She wasn't the type who wanted to be controlled or who needed to be pampered and taken care of. Not anymore. Not again. All she wanted was to be loved. But she didn't think that concept was something most men her age could grasp.

Especially not David. He continually hinted that he could look after her, if only she'd let him. When would he realize that she didn't need or want that? She wasn't a girl who needed to be rescued. She loved life, loved enjoying life to its fullest. And she would rather have a man at her side who appreciated that, not one who tried to squash it.

No. The flirtation was fine, but that was as far as it went.

Even if the sight of him as he waited for her by his pickup made her heart dance.

She pulled up and stepped out of her car. "Did Liz call?"

"That she did. Also warned me that there would be consequences if I didn't send you on your way right after giving you the apples you left behind." He was leaning against his truck.

"You know Liz and her pies." Millie rolled her eyes.

David stood and grabbed the bags of apples sitting on the tailgate. "I sure do. She promised me my own Dutch apple pie too."

Millie opened her trunk for him and watched the muscles in his arms work as he carried the two heavy bags in one hand. For a man his age, he sure had a fine physique.

"Thanks for waiting for me." Millie smiled up at him.

He studied her, shading his eyes from the sun as he always did. "What's got you wound so tight?"

The fact that he'd noticed surprised her. "Have you ever done something you don't want to regret doing even though you know you should?"

There was a look in his eyes, as if he could see inside her soul. He leaned down and cupped his mouth close to her ear.

"All the time. Especially when it comes to you."

Millie blushed. "Now David Jefferies, enough of that."

"You've either done something you know you shouldn't have, or you're about to do it despite knowing you'd be better off not."

She frowned.

"I hear you're about to become a grandma. Or is it *Nana*?" He said casually.

She beamed. "Isn't it amazing! But how did you hear? They're wanting to keep it hush-hush for now. Oh, which reminds me. What type of tea would you recommend for headaches? Claire's getting some really bad ones."

"Peppermint tea. It'll help with the nausea as well. Ginger is good too. My favorite, though, is called skullcap. Let me check to see if I have some left. If not, I'll order it. And . . . as to how I found out, that doesn't matter. I promise not to tell a soul, but it'll cost ya." He nudged her with his elbow, and even though he tried to look serious, his lips quirked at the corners.

She rolled her eyes. "What'll it be this time? More of my oatmeal chocolate chip cookies?"

He shook his head and pulled his arms behind his back. His voice lowered and took on a drawl she hadn't heard in a while.

"Dinner with me. Tonight."

"Tonight?" He'd never asked her out on an actual date before. Sure, they'd stopped for coffee after running into each other in town, but this was more.

She took a deep breath. "Don't you know, David Jefferies, that when you finally ask a girl on a date, you're supposed to give her time to prepare?"

"You've got time. I'd love it if you wore that cute little black top with the pink flowers on the hem, and those jeans you're wearing are just fine." His gaze slid down her body, and for a moment, she felt like a teenager again.

Until she realized what he'd just done.

Told her what to wear. Controlling. Just like every other man in her life. It disappointed her. She'd hoped he was different.

That's not how things worked with her, and it was time he realized that.

"Sorry, David. Tonight, I've got plans. How about I make you a cheesecake to make up for it, though? I'll swing it by in a few days." She shut the trunk and, before he could say a word, got into the driver's seat, closed the door, and pulled away.

A glance in her rearview mirror told her she'd shocked him. He hadn't moved, other than to fold his arms across his chest.

She'd expected him to be angry, but the smile on his face told her otherwise.

"You what?" Liz's mouth gaped open as Mille dropped the apples in the sink.

"Close your mouth, girl, and don't pretend to be so surprised." She rolled her eyes but smiled inwardly. It felt good, after all these years, to say no.

Even if she'd really wanted to say yes.

"You're not a teenager anymore, Millie Jack, so stop acting like one. Not to mention, you've flirted enough with the man . . . why wouldn't you go on a date?"

Millie turned and put a hand on her hip. "Because he told me what to wear."

This time it was Liz's turn to roll her eyes, and Millie didn't appreciate it.

"And what, in heaven's name, did the poor man ask you to wear?" Liz turned on the tap to soak the apples.

"That cute black top with the embroidered flowers that I picked up in Bayfield a few months ago." It was a pretty shirt that made Millie feel at least ten years younger, which, at her age, meant a lot.

"What's wrong with wearing it? The man must obviously like you in it."

"The man"—Millie gave her friend a stern look—"had better like me in anything I put on. But that doesn't give him the right to tell me what to wear."

"Oh, honey." Liz dropped the apples back into the sink full of water and held out her hands.

Millie eyed them with suspicion and then slowly reached out.

"Not every man wants to control you." Liz squeezed her hands tight as her eyes got misty.

"I know that." What was wrong with Liz? "Don't you start crying on me now, you hear?"

"I'm not."

"Yes, you are."

"I'm fine." Liz dropped her hands and turned, but not before Millie noticed her wiping the tears with her apron.

She sighed. Liz was very fragile, and Millie tried hard to help keep her friend's spirits up. That's when it hit her. Today was the anniversary of her son's death. Mark had died in Afghanistan.

Millie rubbed Liz's back.

"I'm okay," Liz said. Millie could hear the grief in her voice.

"Of course you are."

"Give love a chance, Millie," Liz said. "You never know when it may be too late."

"Honey, if I die today, I will die a happy woman. I've dealt with my mistakes, with my past, and moved on. I don't need to be loved by another man, and having that love won't complete me. You know this."

Millie loved who she was. She loved life. She loved how she lived—with abandon, happiness, and peace. She didn't need a man in her life. But, that didn't mean she wouldn't welcome one, if he were the right one.

"What I know, Millie Jack, is that you are a very stubborn woman who believes she can do everything on her own. Well, you can't. There will come a time when you realize that, and I hope to God you haven't pushed everyone away by then."

Shocked at Liz's outburst, Millie dropped the apple she was wiping off, splashing water everywhere.

"I'm sorry," they said in unison, but for two very different reasons.

Millie mopped up the water with a towel, while Liz dropped her knife and began to sob.

"Oh, sweetie." Millie gathered her friend in her arms.

Two years ago today, Captain Mark Dorn, Elizabeth's eldest son, was killed by an IED, an improvised explosive device, while traveling with a convoy in Afghanistan. He was there in a mentoring capacity, which meant he was supposed to have been safe. At least, that's what he promised his mom before he left.

On the day Liz found out about his death, flowers had arrived to celebrate Mother's Day. An hour later, the phone had rung. Liz had thought it was Mark, calling her as a surprise.

It had been his commanding officer instead.

"Elizabeth Dorn, you don't have to be strong with me."

"He liked my apple pies." Liz pulled away, sniffling.

"That's because you make the very best in town."

"I know." Liz managed a smile. "Can you do me a favor now?"

Millie nodded.

"Leave me alone?" She picked up the knife and held it over one of the apples on the cutting board. "I can't handle your mess right now. I'd like to bake my pie in peace, think about my son, and blubber like a baby without feeling foolish. Tomorrow can be all about you."

Millie gave Liz a hug, squeezing her tight. "That's fair. You blubber all you want." Elizabeth Dorn would be okay. She was tough and strong and could weather this storm called grief. She might falter a little here and there, but that was expected. And when she did, Millie would be there, to hold her up and give her a smile.

After all, it's what Liz did for her all those years ago when her husband had died.

MY FEW (BUT AMAZING) CAREER GOALS

1. Make a name for myself.
2. Work for myself.
3. Establish a client list.
4. Create one drawing for myself at least once a year.
5. Create a book of my drawings.
6. Have books I've illustrated land on a *New York Times* bestseller list (or any other list).
7. Illustrate for someone really famous.

FOURTEEN

CLAIRE

Present day

With legs crossed, Claire sat on her bed looking through a box full of stationery she'd collected over the years. Her collection included postcards she'd picked up, along with the odd notecard and stickers to go on the back sides of envelopes.

She'd also collected miscellaneous kinds of paper. Vellum, laid and linen, matte and glossy, even some vintage stationery designs—anything that caught her eye. She loved paper, its texture and heft, loved to draw on it, and adored writing letters.

She'd always been keen on letter writing, despite it being an art whose popularity was rapidly dwindling. As a teen, she'd often sent postcards and letters to pen pals and summer-camp friends. But then the Internet took off, and it became easier to keep in touch via e-mail. These days she only wrote letters occasionally, although always at least once a year for Josh on their anniversary.

Wouldn't it be nice to write letters to her child every year for their birthday? Maybe set them aside, to be opened and read when they were older?

But why wait for a birthday? Why not start now, from the beginning?

She sorted through the papers, looking for the perfect sheet.

She picked one that was soft white with an almost satin finish. She drew her knees up and placed the paper over one of her sketchbooks, so she had a hard surface to write on.

What would she write? How could she express the feelings in her heart for this child—the love, the wonder, the excitement?

She'd never written her son a letter. She'd often thought about it, but she knew that writing him a letter would hurt more than help. Her fear was that if she wrote to him, she'd never get over him, that she would always mourn for what could have been, and that it would hinder her efforts to move forward.

Her hand shook slightly as she held the pen. The only thing she knew about being a mother was how to give up a child. Would she be able to love this one enough?

When Josh first proposed to her, she'd been petrified that he'd find out the truth about her—that she'd had a teenage pregnancy, that she'd given a child up for adoption, and that she was never good enough in her father's eyes. Claire handed the ring back to Josh and told him he deserved someone better.

She would never forget his words. She glanced over at a frame on the wall opposite their bed.

> *Once upon a time, a boy met a girl who made him believe in love.*
> *She changed his world, his heart, and his life.*
> *The happily-ever-after he always searched for was with her.*

She'd melted into a puddle at his words. She'd said yes and kept her fears to herself. But she knew that one day he would leave her. When she finally told him about the baby she'd given up as a teenager, she'd been certain he would call off the wedding and want nothing to do with her. Instead, he'd held her close and told her he'd support her in any decision she made, and that one day, if it was what she wanted, he would love to meet her firstborn son.

She prayed that one day they both would.

Dear child of my heart,

She wrote those words without thought. *Child of my heart . . .* Which child was she writing to?

FIFTEEN

CLAIRE

Present day

D o you think the guys would mind if we stayed the night?" Abby
studied her fingernails as she relaxed in a salon chair.

They'd driven down to London, Ontario, the city closest to them,
for their girls' trip, something they did every three or four months.
Their trips usually consisted of shopping and then recuperating at a
spa before heading back home. Sometimes they would spend the night
in the city. Today, they'd planned a day trip to pick up some maternity
clothes for Claire and indulge in a little pampering.

Claire glanced up from the magazine she was reading. Two weeks
had passed, and Claire's energy had returned somewhat. She still suffered monstrous headaches, but otherwise she was feeling a lot better.
It probably helped that she was about twelve weeks along, which meant
she was passing that first trimester mark.

"We haven't done it in a long time, and we deserve a girls' night,
right?" Abby continued.

"We do. Do you think we could find a hotel so late though?" Claire
reached for her phone to start searching, but when Abby giggled, she
knew.

"You booked us a room already, didn't you? Our favorite hotel?" She couldn't keep the grin off her face. Of course Abby booked them at their hotel, and of course she didn't think to mention it before they'd left earlier today.

"I grabbed a few extra things for you while you were on the phone." Abby gave her a lopsided grin, and Claire just shook her head.

Abby had stopped by the house that morning with coffee and homemade lemon loaf and proposed a girls' trip. Claire hadn't wanted to go. She was behind on her deadline and needed as much time as possible to get caught up, but between Abby's prodding and Josh's pushing her out the door, she'd had no choice.

A client had called just as they were leaving. Claire took the call, and while she had been on the phone in her office, Abby had apparently packed for her.

"Please tell me you remembered a toothbrush at least?"

Abby nodded. "And your hairbrush. And I plucked a shirt and shorts from the folded clothes on your bed, so you don't have to sleep nude. Oh, and I even grabbed some deodorant and a top for you to wear tomorrow." She gave a thumbs-up. "I've got you covered, girlfriend."

Abby held out a palette of nail polish colors and pointed to a bright pink. "Do you think this color will look good?"

"So we'll be twinsies?" Claire nodded toward her own toenails, which were in the process of being painted the exact shade Abby had picked out.

"No," Abby huffed. "I don't know what color will go with my fingernails then."

"You have a French manicure. You can choose any color for your toes. What about that blue you had last summer?" Claire pointed to a segment on the color wheel in Abby's hands.

"That did look good, didn't it? And maybe if we add a little flower design too?" Her smile brightened as the aesthetician working on her feet nodded back at her.

Claire resumed flipping through her magazine.

"So . . . you good with staying the night? I searched online and found some maternity stores that we can check out tomorrow," Abby said.

Claire set the magazine down again. She sipped from her glass of sparking apple juice and looked longingly at Abby's wine.

"Great. I'm definitely up for some shopping. And tonight we can order in, rent a movie, and gossip. We should stop at a bakery and get some cupcakes or something to make it official."

It had been a long time since she had spent time alone with Abby.

Ever since she and Josh had returned from their trip, it felt like everything was all about her. Her exhaustion. Her headaches. Her blood work. Her pregnancy. She knew Abby struggled with talking about what was really bothering her, whether it was her marriage, missing her brother, or something else. Maybe tonight she'd open up.

"I've got all that taken care of. Don't worry." Abby patted her arm. "We've got cupcakes, finger food, nonalcoholic wine for you and the real stuff for me, chips and dip, popcorn, and there's even a mystery box from Sweet Bites. Kat packed it when I mentioned we were off to pamper ourselves, and I noticed Kim slipped in a note too."

"Did you read it?"

Abby shook her head. "Figured we'd read it later."

"We should have invited them. It would have been a fun night."

Abby gave her a look. "Are you kidding? It's been ages since it was just you and me. Girl, we need this." She played with the buttons on her chair and moaned as the massager turned on. "I need this," she said quietly.

Claire reached out and held her friend's hand. She squeezed tight before letting go.

"Do you realize, by this time next year, you'll have a baby in your arms?" There was a wistfulness in Abby's voice.

Claire smiled as she rubbed her stomach. "It's amazing, isn't it? Do you think you and Derek will ever have kids?"

Abby leaned her head back and closed her eyes. "I'm more than happy to live vicariously through you, darling. More than happy."

"So you haven't changed your mind?"

"Nope. And"—she held her hand up—"before you start to give me the spiel about it never being the right time, I get it enough from my mother, thank-you-very-much."

Claire copied Abby and turned her massager on. The rollers going up and down her back felt good.

"Don't you fall asleep on me, Claire Turner."

Claire opened her eyes, and blinked several times. "I'm not."

Abby snorted. "You were asleep for a good twenty minutes. Come on, we're all done and paid up. Time to get to the hotel."

Claire yawned while she swung her legs over the side and glanced down at her pretty toes. She apologized to the technician and handed her a tip before following Abby out to the car.

"I can't believe I fell asleep," she said as they drove to the hotel.

"I was surprised you didn't fall asleep sooner."

Claire rubbed her forehead, pressing her finger in deep. A headache was coming on, and sometimes massaging her head helped.

"You okay?" Abby asked.

"Just a bit of a headache." She reached for her purse and pulled out Tylenol. She put three in her hand and reached for her water bottle.

"Three? Regular strength?" Abby asked.

"Extra."

"A bit excessive for a headache, don't you think?"

Claire shook her head and then popped all three pills into her mouth.

"How bad is the pain?"

"It's sharp, and if I don't do something to kill it now, it'll only get worse."

"So they're getting worse? What's up with that?" Abby gave her a look of concern.

"You tell me. You're the doctor. I assumed this was a normal pregnancy thing."

"Well, as your doctor, I'm advising that you drink more of that tea David found for you and take no more than six of those pills a day. I also want you to keep a record of when they occur. Headaches like this aren't normal, but then, nothing about this pregnancy seems normal." She squeezed Claire's leg. "That's not necessarily a bad thing, by the way."

"Good to know." She rubbed her belly. "When do you think I'll start to show and not just look, you know, like a bloated whale?" She hoped it would be soon. She also couldn't wait for the first flutter from her baby—she heard it was like being tickled.

"You? Probably not till you're almost five months along. You need to eat more first, and since I'm not only your doctor but your best friend, I'm making it my personal duty to ensure you gain that weight. Starting tonight."

"What happened to wanting me to eat healthy?" Claire asked.

"You can start tomorrow. Tonight anything goes."

They arrived at the hotel, and when Abby popped the trunk, Claire couldn't get over the number of bags full of food and drinks.

"Are you sure we're not having a party? Kim and Kat aren't coming later tonight?"

"I'm an emotional eater, Claire. You know that."

Claire followed behind her friend as she walked into the hotel,
arms loaded with the bags of chips, candy, popcorn, and that box from
Sweet Bites.

Claire had tried calling Josh and texting him, but there was no response.

"You know they made that deal, right?"

"What deal?" She checked her phone again.

"The first person to use their phone or even check it has to buy the
other a drink *and* their phones are confiscated by Mike for the rest of
the evening." The look on Abby's face said it all.

"Well that's dumb," Claire muttered before stuffing her phone back
in her pocket. No wonder he wasn't responding.

"That's what I said. But Derek claims it's less distracting. He even
thinks we should try it." Abby laughed as she held her phone in her
hands. "Although . . . really, sometimes I think this thing is glued to
my hands."

Claire curled her legs beneath her. They'd changed into their comfy
clothes and were settled in on the couch in their suite. Abby knew the
manager of the hotel, and he always gave them a deal—often a free
room. She had helped deliver his twins, traveling through a blizzard to
assist with the complications during his wife's labor, and since then, he
treated her like his hero.

"So if the guys don't have their phones, who are you expecting a call
from?" The way Abby kept checking her cell, Claire had at first assumed
Derek would be calling. But obviously, that wasn't the case.

"My mom."

"Your mom? Why?" Claire asked.

Abby grimaced. "She sent me a text earlier, saying a box had arrived
at the house. The return address was odd. Here." She swiped something
on her phone and handed it to Claire. "She sent me a photo."

Claire looked at the box. It was scuffed and dented, with multiple address labels and a lot of stamps all over the box. She used her fingers to enlarge the photo.

"Did that come from Afghanistan?" she asked.

Abby nodded. "That's what I thought too. It looks like it was rerouted a couple of times, sent to a few bases along the way, forwarded to others along the chain of command before making its way to my mom."

Claire handed the phone back. "Do you think it's from Mark?"

"I hope not." She turned her head away. "What type of sister does that make me? But I can't handle more surprises from him."

"Has your mom opened it yet?"

Abby shook her head.

"Is now a good time to talk about it? Or do you want to watch a tearjerker first?" Claire reached for a box of tissue from the table beside her and placed it between them.

In all the years they'd been friends, Abby maintained a wall around her heart. It took a lot for her to cry, and she didn't like to be around people who were too emotional. Claire had learned that the best way for Abby to let out those deep emotions was to watch a weepie. It worked like a charm.

Abby grabbed the remote without saying a word and scrolled through the movie selection until she came upon a romance about two star-crossed lovers who could never be together.

Halfway through the movie, the tears began to fall, and soon Abby was sobbing like a baby, her body curled up as she rested her head on Claire's shoulder.

"I miss him, you know? We always knew he could die, but he was so close to being done, and I thought he'd be okay," Abby said quietly.

Claire handed her some tissues.

"I think my mom is jealous that I got to speak to him last. I think she can't get past that. She'd always been jealous about our connection, but . . . I know it's hard for her, I know that. But he was my twin, Claire. It's like a part of me is missing." Abby's body shuddered as she sobbed.

Claire lightly smoothed Abby's arm. She didn't know what to say. But she also felt words may not be needed anyway. Sometimes the best way to be there for someone is to be quiet and let them talk or cry or just sit in silence. There aren't always words to soothe the tears or erase the pain.

"I knew the moment he died." Abby lifted her head slightly. "Did I tell you that? I could feel it, in my soul. It was like a part of me was ripped away, leaving a hole with ragged edges. Every time I think of Mark, every time I have to repeat his words to my mom, every time she calls me crying, it's like I'm getting ripped open again." She sat up, wiped her eyes and face, and then leaned back, her head tilted toward the ceiling. "God, I'm such a mess. It's been two years. You'd think I'd be over it by now. Derek seems to think so at least."

"Derek's never lost a twin sibling, so he should keep his mouth shut," Claire muttered. Time didn't factor into grief. Whoever said time heals all wounds must have been high on drugs, because even after sixteen years, Claire still missed her son. Still felt the weight of him in her arms when she thought about him.

She wondered if some of the issues Abby and Derek were facing had to do with Abby's grief.

"Millie has been great for my mom. Did you know?" Abby sniffed.

"They've been good for each other. Your mom was a rock for Millie after my father passed. You know she plans to convince your mom to do a cruise?" Claire smiled. She could picture the two women on a cruise ship, taking in all the activities, dancing in the evenings . . .

"My mom? On a cruise? You've got to be kidding me, right? She'll never go for it."

"Why not? They've been talking about it on and off for years, and it might be just what your mom needs—a little distance and a new perspective," Claire said.

"Mark once mentioned we should all do a family cruise together to celebrate his army discharge."

Claire's heart sank. "I had no idea. I'd better mention it to my mom before she goes any further."

They sat there and continued to watch the movie. Abby checked her phone a few times and shook her head in response to Claire's inquiring look.

"You're not crying for me, are you?" Abby nudged her teasingly after the movie ended.

"It's the pregnancy hormones you warned me about." Claire wiped her eyes with a tissue.

"Are you ready for some treats? We haven't opened that box yet." Abby eyed the box they'd left on the little table in the corner.

"Yes, but first, I want to ask you a question." She angled herself toward her friend, one arm across the top of the couch, and readied herself.

"Should I be worried?" Abby asked.

Claire shrugged. "How are you and Derek doing? Every time you guys come over, I notice you taking a deep breath once he leaves the room. What's going on?"

"You noticed, huh?"

Claire nodded and waited.

"I'm jealous of you and Josh, you know? You guys . . . you're solid. Even through all the treatments and negative results, you guys never wavered. You were there for each other, like a team. Josh is one of the good guys. I don't see men like him often. He has stuck by you. He's by your side, no matter what . . . I'm not sure Derek would be."

"Of course he would."

Abby shook her head. "No. I know he wouldn't. You have no idea how many times he's told me that." For a moment, it looked like she was going to cry again. "He looks up to Josh, and I think it's because he knows Josh is a better man than he is."

Claire didn't like hearing that. "That's not true. Derek is a good man, Abby. He may say one thing now, but you don't know how a person will react until they're actually in the situation. He might surprise you."

A look of fondness appeared on Abby's face. She reached out and took Claire's hand. "You know what I do know? That no matter what we go through in life, I'll always have you by my side and vice versa. I don't know what I'd do without you, Claire Turner." She rested her head on Claire's shoulder again.

"And you'll never have to find out." Claire leaned her cheek against Abby's hair. "I feel the same way about you."

SIXTEEN

JOSH

Present day

The moment Josh entered Last Call for his weekly wings-and-beer with Derek, Fran, the owner, accosted him.

"I hear congratulations are in order." She grabbed Josh, pulling him in close for a hug. She smelled of beer, fried food, and—Josh sniffed—lemon?

"Thanks, I think?" Josh pretended he didn't know what she was talking about. "Hey, you smell lemony. New shampoo?" He leaned forward for another lungful. Yep, it was her hair, all right. Smelled just like Claire's, which was a bit pleasant, odd, and distressing all at once.

She blushed. "Still using the one you and Claire gave me. It's my favorite."

"Claire's too." He gave his head a shake. What was he doing smelling other people's hair? And Fran's, of all people. She was Mike's mother. She used to pinch his cheeks and pull his ear whenever he tried to sneak into the pub with Mike for a beer as a teenager.

"She doesn't mind the smell?" Fran asked.

"Who? Claire? No, why would she? You know she loves anything lemon. She's addicted to the lemon drops you make."

"She'd better not be coming in here for those any time soon." A stern frown appeared on her face. "Some women can't handle strong scents when they're"—she leaned closer and whispered—"you know."

Josh chuckled. "Know what?" he whispered back.

"Now don't you be playing those games with me, Josh Turner. I know you better than that." Fran punched him on the arm. "Don't forget who was the one drying your tears when you skinned your knees jumping out of trees with Mikey."

"Aww, come on, Fran. You've got to stop bringing that up. I'm a grown man now. I don't cry over skinned knees anymore." Josh blushed. He secretly loved the teasing. He'd lost his mother years ago, and Fran had taken him in and treated him like her own son.

"Then are you going to tell me, or do I need to drag it out of you?" She folded her arms across her chest and stared at him.

Josh rubbed the back of his neck. "Claire's gonna skin me alive. You know that, right?"

"Because you told me your little secret? Nah. She's gonna wonder what took you so long, and you know it." She pressed her hands to his cheeks before giving him another hug. "I'm so happy for you two." She kissed him on the cheek and then wiped off the lipstick.

"Now, if you're looking for names, I've always loved Britney or Jackson."

"Britney or Jackson." He tried the names out and wasn't a huge fan. "Got it. I'll add them to the list."

She nodded approvingly.

"How did you find out?" Josh asked.

"Oh, honey. How do you think word spreads in our small town? I doubt there's a single soul who doesn't know. We're all just playing along for Claire's sake." With that, Fran stepped past him to chat with a couple who'd just sat down in a booth.

Josh made his way to the bar, shaking his head.

"So how do you want to play this?" Mike asked while drying a beer mug.

"Excuse me?" Still befuddled by Fran, Josh had no idea what Mike was talking about.

"Do you want him to pretend he has no clue about your news?" Derek explained.

Josh sat down on the stool and waited for Mike to pour him a beer.

"Well?" Mike slid the mug toward him.

Josh took a long drink of his beer and wiped the foam from his mouth.

"I'm just trying to think of how to explain this to my wife. She's been trying so hard to keep it a secret."

"She's waiting for that three-month mark, right?" Mike asked.

Josh nodded.

"That's what Mom said." Mike jerked his head toward Fran. "Why not keep Claire in the dark? Don't tell her everyone knows. What will it hurt?"

Derek started to laugh.

"What's so funny?" Mike frowned.

"You need a wife, man. What will it hurt? You keep a secret like this from your wife, and she finds out . . . you're in the doghouse forever." Derek slapped Josh on the shoulder. "If you don't tell her, someone else will, and when she finds out you knew . . ." He shook his head and didn't say another word.

He was right, though. Claire would be upset, not because people knew, but because he knew they knew and didn't tell her. Besides, she was twelve weeks along, so she should be okay with spreading the news.

He pulled out his phone only to have Derek pull it from his hands.

"Dude! You owe me a drink. Mike, you saw that, right? He pulled out his phone and was probably going to send Claire a text." His head turned from Mike to Josh, back to Mike, then to Josh again. "Right?"

He nodded.

"Right is right. You saw it." Derek grinned then handed Josh's phone to Mike before reaching for his own and handing it over too.

Months ago, they'd made a deal to never look at their phones while hanging out together. If their wives needed them, they knew to call the bar or Fran herself.

Usually it was Derek who lost.

"Dude, telling your wife right this instant isn't going to do anything. Besides, she's relaxing and getting pampered, and the last thing Abby needs is a stressed-out, pregnant friend tonight." Derek hunched over his beer, his shoulders curved forward. He frowned.

"What's going on?" Josh took another swig and watched his friend.

Derek didn't say anything for a minute, just stared off to the side.

"She's been pretty down the past week or so. At first, I thought it was the monthly thing, you know, but I think it's more than that. Not sure if it's missing Mark or your wife being pregnant or what."

"I didn't realize you guys wanted kids too."

"That's the funny thing." Derek reached for a handful of peanuts from a basket on the bar, "We don't. Or at least, I thought we didn't. Abs talks about adoption more than anything else, but it's always for a future date, never for now. I thought we were happy with our lives, but then you had to screw it all up for us."

Josh thumped Derek on the shoulder, causing him to spill the peanut shells in his hand. "We didn't screw anything up, so don't put that on us, man."

Josh eyed the beer in front of Derek and wondered how many of those he'd already had.

"I know. I'm sorry." Derek put his hands behind his head and stretched. "Don't listen to me. We're beyond thrilled that you're finally having a baby, and you know you'd better be naming us as godparents, right? 'Cause, dude, that would hurt."

"Hey, I thought I was going to be a godparent. You want someone fun, to teach the little kid what it's like not to be saddled with stress." Mike refilled the peanut basket.

"Mike, no offense, but you are the last person I'd want teaching my child how to have fun." Josh thought back to when they were teens and getting into a lot of trouble. Mike always came up with the ideas, and Josh just followed along. Like when Mike thought it would be a good idea to dress up the lampposts for Halloween by "borrowing" neighbors' underwear from clotheslines. But it wasn't Mike who got caught with a bra in one hand and a staple gun in the other.

"You're still holding a grudge about me taping that "Help Me" sign to the back of your tux on your wedding day, aren't you?" Mike rolled his eyes.

"Just you wait. When you find a woman who'll put up with you, I'll throw you a bachelor party you'll never forget. I'm sure I can hire some of the women from the retirement home to come as strippers." He ducked as Fran's hand slapped the back of his head.

"Don't be so disrespectful, Joshua Turner. You were raised better than that." The frown on Fran's face was quite fierce.

"Sorry, ma'am." Josh struggled not to smile. *The frown on Fran's face was fierce.* That was a good line. Now, he just needed a character with a name that started with *F* . . . Frankie maybe? Would Jack meet a Frankie in Europe? Sure he would. He'd—

"Earth to Josh, do you hear me?" Derek nudged him, making him lose his balance on the barstool. "Dude, you just got your Jack look. You were thinking of your book again, weren't you? I think we need another rule. No work talk *or thought*. Since you broke it first, you owe me another drink." He grabbed his beer, downed it, and banged the empty mug down on the bar.

"I'm not down with that rule, and I think you need to take it easy. How many have you had tonight?" Josh glanced at Mike, who held up three fingers. "How about we get some food? I'm starving."

"Why don't you boys head over to the booth? I'll put the order in for your usual, and you can leave my son in peace, so he can get back to work." Fran slapped the bar top with the towel she kept slung over her shoulder.

Although it was framed as a friendly suggestion, Fran meant business. She stood watching them the whole time, as Josh grabbed Derek's arm and steered him to the booth. She brought over a pitcher of water, two more beers, and a basket of peanuts. "That's your last for a while, so you'd better enjoy it," she warned Derek before leaving.

"She can't dictate how much I can drink," Derek muttered. "I'm a paying customer, and I'm not driving. If I want to fall flat on my face on my way home, that's my business."

"No one is falling flat on their face. What is wrong with you?" This wasn't like Derek at all.

Derek rubbed the back of his neck and leaned back. "I don't know, man. Things at home this past little bit have just been . . . different. I think it's about Mark. It's been two years, man. How long is she going to grieve?" He stared up at the ceiling. "Do you know her mom still calls at night? Still. After two years. Not as bad as before, mind you, back when it was nightly. Now she calls maybe once a week."

"Still?" Did Claire know about this? If she did, she never said anything to him about it.

"Still." He shook his head in what Josh took to be disgust. "Claims she's having a weak moment whenever she calls. All she asks is for Abby to repeat the last words he said to her. Come on. Enough already."

Josh didn't know what to say. He was surprised at Derek's callousness. He'd known Mark, though not well. Mark had been dedicated to the army, to serving his country, and the minute he could enlist, he had. It hadn't just been his career. It had been his life. Sure, he'd passed away two years ago, but you can't tell someone when to stop grieving.

"All I know is that when the girls come home tomorrow, I need Abigail to be happy. I'm unplugging the phone every night from now on and shutting our cell phones off. I don't care if my mother-in-law is having a fragile moment and needs encouragement," Derek grumbled.

"Dude, that's harsh." Josh watched the drops of condensation trickling down his beer mug. Normally, Derek was the wise one, the guy who cheered him up after another negative pregnancy result. It wasn't often he saw this side of Derek—the cold, hard man. What happened to him?

"Have you talked to Liz?" he asked.

Derek snorted. "Till I'm blue in the face. I even called her pastor and got him to come over one night to help her. I know she needs to grieve, and I wouldn't take that from her. But . . . I don't know. Maybe I'm just being selfish. Am I? Being selfish?" Derek shook his head. "Now I feel like a girl, all insecure and crap."

"That's enough." Fran appeared out of nowhere and slapped her hand down on the table. She motioned for Josh to scoot over then sat down beside him.

"Elizabeth lost her son and didn't get a chance to say good-bye. That woman has been trying to appear strong, just like her daughter, your wife. You need to give her some space."

"But how much? It's been two years, Fran," Derek said.

"With the anniversary just passed, don't you think you need to give the women in your family a little break? Stop being such a jerk, Derek. You're better than that."

Derek's gaze dropped. "You're right."

"I know. Now, when Liz calls, do you ever answer, or do you let your wife handle it?" Fran asked.

"It's Abby's mom. I let her answer."

Fran snorted. "Figures," she said. "How about you answer for a while? You say your wife is still grieving . . . maybe it's time for you to be strong for her. Talk to your mother-in-law. Listen to her pleas. Be the son she needs right now. You'll never replace Mark, but you can help her feel less alone." Fran stood abruptly and wiped her hands on her apron.

"You know this, Derek Cox. Smarten up and stop hiding behind your wife. Now, your food is ready. I'll be back."

Josh watched the whole talk with growing astonishment. He'd caught the slight tremble in Fran's hands and knew he'd witnessed the real deal, some tough love.

"She didn't have to be so harsh about it," Derek mumbled after Fran walked away. "But she's right." He raised his head, and Josh saw a steadiness in his gaze for the first time that night. "She's right."

"I can't imagine what it would be like to lose a child," Josh said.

"Mark was a good guy," Derek said.

Josh lifted his beer. "He was the best. Someone to look up to. A real hero."

Derek lifted his own beer. "A true hero."

They drank to Mark and didn't say much else until Fran brought their food. Along with wings, she brought two burgers. "Our special tonight. Hope you're hungry."

"Starving." Derek dug right in while Josh took his time.

"Listen, Derek, man, I'm sorry."

"For what?" Derek picked up a wing drenched in hot sauce.

"For being so selfish. I haven't really been there, as a friend. You guys needed me. Needed us, and we let you down." He thought back to all the times they'd come over for dinner or dessert, or when Abby came over to check on Claire . . . not once had they thought to focus on anything but Claire.

What kind of friends were they?

"The best kind." Derek said and Josh startled, not realizing he'd said it out loud.

"Listen, coming over to your place was like . . . a free zone for us." He fiddled with his napkin. "There were no awkward silences or moments when neither one of us knew what to say about Mark's death, even though it was always hanging there between us. Abby could laugh and not feel guilty, because the goal was to bring a smile to Claire's face.

Or she could be silent and not worry that I was going to ask if she were okay for the millionth time. Don't feel bad." Derek pushed his half-finished beer to the side and reached for his water glass.

"A free zone?" Josh said.

"Trust me," Derek said. "You have no idea."

"Well." Josh cleared his throat. "Either way, I am sorry, for at least not being more aware. But, any time you need the free zone, just say the word and come on over."

"You've got my back?"

Josh nodded. There wasn't a better friend a man could ask for. "Always."

Derek held up his fist. "Likewise. If this pregnancy thing gets to be too much, you know, hormones and stuff, just say the word."

Josh bumped his fist against Derek's. "Deal."

He wolfed down half his burger, amazed at how good it tasted and wondered why burgers always taste better in a pub than at home.

"You are excited though, right?" Derek asked.

Josh nodded. "It's like . . . winning the lottery. We gave up all hope, and then, it just happened."

Derek raised his glass. "Here's to miracles, winning the lottery, and you finally becoming a dad."

Their glasses clinked together, and in that moment, Josh felt like the luckiest man on earth.

SEVENTEEN

CLAIRE

A memory from Bruges, Belgium
First week in April

Claire tugged the blanket up past her head and burrowed as deep as she could.

"Give me a few hours to myself, okay?" she mumbled. Her side of the bed sank, and a second later, the blanket was pulled out of her grasp.

"I just gave you an hour. You were supposed to use that time to shower and get dressed. What's going on?" He wiped away the tears that lingered on her cheeks. "You cried almost all night while you slept, did you know that?" he asked quietly.

"I kept hearing a baby crying." She reached for the blanket, but Josh pushed it further down the bed.

"Breakfast is almost over, but I promised the chef you were on your way down. He's saved you some champagne." He waggled his eyebrows at her.

"Champagne for breakfast?" She liked this little Belgian luxury hotel hidden away on a side street.

"All the mimosas your heart desires. But don't drink too much—we've got a lot of walking to do today. Remember, we wanted to explore the rest of the city, beyond all the chocolate shops."

They'd arrived in Bruges yesterday in the early afternoon and spent hours walking the main streets and stopping in the chocolate stores they came across.

Sampling chocolate in every chocolate shop in Bruges was on Josh's bucket list. With a town boasting more than fifty chocolatiers, there was a lot of stopping and taste testing. He proudly marked it off last night despite complaining of an upset stomach.

"You go," Claire said.

Josh stood up and then reached for her hands, pulling her up with him. "No can do. You're coming with me."

Claire let herself be pulled up and gathered into her husband's arms for a quick hug. The memory of those cries haunted her still. She couldn't let it go.

"I have an idea." Josh led her across the large room, up the stairs to the Jacuzzi. They had been upgraded to a spectacular suite.

"What's that?"

"Let's take today off. From everything."

She looked at him with surprise. "Everything?"

He nodded. "We can just explore. No Jack. No stories. No drawings. No memories. No mourning. Nothing but what each minute brings us."

She let that sink in. "So. From everything."

"Everything. We'll take life moment by moment, hour by hour, for one day. Remember when we used to do that?"

The sound of that cry from her dream faded as what her husband proposed took shape in her mind. "I can do that. Moment by moment."

"Good." The smile on his face was bright and wide, and his eyes lit up with excitement. "I hear there's a convent that we should explore, and then we need to head to the Church of Our Lady to see *Madonna and Child.* And if we have time, we could stop in at Choco-Story, the chocolate museum . . ."

Claire shook her head. "Oh no. No more chocolate. You promised yesterday." She shook her finger at him. "*One day,* you said, one day to get it out of your system. One day to fully experience a chocolate town. No more." If she had to smell another chocolate shop, the nausea would be too much.

"But if we happen to pass by . . ." His voice trailed off.

"Of course we're going to pass by a shop, there's one every few stores. No, Josh." She patted his belly. "Just think of all the walking we have to do to work off all that chocolate from yesterday alone. No way. But, didn't you promise me some original Belgium waffles and beer?"

He licked his lips and rubbed his stomach, hamming it up, which got her chuckling. She knew he was trying to take her mind off the heaviness in her heart and put a smile on her face.

For a moment, she felt guilty for smiling.

"Just one day," Josh said quietly, as if reading her thoughts.

"One day."

If ever Claire had fallen in love with a town, it was Bruges. This medieval village was full of charm, character, and a stillness that soothed her soul. What would it take for them to live here, at least part time, or perhaps visit every year? All she would need was a month, at least a month, to allow the peace she'd found here to fill her up, to help her move forward.

There was one place in particular she wanted to revisit, over and over again.

The Beguine convent. There was a sense of peace within the grounds that took her breath away. The moment they crossed the huge doors into the garden area, she felt it. The quiet. The stillness. It eased her heart, filled her with warmth, and all she wanted to do was sit among the yellow daffodils and just be.

The square garden was surrounded by a group of white buildings. A few of the doors were open, and if you were nosy enough to look in, you would find nuns going about their day.

She wanted to draw the scene, color in the flowers, the trees, shade in the houses . . . maybe one day she would. She knew Josh had taken quite a few photos of the gardens and homes, even of a nun as she walked along the pathways. Perhaps she'd work on a drawing tonight in her sketchbook. She should try to find an art-supply shop, since her sketchbook was almost full.

"So we've seen the *Madonna and Child* and now the convent. What else would you like to do today?" Josh held her hand as they stopped on a bridge and smiled down at the boats full of tourists passing beneath them.

"Let's just get lost." Claire shoved the small map into her handbag. "I want to grab a postcard to leave on the board at the hotel—leave our own little touch to add to the quaintness. Who knows? Maybe one day we'll come back when we're old and gray and find it still there among the others. After that, we can find a pub or restaurant, sip on some Belgian beer, listen to local musicians . . . let's just get lost. For a moment."

"For an hour," Josh said.

"For the rest of the day." Claire smiled up at him. She wasn't burdened with sadness. Her heart was light and happy, and that's how it should be. They were in this amazing medieval town full of history, and they should be enjoying it rather than living in the past.

She breathed in deeply.

She would live in the moment. If only for today.

EIGHTEEN

CLAIRE

Present day

C urled in her large reading chair in her office, Claire doodled in the margins of her notebook and reread the last page she'd just written.

She'd woken up this morning, headache-free for the first time in over a week, and went right to work. Josh was out for the day running errands, so she had the house to herself, which was liberating. For the first time in a long time there wasn't someone hovering over her, making sure she was okay.

She was more than okay, and she wished people would start believing her.

Armed with coffee and fresh fruit, Claire had completed two designs for the latest Jack book and then decided it was time to start her own project. She couldn't believe she was really doing this.

She reread the lines she'd written and wondered how Josh did this day in and day out. How did he come up with words that not only encouraged children to want to read but that also engaged their imagination at the same time?

This wasn't a Jack book. It couldn't be. She wanted to write a story about a little girl named Zoe or Lilly or Rose or something else. She couldn't decide on a name. It had to be perfect, something that would make a lasting impression. But coming up with that perfect name for a character was proving to be just as difficult as coming up with a name for their own baby.

Josh's most recent suggestion was Zara or Tyrone.

Again, not the perfect name.

"Who are you in there, little one?" Claire rubbed her belly and thought about all the names Josh had added to his list so far. He didn't want to know the sex. He would prefer to be surprised, but not Claire. She wanted to know. She needed to know.

She thought, or at least hoped, it would be a girl. A daughter she could dress up in pretty outfits with ribbons in her hair, a little girl who could wrap her daddy around her finger, a beautiful angel to melt the hearts of everyone with her sweet smile.

This wasn't a do-over for her. It wasn't a way for her to make amends or to fill a hole in her heart after giving away her little boy. If she had a boy, she worried she'd search for the same look in his eyes that her son had, for the familiar twist of his mouth when he yawned, or the little dimple in his chin.

That wouldn't be fair to Josh or this baby.

Claire rubbed the back of her neck as a headache formed. She groaned as she kneaded a tight area and wondered how long she could go before needing Tylenol. She was really starting to hate these headaches, hated the constant dull throb she woke to and the piercing pain that grew sharper throughout the day. She tried not to complain though, knowing if this was the only drawback to being pregnant, she was doing pretty well. At least she could eat when she was hungry, and she didn't have the nausea most complained about.

She looked down at the words she'd written.

When xxx (note to self: need the perfect name, but
don't ask Josh) dreamed, it was of castles and unicorns
and tiny little fairies that tickled her toes so she would
laugh. Her laughter was magical, and the little fairies
needed her magic.

Something about her idea was off. Why did she have to be dreaming? Why couldn't the little girl she wrote about actually live in a land
where her laughter was really magical?

Claire tapped her pen against the notebook and thought this
through. In her mind, she could see the drawings to go with the story—
castles with turrets that glittered with pink diamonds and unicorns that
flew through the sky. She could picture Josh reading their daughter the
story and stopping to tickle her toes so their little girl would laugh, just
like in the story.

Claire leaned back in the chair, gently rotating her head to work
out a kink in her neck, and then she smiled.

Claire set the notebook aside and made her way to the baby's room,
where she'd left the journal Josh had bought her. Each day she would
add more items to her bucket list as they occurred to her, and she had
no doubt she'd run out of lines in the journal before their baby arrived.
Maybe she should start a yearly bucket list with the baby in mind—
things to do before she turned one and then two and so on. That might
be a better idea and keep things cleaner.

Her doorbell rang, and before she was halfway down her stairs,
she heard the door open then close and her mother calling out to her.

"Don't get up. I'm only dropping by to leave you some fresh fruit
salad." Millie almost jumped when she reached the steps and caught
sight of Claire.

"Too late," Claire said. She took the bowl from Millie and headed
into the kitchen. "Thanks for the fruit salad. I'm craving kiwi and

strawberries. Please tell me there's kiwi and strawberries in here." She smiled at her mom before opening the lid and popping a berry into her mouth.

"Gloria even sent along a little container with extras in case she didn't add enough in there." Millie pulled out a small food-storage container from her purse and put it in the fridge.

"I'll have to thank her tonight." Claire pulled a fork out of the drawer and began to eat the salad, suddenly starving.

"Dinner plans?"

"I hope so. Josh won't be home till later, and I really don't feel like cooking. Besides, it's been a while since we've been there, and now I have an excuse." She continued to scarf down the fruit salad and was amazed at how delicious it tasted.

"How are you feeling today?" Millie filled up the teakettle and set it on the stove. Claire assumed this meant her mom was here for a visit.

"Not too bad. Not as tired, which is great."

"Headache again?" Her mom turned on the hot water tap and rinsed out the teapot that sat on the counter.

"Right now, yes, but when I woke up, no. It was nice not to wake up to a jackhammer in my brain the moment I moved." She could already see where this conversation was headed, because no doubt it would be the same thing Josh and Abigail had been telling her.

"I don't think these headaches are normal, Claire. How is your vision? You should go in and see Abigail about them." Millie set the teapot down, now full of hot water, and waited for the teakettle to boil.

Millie liked to make tea in a specific way, and Claire loved it. She'd been thrilled when they stayed at the Blossom Lane Bed and Breakfast in London and realized her mother made tea correctly.

"What does my vision have to do with my headaches?" She was fine. Why wouldn't people believe her? Just yesterday she'd read that headaches were quite common for pregnant women.

"I'm serious," her mother reiterated. "Why don't you call the clinic now and see if she can see you. I'll drive you in."

"I'm okay right now, but thank you." Claire reached for the small bottle of pills she kept on the counter and shook two into the palm of her hand.

"If you don't, I will." Millie, her lips a fine line, eyed Claire while she swallowed the pills.

"It's just a headache. I wish everyone would leave me alone about them."

All Millie did was arch her eyebrow and give her that look, the one that said, *Who do you think you're fooling?*

"I had headaches before, if you remember."

Millie shook her head firmly and looked away.

Claire sighed. "Fine. I'll call."

"Thank you." Millie handed her the phone and waited for her to dial.

Claire rolled her eyes. Rebecca answered and told her Abigail was completely booked. Claire started to ask about tomorrow, but Rebecca surprised her and said Dr. Shuman could see her. Normally Dr. Shuman was the one booked, being a town favorite for young and old alike.

Millie was thrilled. She grabbed her keys and bustled Claire out of the house faster than she'd ever seen her mother move before.

"If anyone will know what is going on, it's Dr. Shuman." Millie reached over and squeezed Claire's hand. "Soon, everything will be okay."

Claire reached for a strawberry lollipop on Dr. Shuman's desk. Some things never changed, much like his office. Ever since she was a child, he'd served as the town's main family physician until their hospital was built and more doctors arrived. He maintained his small clinic on the outskirts of downtown, and then Abby joined him. Other than a half-full jar of lollipops and a notepad of paper, his desk was spotless. She didn't think she'd seen him with a messy desk, ever. His walls were full of pictures drawn by his patients, both children and adults, on the notepad he kept on his desk.

While waiting for him, Claire reached for the notepad and the pencil beside it and began to draw. There were already a few of her drawings on his wall, but she couldn't help herself.

By the time he arrived, she'd not only drawn her picture but she'd added it to the wall, mixed in with other squares.

She rather liked her drawing today.

"I couldn't believe it when I saw your mother out there. Reminds me of when you were just a little girl in pigtails. And now you're about to have your own." Dr. Shuman shook his head. "Time certainly flies by, doesn't it?"

"Who would have thought Millie would still be dragging me in to see you?" She smiled while he sat on the corner of his desk, her file held in his hands.

"Who indeed? Must be pretty serious for you to be so stubborn. But then, you always did hate coming in to see me." His left eyebrow rose.

"I just don't like doctors' offices, that's all." Claire shrugged.

"So what brings you in today, then?"

"My headaches. Abigail told me to come in if they got worse."

Dr. Shuman moved to his chair behind his desk and opened her file.

"How often do you get them?"

"Daily. It's rare I don't have one, actually."

"Do you have one now?" He scribbled in her file.

Claire nodded. "Just starting. Today was probably the first time in the past few weeks I didn't wake up with one."

He sat back in his seat. "What are you taking for them and how much?"

"Tylenol, extra strength, and Abigail told me only six a day, if necessary." She couldn't look him in the eye.

"I didn't ask how many Abby told you to take, now did I?" He took off his glasses and held them in his hand.

She winced. "When it turns into a migraine, I can take up to eight or ten pills. Well . . . I could take more but—I'm also drinking tea. Lots of tea."

"Tea is good. You have a baby to take care of now. You need to think about what you do, what you eat or take, and how it affects that little one inside of you."

Claire hung her head but then looked up and smiled. "It's pretty amazing, isn't it?" she said.

Dr. Shuman nodded. "Pretty amazing. I helped deliver you, and you can bet your bottom dollar I'll be in that room with Abigail to see this little one too. I'll need to add your photos to my family wall."

One of the clinic's walls was full of photos of babies being held by either Dr. Shuman or Abigail. It was a wall the clinic was very proud of, and Claire couldn't wait to have her little one on there too.

"Other than your headaches, any other symptoms? Are you still tired? How about your appetite? Getting any morning sickness?" The look on her old doctor's face was quite serious.

"Exhausted, but not as bad as before. I'm not really all that nauseated either, but that's a good thing, right?" She bit her lip.

"There's old wives' tales that the sicker you are, the healthier the baby, but your own mother is a prime example that's not always the case. You're not worried, are you?" He leaned forward and clasped his hands together.

"What about the headaches? I never got them before this, so could it just be . . . ?" Her voice trailed.

"Pregnancy hormones?" he asked.

She nodded.

"It's possible. You're starting the second trimester, and it is quite common . . ." He hesitated as he looked over her file. "Your blood work looks fine. Abigail has left a note here, though, that she's concerned about your headaches." He sighed and leaned back. "I'd like to send you for an MRI."

That caught Claire off guard. "An MRI? For headaches? Don't you think that's a bit extreme? Is that harmful to the baby?"

Dr. Shuman stood up and walked toward her, taking a seat on the corner of his desk again.

"There are studies that show MRIs are completely safe during pregnancies. Nothing for you to be worried about. I'll have Rebecca set it up." He leaned forward and clasped her shoulder. "I'll be right back."

Claire took a few deep breaths to calm herself. Everything was fine. Her baby was fine. She was fine.

She took out her phone, her hands shaking slightly, and sent her husband a text message.

At doctor's for headaches. Millie dragged me here. Getting an MRI.

She knew Josh was out running errands, but she wasn't sure where he was.

Do you need me? I can be there in ten minutes. Are you okay?

Was she okay? Great question.

She wasn't one to get excited over the little things, but this didn't feel so little. She glanced at her medical file sitting on the desk and pulled it toward her. The fact that Abby had left notes about her headaches bothered her.

On a sticky note, Abby had the following written down: *Worsening headaches. If come in, do a scan. Safe.*

Claire pushed the file back and tried to calm herself, but she jumped at the slight knock on the door.

"You okay in here?" Abby popped her head in.

Claire turned slightly in her chair and shook her head. She tried to answer but knew the moment she did, she'd start crying.

"I'm sorry I couldn't fit you in, but I'm glad you're here. I just heard Will ask Rebecca to get you an appointment at the hospital today for the MRI." Abby stepped in and closed the door behind her. She squatted down so she was eye level with Claire and reached for her hands.

"I read your note." Claire was proud of herself for not crying. "You're worried about me?"

Abby's grip tightened. "I'd rather be safe than sorry. I'm not liking these headaches of yours."

"But they're normal for pregnant women."

Abby shrugged. "I hope it's just a hormonal thing, but let me just be a doctor right now, okay? We need to be sure."

Claire looked up to the ceiling and let out a long breath. "So I shouldn't be worried?"

Abigail stood up. "Tell you what, if it turns out to be nothing and it's just hormones, I promise to throw you the absolute best baby shower anyone in this town has ever seen."

"You're going to do that regardless." Claire managed to smile.

"True. Okay, how about I'll throw you the best baby shower ever, and we'll do the ultimate girlfriend weekend before you get too far along in your pregnancy?" She stuck her hand out.

"Fine." Claire shook her hand. "But you also owe me your famous fried chicken for dinner. Tonight."

"Tonight?" Abby's voice rose. "Did I forget to mention my schedule is full all day, and I'll be completely fried by the time I get home?"

"Don't care. I'm the pregnant friend you're stressing out. Fried chicken. Tonight." Claire gave her a stern look.

Abby sighed. "Fine. If it means you're eating, then I can't complain. But it won't be till after eight o'clock. And I expect you to bring wine and dessert. Maybe some pie from Sweet Bites?"

The door opened and Dr. Shuman walked in. "Abigail, you're not bothering sweet Claire, now are you?"

Abby smiled. "Not at all. I just managed to finagle some pie out of my good friend there, that's all. I'd better go. Mrs. Getschen is probably waiting for me to take a look at her bunions again."

"Room five," Dr. Shuman said. He held the door open and waited until it was just the two of them. "Now, Rebecca was able to work her magic, and they can get you right in. It'll be completely painless. You'll need to lie still for thirty to forty minutes, and then I should have the results within a few days."

"But there's no harm to the baby, right?" Claire needed to be reassured.

"No harm, I promise. Just do me a favor? No more than six Tylenol if you can help it, okay?"

Claire groaned. He obviously had no idea how bad her headaches could get.

Her phone buzzed. *I'm here. Chatting with your mom.*

"Josh is here." Any tension Claire felt disappeared knowing he was there with her.

"Now there's a good man. Just what I like to see." Dr. Shuman opened his office door for her. "You make sure he takes good care of you, or he'll have me to deal with. Trust me, I can make sure his next checkup won't be so gentle."

NINETEEN

CLAIRE

Present day

Claire's hands were visibly shaking. If it weren't for Josh holding her up, she'd probably collapse into a puddle.

Ever since the MRI, she'd been a bundle of nerves.

She knew everything was fine. Although she felt anything but.

She had an appointment for this afternoon to get more blood work done. Abby figured the results of her brain scan would be in and reassured her there would be nothing to worry about.

Easy for her to say.

"Need a refill?" Julie Peters, owner of the Odd Cup coffee shop, stood at their table, carafe of coffee in her hand.

Claire shook her head, holding her hand over her mug, but Josh held his up.

"You make the best cup of joe, Julie." Josh sipped at his liquid gold. "When are you going to start letting us buy beans here?"

He'd been asking the same thing for the past two years. And for two years, Julie gave the same answer.

"And not see your handsome face? Never." She winked at Claire. "How are you feeling? I have a special rooibos blend to help with the nausea you should try."

"Thanks, Julie, but I think I'm far enough along now that I should be safe. Fingers crossed."

"Really?" She sounded surprised. "Have you talked to Abigail about that? My mom used to say the sicker you felt, the better."

Claire struggled to keep the smile on her face. Ever since word got out about her pregnancy, she'd had a whole assortment of advice given to her.

"My mom was never sick, so hopefully it's a family trait."

That appeared to mollify Julie. "Well, that would make sense. I can't tell you how excited everyone is about your little one. If anyone deserves to be parents, it's you two. Have you thought of names yet?" She leaned forward. "There's a bet going on over at Last Call about the sex and name. Did you know?"

"Really?" Josh said.

"Really. Mike's the man to talk to. I've got my money on a girl named Emily," Julie said as Claire glanced at the time and then stared out the window. The seconds crawled, and she was antsy.

"Let me finish my coffee, and then we can head over." Josh watched her, and she noticed new worry lines around his eyes and forehead.

This must be just as stressful for him as it was for her, but he was trying his best to stay upbeat for her.

"What if something's wrong with the baby?" Claire whispered.

Josh's eyes widened at her words, and then he shook his head.

"There's nothing wrong. They would have wanted us in right away if there was." Josh forced a smile, but Claire heard the false hope. Even he was worried.

By the time they walked through the front doors, her hands were trembling, her mouth dry, and all she could think about was that something was wrong with the baby.

"Nothing is wrong with the baby." Abigail accosted Claire the moment she walked into the empty waiting room and gave Claire a hug, holding her tight.

Claire searched Abby's red-rimmed eyes. "Why the tears then?"

Abby shook her head, lightly touched her arm, and struggled with her words. This wasn't the Dr. Abigail Cox everyone knew and loved. The woman who remained calm and strong for her patients, who made it her mission to never break down while at the office—who firmly believed that her patients needed her to be strong, and so strong she would be.

"Abigail, what's wrong?" Josh asked.

Abby just shook her head and then gripped the white jacket she wore over her shirt and jeans.

"I saw you from the windows and just wanted to give you a hug. Come on, let's go get that blood work done before you see Dr. Shuman."

Abigail wouldn't meet her eyes. Claire glanced at Josh to see whether he noticed.

She never thought Abigail would lie to her. She never did when any of the fertility treatments came back negative. But right now, in this moment, Claire knew, in her heart of hearts, she was being lied to.

Her legs wobbled as they walked toward one of the patient rooms. No one spoke while Abby took five vials of blood, listened to Claire's heart, and checked her blood pressure.

"How are you feeling? Still exhausted? How are the headaches? Any cramping or nausea?" Abigail rattled off her questions.

"Not sure. Absolutely. I have a headache now. No cramping, and Julie says that being nauseous while pregnant is actually a good sign. Should I be worried?" Claire asked.

"Did you have morning sickness last time?"

There were only a few people who knew about her previous pregnancy. Abigail was one of them. As her doctor, it made sense, especially since they'd gone through years of infertility treatments.

Claire shook her head.

"Then I wouldn't worry. What does Julie know? And what do you mean by *not sure*?"

"You asked how I'm feeling. I'm not sure. How am I supposed to feel? I'm nervous, scared, tired, and irritated. Is this just pregnancy hormones or something else? Should I be afraid? I can't shake off the feeling that something is wrong. Were you wrong? Should we not have done the MRI because of the baby?" Claire's pitch ratcheted upward the more questions she asked.

"I think what you're feeling is normal. I'm sorry this has been so stressful for you. Please believe me—the baby is fine. Your ultrasound is in a few days, and you'll see for yourself. Have you thought about whether you want to know the sex yet?"

There was the Dr. Abigail Cox that Claire expected to see. Her voice was composed, authoritative, and with enough of a hint of a smile to calm her.

"We want it to be a surprise," Claire said. "Well, Josh does at least."

"Are you sure? It's okay if you change your mind at the last minute, lots of couples do."

"And spoil the fun?" Josh asked. "Did you know there's a bet going on about both the sex and the name?"

Abigail blushed.

"What did you pick?" he asked.

"I can picture a little girl with her daddy, can't you?" Abby grinned and then quickly sobered. "Will is probably waiting in his office for you. I'll see you after, okay?"

"Sure." Claire cleared her throat. "Do you, uh, know the results?"

She wasn't sure if Abby heard her, though. She'd opened the door and rushed out before Claire even had a chance to stand up.

"Let's get this over with." Josh sighed and led the way. They followed Abby to Dr. Shuman's office down the hall.

Dr. Shuman sat at his desk, looking over what Claire assumed was her file. The door to the bookcase behind his desk was open, and the monitor normally hidden away had been pulled out and turned on. Two scans of what Claire assumed were her brain appeared on the monitor.

He stood when they entered.

"Abigail, if you don't have any patients, I'd like you to stay, please," Dr. Shuman said.

Claire remained quiet and watched the facial expressions of both her best friend and her family physician. Something was wrong. She turned her attention to the scans on the display, and tried to detect anything odd about how her brain looked.

"How's your headache today, Claire?" Dr. Shuman asked as he sat back down behind his desk. "On a scale of one to ten."

"Four." Which meant she'd also had about four pills by now to dull the throb she'd woken up with.

"The headaches are just hormonal, right?" Josh asked.

Claire waited to hear the confirmation. She needed to hear Dr. Will say yes. She leaned forward, ready for his answer.

"Not exactly."

Claire sat back and sighed.

Dr. Shuman tapped his index fingers together, as if thinking of his next words.

"I've learned throughout my years that there's no sugarcoating unexpected news. Claire, you have what is called an anaplastic meningioma, a grade-three brain tumor."

The words swept Claire away. She felt like she was drowning. Dr. Shuman continued to speak, but she couldn't make out the words. They were garbled and distorted.

The tips of her fingers began to tingle and freeze, the coldness crawled along her veins, up her arms and into her chest. She couldn't breathe. She struggled to make her lungs work, to draw in air and push it back out, but they were frozen as well. Her body floated over the chair she sat in before things began to spin wildly around her. She tried to reach out to Josh, but he seemed so far away, and then everything disappeared.

TWENTY

JOSH

Present day

He caught her before she fell.

"Claire." The skin of her arm was cold to his touch. "Claire." He called her name over and over, while he held her at an awkward angle. She'd slumped forward and to the right, toward him.

Abby rushed forward and helped, getting her to lean back in the chair, and then just looked at her.

"Do something." His wife just fainted. She has a brain tumor, and she fainted. That must mean something. Why wasn't Abby helping her?

"Claire? Claire, honey? Can you hear me?" Abigail said softly, her hands ran up and down Claire's arms, as if trying to warm her up.

Josh looked at Dr. Shuman, feeling helpless and angry at the same time. "Is this because of . . . because she has . . ." He couldn't even say the words.

He'd heard Dr. Shuman loud and clear. He knew exactly what "anaplastic meningioma, a grade-three brain tumor" meant. Cancer. Something his own mother had died from. Although hers was stage four, and by the time they'd caught it, it had been too late.

"Has she fainted before now?" Dr. Shuman asked.

"No. Just headaches, and she sleeps a lot." Josh leaned forward, buried his head in his hands. "Why didn't I see this sooner? I know the signs. I should have seen this." His whole world was being swallowed up, and there was nothing he could do about it.

His wife stirred, and Josh bolted upright in his seat.

Her lashes fluttered, and she turned to him, her eyes reaching out. For him.

"There we go." Abigail stood but kept Claire's hands within hers. "I think that's the first time I've ever seen you faint."

He could hear the false cheer in Abigail's voice, but it was the look of apprehension on her face that scared him the most.

If Abigail was worried, then things weren't good.

"Josh? I want to go home. Please?" Claire pulled her hands out from Abigail's grip and reached out for him.

He stood, gathered his wife into his arms, and held her tight. "Are you okay?" He kissed the top of her head. "I need to know you're okay," he whispered for only her to hear.

She nodded, but her body tensed as she stared at Dr. Shuman.

"Claire, why don't you sit down?"

His wife's body shook in his arms. "Let me take her home," Josh said.

"We need to talk about this." Dr. Shuman shook his head and stood, bracing his hands on his desk. "Please, I know this is overwhelming and"—he breathed in deep—"scary, but you're not alone."

"It's okay," Claire whispered. "I'm okay." She returned to her seat but held on to his hands. Small tremors swept through her body.

"I'm sorry." She shook her head. "The last thing I heard you say was that I have a tumor." She swallowed past that word but kept her focus steady. Her grip on his hand tightened, though.

"Claire, your headaches are the result of a grade-three tumor that is putting pressure on your skull at the base. I wish I could tell you they are due to pregnancy hormones, but I can't." The doctor sat back down but leaned forward, resting his elbows on the desk, and watched Claire intently.

"What does *stage three* mean?" she asked.

"Some cancers disappear after treatment—whether it's through surgery or radiation or even chemotherapy. Some may grow back. Stage three means that, regardless of treatment, chances are strong that it will grow back."

The silence in the room while they all watched Claire process his words was palpable.

"So I have cancer in my brain, and you're telling me it won't go away." She gave a slight nod of her head. "What about my baby? Are there concerns? Can we get that ultrasound done right away so we can check?" She placed her free hand over her belly.

"What are our options?" Josh twisted in his seat to look at Abigail and Dr. Shuman. He read two different scenarios on their faces. Abigail seemed uncertain, and Dr. Shuman seemed determined.

"Claire, the baby is fine." At least Abigail's voice was reassuring.

"I'm going to be honest with you." Dr. Will cleared his throat. "If you weren't pregnant, I'd recommend immediate surgery followed by radiation."

"But?" Josh asked.

"Josh, radiation is dangerous for the baby. There are too many risks involved."

"What do you mean risks?" Claire scooted forward in her chair, her focus intent on the doctor.

Josh placed his hand along her back. He needed to feel connected to her right now.

"You're at"—Dr. Will checked the file before looking up—"seventeen weeks right now, which means we're almost past when normal miscarriages occur, but you're not far enough along to rule out that possibility. I—"

"Miscarriage?" The words sounded like they were strangling Claire. "When is the risk over for that?"

"About twenty weeks. I would suggest waiting until you're further along, but the dosage you need is too high."

"Too high for . . . ?"

"There could be substantial risk of major malformations like neurological and motor deficiencies."

Claire nodded, sat back in her chair, and took a moment.

"So we wait until the baby is born. Right?"

"Wait?" Josh didn't like the sound of that. "Can we? Is the tumor growing?" He shook his head. "It's not worth the risk."

Claire turned to him. "The baby isn't worth the risk? Is that what you're saying?"

Josh rubbed his hand over his face. "That's not what I said."

"What we're going to do is called active surveillance. We're going to monitor the tumor, and see if it grows. If it doesn't, then we have time." Dr. Shuman's gaze softened as he looked at Claire.

Josh tried to process his words.

"So *we're doing nothing* is what you're saying. She could die, but we're going to do nothing about it?" His voice rose as the reality of what was happening hit him square in the gut. He could lose his wife, his soul mate, the one person who made his life make sense—because she was pregnant.

"She won't die, Josh. I won't let that happen." Abigail spoke the words he needed to hear, but in this moment, he wasn't sure he believed her.

"I'm not going to die, Josh." She looked at him, and what Josh read in her gaze humbled him.

Here she was, the one with a brain tumor, the one who could die, and she was comforting him.

What was wrong with him?

"So when you say monitor, you mean more MRIs?" she asked.

"Yes. And we'll keep a close eye on your symptoms, how you're feeling. I'd like you to start keeping a record, a journal." Dr. Shuman pulled out a small notebook from a desk drawer and handed it over. "Every day, I want you to write when you get a headache, how long it lasts, and rate it from one to ten. Also detail how are you feeling, your energy level, what you're eating, and so on. There's never too much data. Abigail and I will work together, so you can show it to her weekly and to me every month or so when you come in. If there is anything she sees that we need to look at more closely, we'll deal with it then."

Claire thumbed through the notebook and then nodded. She handed it to Josh to look through. It was a daily journal, with areas at the top for the date, symptoms, and diet, and then a smaller area at the bottom of each page for special notes. It was laid out in a practical way, and for his note-taking wife, exactly what she needed.

"I know it's a lot to take in, and I'm sure you have questions. But why don't you go home and rest, and Abigail will stop by later." Dr. Shuman glanced up at Abigail.

"Absolutely. Why don't Derek and I come by, and we'll bring dinner too? We can talk things through and create a plan. You'll be okay, Claire. I promise." Abigail stepped away from the counter she'd been leaning against and pulled Claire up into a hug. "I promise."

Josh stood alongside his wife but remained where he was as Abigail led Claire out of the room. He turned to the doctor and stared at him until he knew Claire wasn't within hearing distance.

"Tell me straight. My mother died of a stage-four brain tumor, so I know what this looks like. She's going to die, isn't she?"

Dr. Shuman pinched the bridge of his nose and let out a long breath.

"I love that girl as if she were my own. You know that, right? She's not dying on my watch, Josh. I can promise you that."

"What about the baby?"

Dr. Shuman's shoulders dropped, and in that moment, the elderly doctor looked old.

"I'm not going to lie. Things would be simpler if she weren't pregnant. Like I said, I'd have her in for surgery and radiation treatment right away. She'd have a better chance if we did."

For a moment, Josh was speechless.

"So you're saying she should have an abortion?"

Dr. Shuman shook his head. "No, I'm not saying that. If that is what you both decide, then we can discuss what that looks like. But I think the active surveillance is our best option right now." He clasped Josh on the shoulder. "It's a lot to take in. If you need me, call me anytime. We'll get through this, Josh, and both Claire and your baby will be fine."

The memory of his mother, of the way she wasted away, of what her life was like those last few months hit him hard.

"But you can't promise. I know. I've lived through it. I know what brain cancer is like. Claire . . ." his throat thickened, and it was hard to get the words out. "She's my life. She can't die. Do you understand? I don't care what that looks like, but she cannot die."

He was over the moon to be a father, to know that their dream of being parents was finally coming true, but he loved his wife more. He prayed he didn't have to make that choice, that he could have the best of both worlds. But if he had to, if it meant Claire's life or their baby?

There was no choice. Not for him.

TWENTY-ONE

CLAIRE

Present day

Little was said between her and Josh as they drove home. Once in the house, Josh trailed after her like a puppy dog, while Claire poured herself some iced tea.

Dr. Shuman's words swirled around in her head, and she was trying very hard to ignore them.

"Why don't you go lie down, and I'll bring your drink out?" Josh hovered by her.

"I'm fine," she snapped.

"You're not. Your hands are shaking so bad you're spilling tea all over the counter." Josh took the pitcher from her and set it down. He cleaned up while she just stood there, stunned.

She held out her hands. He was right.

"I'm fine," she repeated.

Josh tossed the paper towel in the garbage. "You're not fine. I'm not fine. There's nothing about this that is fine."

"Don't," Claire whispered it like a prayer. *Don't do this. Don't lose hope. Don't let it overwhelm you. Don't let it destroy us. Don't accept it.*

Don't accept it. Because she couldn't.

She didn't have a brain tumor. She couldn't. All she had were head-aches caused by pregnancy. That's when the headaches started—close to the time she became pregnant. That had to count for something, didn't it?

Her phone buzzed, and she pulled it out of her pocket.

We're on our way.

"I need you to be strong for me right now, Josh. For us. I need you to help me understand what is going on, what is happening, because I can't." A flood of tears broke loose. "I can't." She cried harder.

Josh's arms were around her within moments, and she felt safe. Claire rested her head against his chest and let the tears flow.

"It's going to be okay. It has to be."

Claire looked up and noticed the tears that glimmered in her hus-band's eyes. His gaze was haunted, the memories he pushed to the side no longer willing to hide.

"I'm not going to die," she whispered.

"You're not," he whispered back.

"Abby is on her way." Claire pulled back slightly and wiped her face with her hand. She took a deep breath. She knew that if she let it, she would give in to the weight of what they'd just been told. But she couldn't. She wouldn't. She needed to be strong. For her baby. For her family.

One look into her husband's eyes confirmed that for her.

"I can't lose you," Josh said.

"You won't."

Claire pulled out a chair from the kitchen island and sat. She held her glass between her hands and stared at the liquid, lost in her own thoughts.

"I spoke to Dr. Shuman before we left." Josh sat down beside her, his body angled toward her, his hand on her leg. "If you weren't preg-nant, he'd recommend surgery. Immediately."

She shook her head.

"But I am pregnant, so that's not an option."

"But what if it were—an option?"

What was he saying?

"I'm pregnant, Josh." As if she had to remind him. She placed her hands over her stomach and gently rubbed.

His gaze tore from hers, and he stared up at the ceiling, his leg bouncing. She knew the signs. He was agitated.

"Claire. It's still early. We could try again, we—"

The sound of her hand hitting his face, the loud slap of her palm hitting his cheek filled the room, startling them both.

"I'm sorry," she said, her hand suspended in the air as he stared at her with disbelief.

Why did she just apologize? He should be apologizing to her. To their child. What was he thinking?

"Don't do this," she pleaded with him, her voice soft despite the sliver of anger that worked its way into her heart. "It's not an option, Josh. It's not."

He was asking her to kill their child, the child they'd prayed for, dreamed about, cried over. Their miracle baby. How could he ask that of her?

"I choose you, Claire. I will always choose you. I need you. This will kill you. I know." He pushed his chair away and stood. *"I know!"* he cried out, his face stark with pain. The imprint of her hand on his cheek stood out against the whiteness of his face.

"There doesn't have to be a choice."

"There's always a choice. And you've already made yours, haven't you?"

The doorbell rang before Claire had a chance to respond. Josh threw his arms up in the air as he went to answer it. "Maybe Abby can talk some sense into you," he snapped as he left to answer the door.

Abby's eyes were rimmed bright red and tears fell as she rushed toward Claire for a hug.

"I'm sorry," Abby said. "I'm so sorry."

"Don't you dare apologize. This isn't your fault."

"I know, but—"

"Stop," Claire interrupted. "If you want to cry or feel sorry for me, then do it at home. But not here. Okay? I don't need tears. I don't need pity. I'm going to fight this. I'm going to have this baby." She glared at her husband. "And I'm going to be fine. Do you hear me?" She looked directly at both Abby and Josh, her eyes boring holes into them.

Josh was just in shock. He had to be. That could be the only reason for him mentioning abortion. The *only* reason.

"Where's Derek?" Josh asked.

"Right here." Derek stood in the doorway, his arms full of small boxes Claire recognized were from the bakery in town. "Apparently what I have in here might be considered a peace offering?" His brow rose as he walked into the kitchen and set the boxes down. "The tension in this room right now is taut. Come on . . . Claire isn't dead. Not yet, at least." He shot a knowing smile toward Claire, who appreciated his dry humor while everyone else gasped.

"Seriously, Derek, that was uncalled for." Abby looked daggers at him, while Josh's face hardened. He yanked a cold beer from the fridge and almost threw it toward Derek.

"Whoa, calm down. Abs, you're the last person Claire needs to be giving her a pity party. Be the doctor you are. Come on. You were the one who said you weren't going to lose it, so suck it up." He opened up one of the boxes and pulled out a cream-filled éclair.

"Dude." He held it out to Josh. "I'm here for you. Let's go drink our beer outside while things calm down a little. I know you, and you need a plan. So"—he looked each of them in the eye—"let's figure this out." He handed a small box to Claire and showed her the cream puff inside of it. "Deal?"

"Deal," Claire said. She gave him a hug, so grateful to him for being so levelheaded about it all. She would do whatever it took to fight this. Today, they would come up with a plan.

With the boys outside, Claire pulled apart her cream puff and made sure there were equal amounts of whipped cream on each puff pastry before handing half to Abby.

"Can I be all mushy for one more minute?" Abby asked.

"Nope. I'm . . . I'm going to ask something of you, and you're not allowed to say no." Claire took a bite of her halved cream puff, mentally stuffing all the fears and worries she had into a box and storing it deep inside herself.

"Ok." Abby gave a shaky laugh and set her cream puff down, giving Claire her full attention.

"I need you to be my cheerleader. Both with the pregnancy and this tumor. Okay? You can be my doctor too, as long as you keep the worry and fear to yourself." She set her own pastry down and stared at her friend.

"Under no circumstances are you ever going to suggest my life is more important than my child's. Ever. Understood?" Claire had never been more serious in her life.

Abigail nodded. "Claire," she said as she reached her hand out, "our plan of attack will be to save both you and your baby. There's no either-or, not in my mind."

Claire slowly closed her eyes and let out a deliberate quiet exhale. "Thank you," she whispered.

"Josh is freaking out, eh?"

When Claire opened her eyes, she noticed a slight smile on her friend's face.

"Freaking out?" she repeated. She glanced out the window and watched as Josh leaned forward, his head in his hands and his shoulders shuddering. She hated seeing him like that. "That's putting it mildly. I think he thinks I should have an abortion." She choked on the words.

"You can't fault him for his reaction, honey. Let him process it. That's what Derek is doing outside with him. Giving Josh the out that he needs to come to grips with the news."

"You guys are true friends. You know that, right?" Claire said.

"I know." Abigail flashed a grin at her as she snagged a bite of her cream puff. "I'm such an awesome friend that I'll even share the extra cream puff I brought with me."

Claire snorted. "If I'd known there were two, I never would have shared."

"Again, just a sign of our awesome friendship." Abby sighed with immense satisfaction as she finished her portion. She looked at Claire. But when tears welled in her eyes, she quickly looked away.

Claire bit her lip and turned her gaze away. She wasn't going to lose it now. She couldn't. Maybe tonight, when she was alone in the shower, where Josh couldn't hear her sobbing. Maybe then she would let the force of this hit her.

"I'm going to be okay, right?" Claire's voice quivered.

"Absolutely. I promise we'll get through this." The conviction in her voice soothed Claire's fears a little.

"This active . . ." She couldn't remember what Abby had called it earlier. In fact, she didn't remember much about what they'd talked about.

"Active surveillance. I really do think it's the best thing to do right now. We'll keep an eye on your headaches, how things are going, how you're feeling. The goal is to get you far enough along in the pregnancy without . . ." Abby glanced away again.

Claire handed her a tissue as she read between the lines. "So, I'm twelve weeks now. What's the earliest the baby can be delivered?" She was surprised at how calm she sounded.

"I would like to see you go full term, Claire. That is the goal."

"How do we get me there without radiation or chemo or surgery?" While she didn't remember much of what had been said in the doctor's office, she did remember that part.

"We start off with you promising to be honest with me. No lies. No stretching the truth. No hiding how bad things get because you are afraid of what action I might take. I need you to be honest and to trust me."

"Of course I'll be honest." That was a given. Why wouldn't she?

"I need you to rate on a scale of one to ten how bad your headaches get. You said earlier you were at four. That is manageable. But if you get to an eight, then it's time we stepped in. Do you understand?"

Claire shook her head. "I will do anything to protect my child." She lightly rubbed her belly, "That's what's important. So if I have to deal with an eight, then I will."

"No you won't. An eight for most people would be close to a ten, and it means it's too late. That's not acceptable."

Claire let that sink in. "So the goal is to not get to an eight."

Abby nodded. "There's lots we can do to help keep the headaches manageable."

"Like herbal stuff, right? Teas, vitamins . . ."

Abby smiled. "Yes, that will all help. Massages will help, and there's a chiropractor at the hospital that will be good as well. He uses alternative treatment methods rather than the spinal manipulation. He's also well known for treating neck pain. He only comes to the hospital once a week, but I'll give him a call."

"What kinds of other methods does he use?" She wasn't too sure she liked the idea of seeing a chiropractor for a tumor. It just didn't sound . . . right.

"It's called an activator technique. Rather than manipulate your spine with sharp twists, he'll use a spring-loaded tool to deliver precise adjustments to your spine. Which means, he won't touch the tumor at all. It's safe, trust me." The conviction in Abigail's tone soothed Claire.

Okay, she could do this. She would do this.

"Should we go join the boys?" she suggested. She noticed Josh seemed a little more relaxed. He was sitting back in his chair, his hand wrapped around the bottle of beer.

Once outside, she put her hand on his shoulder and squeezed. He set down his bottle, pulled her around, and then sat her on his lap, his arms wrapping around her as he held her close. His lips nuzzled her neck before he whispered I love you in her ear.

"I'm not sure what you ladies were discussing inside, but I came up with a brilliant idea," Derek said.

Claire caught the way he watched her, as if judging her emotional response. She gave him a smile, letting him know she was okay. She was. For now.

"What's the brilliant idea, hotshot?" Abigail sat in the chair next to her husband.

"You need a pregnancy bucket list."

When no one said anything, he continued. "You have a list for everything else in your life. Why not this too? Something to keep your focus on besides the tumor."

Claire liked the idea, and it did make sense. A lot of sense. She pushed herself up from Josh's lap and headed inside. She had just the notepad to write out this new bucket list too.

"Did I say something wrong?" she heard Derek ask.

She went to her office and pulled out a small notebook she'd been keeping for something special. The notebook was a soft-pink color with an embossed saying on the cover.

Failure only happens when you give up.
So don't.
Ever.

It was perfect for right now. She grabbed a pen from her desk and smiled at it. Alice had given it to her at their book signing. It was a small green pen with the words *Wild at Heart* on it and an antler charm hanging from the top. It made her smile.

"Everything okay?" Derek asked when she rejoined the group outside.

She kissed the top of Josh's head and pulled up a chair beside him. He frowned, but she didn't want to sit on his lap again. It was time to get down to work.

"Your idea of having a bucket list is perfect. I want there to be realistic goals on here, though. Things I can mark off as we go. I want to fill each page with normal ordinary things one would do while being pregnant, along with the things I need to do"—she glanced at Abby—"to keep my doctor happy."

"I think the last entry on there should be to hold your child in your arms and kiss him or her for the first time." There was a sheen in Derek's eyes when he said it. He looked down at the patio a moment and then took a sip of his beer.

Claire turned to the very last page and wrote down exactly those words.

"The first thing on your bucket list should be . . ." Josh tapped his chin in thought.

"Read that mammoth of a pregnancy book that you bought," Abby suggested.

"Good one." Claire smiled and wrote it down. She did need to read it.

The ideas began to fly, and Claire wrote them all down in her book. From taking daily walks to getting weekly massages to eating healthy food—by the time they were finished throwing ideas out there, she had multiple pages filled.

Abby made her dedicate a page to the massages, with the idea that she was to record the dates she got them, to keep herself accountable.

"I think you should add one new outfit each month, just to help with your self-esteem," Abby mentioned.

"What's wrong with my self-esteem? I think I look fine."

"Of course you do, honey." Abby leaned forward. "But any excuse to go shopping for clothes is a good one."

Josh groaned as Claire happily added it to her list. Her stomach grumbled.

"Sounds like that's my cue to get dinner started. Will you guys stay?" Josh asked.

"We could go out," Derek said.

The idea of going out in public stole Claire's breath. She gave her head a small shake.

"Or we could order in. How about Chinese? It's been a while since we've had that," Derek offered, as if sensing something was wrong.

"Claire?" Josh put a hand on her arm, gently stroking it as he looked at her with concern in his eyes.

"I just . . . I just want to stay home for a bit. Is that okay?" She didn't understand where the panic came from at the mention of going out, but she could only assume it was from being overwhelmed.

Despite her smiles and outward calmness, on the inside, she was anything but. She felt wound up tight, like she could break at any moment.

"Honey, it's been a long day. Why don't you go have a hot bath, relax, and let Josh pamper you for a bit. Derek and I don't need to stay. I'll check in with you tomorrow."

Claire nodded, thankful for Abby's gentleness.

"Thank you," she said. "You guys are the best."

"We'll get through this. I promise." Abby gave her a tight hug. "You're not alone, even if it starts to feel that way. You're not." She held Claire by the shoulders, her grip strong. "I'm in your corner."

"So am I," Derek said. "Even if it's to remind you to smile and laugh a little."

It wasn't until after they'd left that Claire let the tears fall.

Josh picked her up in his arms and carried her into the house, where they sat on the couch together, snuggled up close.

"I need to tell my mom," Claire said, her fingers wrapped around the collar of Josh's shirt.

"Not yet," he said as he played with the ends of her hair. "Let's just have the night, okay? Where it's just us in our own little world. If you call Millie now, she'll be over here within minutes, and we won't have this chance to breathe."

"She's going to be hurt I didn't call right away," Claire mentioned, feeling a little guilty.

"That's her problem then. Not yours. Call her tomorrow, or send her a text and tell her to come for breakfast."

Claire liked that idea.

"Why don't you go have a bath, and I'll get supper started."

"I'm not really hungry, Josh." When she said not really, she meant not at all.

"I know. But . . . you need to eat. We need to keep you as healthy as we can. Not just for you but for the baby as well."

Claire stared into his eyes, trying to read behind the words. Was he okay with her decision to focus on the baby then? To not give up on this little miracle of theirs?

"Okay," she whispered. She wasn't sure where he stood yet, but maybe he also needed the time. Time to adjust, to accept, and to come to terms.

Although, how they were supposed to accept the fact she could die from a brain tumor was beyond her.

TWENTY-TWO

MILLIE

Present day

Millie buzzed with energy, but the right kind of energy.

She needed to breathe, to remain calm, to take in what her daughter had just thrown at her, and figure out a way to make this right.

Right now, in this moment, Claire needed her more than ever.

"Okay, so if I'm hearing you right, you're refusing any sort of treatment because it could hurt our baby. So what we need to do is figure out some alternative ways to fight this tumor and keep my grandbaby safe. Right?"

Claire nodded.

Millie wasn't sure if she agreed with this. She also had a feeling her daughter wasn't telling her the whole truth.

"What do you need from me?"

Claire leaned back in her chair, holding the cup of coffee between her hands, and her weak smile wavered. "Support me. Be there for me. Don't let me lose hope."

A ball of lead settled in Millie's stomach. Her daughter sounded like she'd already lost hope, and that wasn't good. If that were the case, then she would squash all her fears and worries into a box and stuff it in the remotest closet she could find deep within her heart.

"I'm here for you. Whenever you need me. I'll be your biggest supporter. How is that tea from David working?" Her words ran together, but hopefully Claire didn't notice.

At her daughter's grimace, Millie chuckled, thankful that Claire focused more on the tea and not her nervousness.

"Add some sugar to sweeten the taste if you have to."

"If you tell me to suck it up, I'm going to get upset."

"You forgot to add the *buttercup*. It's 'Suck it up, buttercup,' sweetie. And no, I won't say that. You've already done it for me." Millie worried her hands together, squeezing her fingers tight beneath the table.

"So what happens next?" she asked.

"What do you mean?"

Millie jumped up from her seat to fill her cup with hot water. She dunked her tea bag repeatedly, needing to move, to do something other than just sit there.

"What are the next steps? What do you do now? I feel like there must be something we can do instead of just watching you . . ." Her voice trailed off.

"Don't. Don't watch me, not like that. I'm not a lab rat or on my deathbed. I have headaches, and I'm pregnant. I want to enjoy life as much as I can. So there's nothing we need to do other than what we normally do. I'll write in a journal every day, Abby will monitor how bad my headaches get, and you'll help me prepare for this baby, while Josh and I work on our stories."

"So it's life as usual."

Claire nodded. "You got it. That's all I can do, Mom. I won't fall apart. I can handle this."

"I know you can, honey."

Her daughter was a strong and calm person, and she admired that. But what if her daughter was mistaking that strength for avoidance?

This wasn't just a headache she had to deal with. A stage-three tumor wasn't something to ignore, and yet, she had a feeling that's exactly what her daughter wanted to do.

"Do you remember what I used to do for you when you had headaches before?" Millie asked.

"You mean when I was pregnant before? At the cottage?" Claire knitted her brow in concentration. "You used to massage my head for me, didn't you?"

Millie nodded. "You should start getting weekly massages and have someone do cranial on you. I know you have to be careful about the placement of the tumor and everything, but if Dr. Will or Abby could share your MRI scans, it might help them help you better?"

It wasn't much, but if she could find small ways to help her daughter through this, then she would. She checked the time and realized it was almost noon. If she left now, she could stop in town and see if Dr. Will was having lunch at the pub. If so, she'd have a few words with him, and maybe he'd give her a better understanding of what was going on.

"Honey, do you mind if I head out? I'd like to find David and see if he has any other teas to help that are better tasting. I'm sure you have some drawing you need to get back to. Why don't you join me for dinner tonight? Maybe the Wandering Table? I can see what Gloria has on the menu." She caught the panicked look on her daughter's face. "What's wrong?"

"I'm not . . . ," Claire said, and then cleared her throat. "Um, I'd rather just stay home if that's okay?"

Surprised, Millie touched her hand to her throat, not liking what she heard in her daughter's voice.

"Since when did you turn down a meal you or Josh didn't have to make? You love Gloria's cooking."

Claire went to stand in front of her patio door, looking outside, and not at her.

"Claire? What's going on?"

Her daughter's shoulders lifted and then dropped. "Nothing. I just . . . I just want to stay home for now. I want things to be normal, I need them to be normal, but I know it's not." She turned, a haunted look in her eyes. "Here, at home, I can pretend things are and that I'm in control. But when people start finding out . . . they're going to look at me with pity. I don't . . ." Her head dropped forward and Millie rushed over, placing her arms around her daughter, holding her close.

"Everyone in town loves you. You know that, right?" Millie said softly.

Claire nodded.

"They'll be sad, and some will be uncertain what it means, but other than that . . . I'd be shocked if you didn't see people only wanting to give you support, whether it's a smile or a hug or words of advice. Some might even ignore the fact you have a tumor and just focus on your growing belly, so happy that you'll soon have that baby you've been praying for."

Claire didn't say anything for a few moments, but then she turned in Millie's arms and hugged her back.

"I just want to be a mom, to hold my baby, and know he or she is mine. Forever," Claire whispered.

The words tore at Millie's heart, more than she thought possible even after all this time.

Should she confess, as Liz had been bugging her to do, about her correspondence with Marie and her drawer full of photos and drawings from Jackson? Millie struggled with this, not knowing whether telling Claire was the right thing to do.

It might bring back too many memories. Memories she didn't need to deal with right now, not with everything else going on.

"You will, hon. You will."

"I wonder if he'd care to know he was about to be a big brother? Maybe he already is, and it wouldn't be a big deal."

Millie took a deep breath and forced herself to say the words she'd often thought about over years. "Have you ever thought about trying to find him?"

"Of course I have. All the time. But I made a decision years ago to let him live his life, with his family, free of the complications of adding another mother who loves him to the mix." She bit her lip and looked down at the floor. "I do hope that he'll want to reach out to me when he's eighteen, though. That . . ." She shook her head and inhaled slowly. "It would be another dream come true."

Millie nodded and held her tongue. It would be so easy to ask her if she'd like to see photos, but then she'd have to explain how she's been in touch with Marie all these years. How could she explain that? As far as her daughter has been concerned, Millie never wanted anything to do with her grandson. And as hard as it had been to maintain that facade, facing her daughter's anger at this moment, when she had not one but two ticking time bombs in her body . . . No.

Her decision was made. She'll wait till later, after Claire had her surgery, after her grandchild was born, when things calmed down, and Claire could handle it emotionally.

It might not be the right decision, but it was the best one she could come up with for now.

Will Shuman walked down the street toward where Millie stood, arms crossed over her chest and ready to have words with the man.

"Millie," he said. His back looked hunched, and his feet shuffled against the sidewalk.

"You look old, William."

"I feel it. I think it's time I retire, move to my little cottage up by Tobermory, and fish."

Her brows rose. "I don't think so."

"Excuse me?"

"You think I'm going to allow you to abandon me and my family when we need you the most? Come on, William, you're better than that. You don't leave a patient behind."

"Abigail is an excellent doctor. Your little girl is in good hands."

"Abby is also Claire's best friend and is bound to find the two roles a struggle on the best of days." Millie wasn't going to let him give up, not on her daughter. "She needs you. Besides . . . you've got to be there when my grandbaby is born."

Will huffed then blew his nose. "You're a stubborn ol' mule. You know that, right? Especially when it comes to that girl of yours."

Millie's arms relaxed to her side. "That daughter of mine has been your favorite patient since she was a little girl, and you know it. She was the one who started that wall of drawings, and you need a picture on there from her baby too. Which means you've got a few more years left in you before you try fishing full time. Am I right?" She smiled up at him, knowing she was right and he was full of hot air.

William shook his head. "Of course you are," he said. He walked past her toward the door to the pub and held it open. "I'm a hungry man, Millie, and I don't want to discuss this out on the street. Are you coming in, or will I find you waiting for me outside my office later?"

"Now then. No need to get snippy with me." She followed him to a table off in the corner.

Fran waved from the bar, and Millie waved back. By the time Fran made it to their table, she had two glasses of water and a pot of tea on a tray.

"Doc, the usual?" she asked as she set the beverages down, with the tea in the middle. "Millie, good to see you. Interested in my homemade cream of mushroom soup today?"

"Girl, you know I don't like mushrooms," Millie said. She and Fran had a bit of a rival going on. Each year at the local fair, they both entered their recipes and baked goods, and every year they tied for first.

Millie believed people were just afraid of not letting Fran win, but it annoyed her every single time.

"One day you ladies will kiss and make up," William mumbled as he poured tea into both their empty cups.

"That's the day Lake Huron will freeze over completely."

Don't get her wrong, Fran was a lovely lady and a pillar in their small town. But would it hurt her to not enter the same categories Millie did for once?

"Now." William leaned back. "Tell me what Claire told you. I was worried she didn't get a chance to take it all in, and I was expecting her to call me."

"Abby spent some time with her yesterday."

"Ah." William nodded. "That's good."

"How about you just tell me what I need to know. My daughter is pretending nothing is seriously wrong with her." Millie leaned forward, pushed her water glass out of the way, and put her forearms on the table. "Is my daughter going to die?"

William took a sip of his tea and then removed his glasses, resting them on top of his head. "Not on my watch."

"Is that a doctor talking or a friend?" Millie needed to know the truth, no holds barred and all that stuff.

"She's not going to die, Millie. I can promise you that."

"Then how serious is it?" She played with the cutlery wrapped tight in a napkin, unable to keep still.

"She's got two tumors—brain and spinal cord. They are grade three, which is serious. If she weren't pregnant, I'd suggest surgery and then radiation. But I won't put that little baby of hers at risk."

"So you're placing my daughter's life at risk then?"

He shook his head. "I need you to trust me, Millie. I love that girl as if she were my own. You know that. I couldn't be more proud of her if she actually were mine." Tears glistened on his cheeks as they ran down his face, but Millie gave it no thought. The old man cried at the simplest of things on the best of days.

"Then what are you going to do? And don't give me that nonsense about watching her and keeping track of her headache pain. You know that girl has a high tolerance. And if she feels being honest with you will put her baby at risk, she'll keep her mouth shut." Millie's lips pursed in frustration.

"Just like her mother."

"What's that supposed to mean?"

William sighed with frustration, and it irritated Millie to know it was directed at her.

"I know a certain woman who put up with a lot to protect her child too. Claire comes by it honestly."

Millie took that as a compliment, whether he meant it that way or not.

"You still haven't told me what the plan is. And"—she held out her hand when Willian began to object—"don't bother telling me there is no plan, because I know you." She leaned forward again. "I'll tell you what I think the plan is. You're going let her pregnancy progress until it's safe for the baby to be born. Probably via caesarean, so after thirty weeks. Right? Then you're going to whisk her off to surgery and thus save them both at the same time." She sat back, folded her arms across her chest, and smiled at the look on his face. "Tell me I'm wrong." She challenged him.

He shook his head. "I'll do no such thing. Of course, that's what we're going to do. Claire explained all that to you, I'm assuming. There's no hidden agenda here, Millie."

She raised an eyebrow. "What happens if the tumors grow? Still just going to passively watch her?"

"Of course not." Will sounded offended.

Good.

"So then what? What if you have to make the choice between my daughter's life or my grandchild's?" As much as Millie hated to admit that might be a possibility, someone needed to, because she had a feeling her daughter wasn't facing reality.

William rubbed his face with both his hands and groaned.

"I'm praying that won't happen," he said.

"We both know God doesn't always answer prayers," she said quietly. She'd lived a lifetime learning the hard way that God's ways were not always her ways.

"What do you want me to tell you, Millie?"

"I want you to tell me you will do everything possible to ensure my daughter doesn't die. Everything. Do you hear me, William Shuman? I do not care what needs to be done. My daughter's life is nonnegotiable."

The words twisted their way out of her very soul, and the moment she voiced her fear into existence, she knew deep in her heart that while she was reacting as a mother, so too was her daughter.

TWENTY-THREE

CLAIRE

Present day

> *Dear child of my heart,*
>   *There will be times when you're faced with diffi-*
> *cult decisions, some harder than others, but all test your*
> *strength, your determination, and your heart.*
>   *Above all else, trust your heart.*

In the large chair in her office, which overlooked her backyard, Claire recalled those words she'd written on a postcard while staring out across the Tyrrhenian Sea in Positano, Italy. Casa delle Memorie, the small family-owned bed-and-breakfast, had welcomed them with open arms, and Claire had been lulled by the tranquility of the area, never wanting to leave.

She wished she could go back. What would it be like there now, in the fall? To stare out across the waters, to be surrounded by the warmth of the people, and to marvel at the heritage and culture she'd fallen in love with.

She should write Rocco and Miima, the family who ran the little bed-and-breakfast they stayed at for a week, and let them know about her pregnancy. Miima would be ecstatic.

Claire reached down for a box she kept close to her chair. It was full of hand-drawn postcards she'd made a few years ago. Sending one of her postcards to Miima would be perfect, especially considering the large wall of postcards they kept in each bedroom.

When they'd first walked into their bedroom at Casa delle Memorie, they'd marveled at the small hallway that led to their suite. The hallway was covered in postcards from others who had stayed there. Once she saw that wall and listened to Miima's story about how it started, the name of the bed-and-breakfast suddenly made sense—House of Memories.

> *Ciao Miima,*
>
> *I'm lost in memories today and find myself dreaming of your beautiful garden, where we would sit and make up stories for one another. Do you remember the last story you told me, the one where we came back to visit and introduced you to our child?*
>
> *That story is about to come true! Our little one is due in January.*
>
> *It may take a few years for us to come back to visit, but when we come, we won't be alone. I can't wait to show our child your memory wall and see if they can find the postcard I left there.*

Claire suddenly had an idea.

> *Your memory wall has stuck with me, and so I've decided to start my own in my office . . . a postcard from all the places we've been and from those we love who live abroad.*

*Forever . . . your very pregnant and glowing with
happiness Canadian friend,
    Claire*

She could almost imagine Miima's giddiness when she received her postcard. She and Rocco, her husband of almost fifty years, would open a bottle of wine from their own vineyard and raise a toast to not only her happiness but her health as well.

She could really use that toast right about now. She was almost at twenty-two weeks, the halfway mark of her pregnancy. She wished this were a normal pregnancy, where she could revel in each week, cherish the time her baby grew in her womb, and enjoy every moment, but she couldn't. All she could do was count down to when things would be safe for her baby and she could begin treatment. If she began treatment.

Claire stood up carefully so the room wouldn't spin, which had started happening recently, and began to pace in her office. She wanted to create her own memory wall. She had boxes of postcards, letters, drawings, and other small items not just from their own travels but also from readers who fell in love with their stories. She should have thought of this years ago . . . instead of pulling out the letters and drawings from young readers when she needed a boost, she should have placed them on her wall, right in front of her desk, where she could see them all the time.

She found a roll of cork that was left over from a project Josh hadn't followed through on. It took a couple of hours, but when she finally she stepped back, she smiled with satisfaction. She'd play some more with the arrangement of some of the letters, drawings, and postcards, but for now, it was perfect.

Not only was it an inspiration, it was a reminder.

To never give up.

She rubbed the back of her neck, rolling her shoulders as she did so, and regretted not taking the pills for her headache earlier. Just as she swallowed three of the coated capsules, their front door slammed shut downstairs.

"Helllloooo." Josh's voice carried up the stairs.

Claire checked the time. He'd left this morning on a drive, something he often did when he was stuck on a scene. His drives could take him anywhere and would range from a few hours to all day. He was home sooner than she'd expected.

"Up here." She stood in the doorway and called down.

Her husband ran up the stairs and enfolded her in a hug and then gave her a loud, smacking kiss.

"Someone's in a good mood," she teased. "I figured you'd be home in time for dessert."

"I made my way up to the Smokey Head nature reserve, sat on the rocks, and stared out into the bay. It didn't take long for the story to play out in my mind. We should go back up there, make a day trip of it. I forgot how beautiful it is there, especially this time of the year. The leaves are all turning, and there's a refreshing crispness to the air that does a body good."

A day trip away from everyone they knew, where she could enjoy being outside, breathe in the lake air, and not worry about running in to someone she knew? Count her in.

"Whoa." Josh noticed her wall and whistled. "Someone's been busy. You know what this reminds me of?"

"Casa delle Memorie," they said in unison before laughing together.

"I wrote a postcard to Miima, telling her the news. I figured she'd love to know."

Josh placed his hand on her belly but didn't say anything. He didn't talk much of their baby anymore.

"How are you feeling?"

"I'm okay. About a three." She gave the number before he even asked, not letting herself reflect that she was telling him how many pills she'd taken rather than how bad the headache really was. "What do you think of Leah or Rosa for a name if we have a girl?"

"Someone's been thinking about Italy." A smile appeared finally, and she relaxed a little.

"Maybe a little."

"So, just a three, huh? That's pretty good."

Claire picked up a mug of tea she'd been drinking all day. "I think I found a way to drink that awful skullcap tea from David. I've been sipping at it all day. Maybe it's actually helping."

"Any naps today?"

Claire smothered her frustration and shook her head.

"We should celebrate then." He hesitated and looked at her. Claire's breathing quickened. He was about to say something or ask something she wouldn't like. She knew it.

"What about a picnic down at the pier?" he suggested.

Before she had a chance to say no, he placed a finger against her lips.

"We can find a secluded area away from any of the tables or family areas. Sit by the water, listen to the waves, and stare into each other's eyes and—"

"No." She didn't even let him finish. She turned from him and picked up a pile of papers from her desk, going through them without really seeing them.

"Claire, you haven't left the house in weeks," Josh said quietly.

"Not true. I was out twice last week and once so far this week." She tightened her grip on the papers.

"To go to the hospital for your appointments. But you turn down the girls' invitations for coffee, you make your mother come out here, and you rarely answer the phone anymore. This isn't healthy. You're . . . ," he said with a sigh, "isolating yourself, and I don't like it."

She shook her head. "You don't understand."

When her husband didn't respond, she set the papers down and turned to face him.

"You're right," he finally said. "I don't." He swallowed hard and reached for her hand. "I don't understand why you're pulling yourself away from everyone who loves you. If you don't want to tell people about the tumors, fine. You don't need to. But these are your friends. They want to celebrate this pregnancy with you. They miss you, and I can only make so many excuses for you before they start to get suspicious."

"I can't." She physically couldn't. The idea of going out in public, of having to explain her headaches or worry about not getting stressed, seeing the pity on people's faces after they found out . . .

"I need more time, Josh," she pleaded.

His face fell, and she hated that she was doing this to him, putting him in a position where he had to keep lying for her to all their friends, but she didn't know what else to do.

She wasn't ready. Not yet.

"Besides, we're under some tight deadlines, so it's not like this is anything abnormal."

"They're not *that* tight, Claire. Unless you haven't started on your drawings. But you have, right?" His eyes narrowed as he studied her.

She shrugged. "Somewhat. I'm a bit behind . . . probably two chapters. The headaches don't help." It also didn't help that she was focused on a certain side project her husband had no idea about.

She'd been struggling with her story idea, not feeling the connection, but today, while working on the memory board, she'd had an idea. Why not write her child a story about their time in Europe? She could share her passion for traveling and leave their child a message at the same time. At every place they stayed, Claire had left something behind—a letter, a postcard, a drawing.

Claire would love to take their child on an adventure, to go back to the places they'd visited and loved. But, if something happened, and Claire couldn't be there . . . she could use her story to do the same thing, essentially.

As much as she didn't want to admit it, she had to face the fact that things might not go as planned, that by the time she could undergo treatment, it might be too late.

TWENTY-FOUR

MILLIE

Present day

Millie sipped her hibiscus tea at the Odd Cup and slathered some of Julie's homemade strawberry jam onto her vanilla cream scone while she waited for Liz to arrive.

"How is Claire? I haven't seen her in ages. Is she showing yet? How far along is she? You need to tell that girl to come in, and I'll make her something special. Oh, and tell her I added something to my shelf with her in mind." Julie pulled out a chair and sat down. She pointed to the wall off to the side.

Millie's eyes scanned the items on the shelves. Everything had a beach or homemade feel to it, from white lanterns to seashells, to . . . ah. Millie smiled. "Where did you find that black sheep? Claire is going to love it."

"There's a little shop in Bayfield that just opened, and it has a whole selection of sheep curios. I mentioned we had a famous author who collects black sheep and just happened to be pregnant, so the owner's on the lookout for some baby items."

"No doubt you'll be Claire's new favorite person. She looks fabulous, by the way. She's about twenty-four or so weeks now and complains that her soccer-ball-sized belly will soon look like a beach ball."

Julie chuckled. "You warned her it gets worse, right?"

"Oh no." Millie's eyes grew in size. "You know my daughter. She's been reading all those pregnancy books and thinks she knows how everything will go."

"Seriously though, is she okay? I'm not the only one who's noticed her absence. Or is she on a deadline?"

Millie took a sip of her tea and then ate a small piece of her scone.

"She's good, and yes, she's got a lot of projects on the go. That's probably why she hasn't been in." That's as good an excuse as any. Claire wasn't ready for people to find out about her tumor. But, how she expected to keep that a secret was beyond her. Eventually, someone was going to talk, whether a patient Claire bumped into at the hospital or one of the nurses or . . .

"You started without me?" Liz arrived, a big purse slung over her shoulder, and frowned at the scone in front of Millie.

Julie stood and held the chair out for Liz. "I've got a new strawberry cream tea that just came in. Would taste good with a scone."

"Sounds perfect." Liz smiled up at Julie before she sat down.

"New bag?" Millie liked the hot-pink color of the bag. Liz loved her bags, whether large purses or small handbags, and she had a large walk-in closet full of them.

"Just arrived in the mail. I think it's my new favorite. How are you doing?" She sneaked a piece of Millie's scone and moaned as she took a bite. "We need to take Julie out one night and get her drunk enough that she'll spill the secret to her scones. Mine never taste like this."

Millie laughed. "Julie drunk? Have you thought about asking for her recipe instead? I don't think I've ever seen her with a drink in hand."

Liz grumbled something in reply, but it was too low for Millie to catch.

"To answer your question, I'm fine. How are you?"

"Don't lie to me, Millie. I know you better than that." Liz challenged her.

Millie shrugged. "How am I supposed to be? My daughter is suffering, and there's nothing I can say or do to convince her that her life is important too."

Truth be told, she was angry. Angry at Claire for being so stubborn and pigheaded. Angry at Josh for not being able to talk some sense into his wife. Angry at Abigail, who wouldn't push Claire to get treatment, and angry at William for not insisting from the very beginning that her daughter have surgery.

More importantly, she was angry at herself for being so frustrated with her daughter. Claire needed her support, and given how hard it was getting with the worsening headaches, Millie needed to get past her anger and figure out a way to handle this.

"Millie, I love you. We've been friends forever and through a lot of things life has thrown our way. But you need to respect Claire's decision and find some measure of peace in all this."

Millie wrapped her hands around her lukewarm tea mug. "Peace? I will never find peace in knowing my daughter is willing to die."

"To protect her child. You would do the same thing," Liz said quietly.

"I . . ." She wanted to argue, to say she wouldn't, but Liz knew her too well. If she could, she would willingly give her life for her daughter. She'd already lived a long life and was content with where she was, but her daughter had so much more life to live.

"I will fight for my daughter, the same as she is fighting for her child. You can't ask me to stop doing that," she said instead.

Liz reached her hand across and gripped Millie's tight. "Of course not. If I could turn back time and find a way to keep Mark alive, you better believe I would. I would have faked an illness or begged him to leave one tour early. I would have done something, *anything*, to make sure he was still alive today." Liz sighed. "But Claire is more than just a daughter now. She's also a mother with the need to protect her child."

"It's hard, Liz. So hard," Millie whispered, suddenly feeling very choked up. "She still won't leave the house. Did Abby tell you that?"

Liz nodded. "Other than her appointments, Abby said she's basically housebound."

"She—"

Julie approached, holding a tray full of goodies. She set a hot pot of tea down in front of Liz, and then refilled Millie's pot.

"I saw Liz sneaking bites of your scone, Millie, so I brought an extra that you both can share. My treat. I'm also going to pack up some fresh baked goodies for Claire. Will you take it to her? Tell her it's my contribution to that beach ball look she's going for." Julie grinned and then headed off to another table of customers.

The Odd Cup was a great little spot in town and was slowly becoming more popular with tourists and visitors. During the summer months, it turned into a zoo, and Millie would only come first thing in the morning, before the crowds.

"You were saying," Liz prodded.

"She seems to think the stress of being out in public would trigger a headache, so her goal is to limit the amount of stress her body has to handle." Millie rolled her eyes.

"You don't agree with her, I take it."

"Her whole life is one big ball of stress right now. What she needs is to be surrounded by those who love her, who want to support her . . . but she doesn't see it that way. I should just force her to . . . I could arrange for a community baby shower, and then she'd have no choice but to come out of hiding."

Liz kept quiet, but Millie could see the hamster wheel in her brain going full speed.

"That's not the right way to deal with this, and you know it. The real issue, I think, is that for a woman used to being in control . . . that choice has been taken away from her thanks to the tumors. She's scared, Millie. You know that."

Millie nodded.

"Is she having panic attacks again?" Liz asked.

Stunned, Millie sat back and thought about that. When things got to be too much for her daughter, she pulled inside of herself to the point of becoming separated from reality. She did it when Millie dragged her to Europe to help heal her heart, she did it after her father died, and each time she received a negative pregnancy test.

"You know, I'm not sure. As bad as that sounds."

"Don't beat yourself up over it, Millie. She . . ." Liz stopped and a big smile spread on her face. "Well, look who's here."

Millie twisted in her seat to see David walking in with a gift bag dangling from his fingers.

She couldn't help but smile up at him.

"Hope I'm not interrupting, ladies," he said.

"Not at all." Liz pointed to a chair. "Why don't you join us?"

David didn't sit until Millie nodded. Liz nudged her beneath the table with her foot and then cleared her throat.

"I actually have a few errands to run. Why don't I let you kids enjoy a cup of tea." Liz pushed her chair back.

"Seriously? You're leaving?" Millie wanted to glare but held back.

"I'll only be a half hour. Think you can keep her entertained that long, David?" The smirk on Liz's face had Millie simmering.

What was Liz doing? No, she knew exactly what she was doing: meddling.

"I don't need entertaining." Millie narrowed her eyes at her laughing friend and then smiled at the man beside her. "But spending time with you is always a pleasure."

She ignored Liz's good-bye and sipped her tea instead.

"You're looking nice today, Millie Jack," David said once they were alone.

"Buttering me up, are you?" She looked at him over the rim of her teacup, struggling to keep the smile off her face.

"Looks like you might need it. I haven't seen you this tense in a while." He studied her, as if trying to figure out what was wrong.

She wished she could tell him. There was a part of her that wished she could lean on him, share what was going on, and use him as a sounding board, but Claire had begged her to keep things a secret. Including David.

"You obviously aren't seeing enough of me," she said quietly.

"I've been saying that for a long time now." Despite the stoic look on his face, she could hear the glint of joy in his voice. She gave him a small smile before she sighed.

"I brought you a gift." He set the gift bag on the table and nudged it toward her.

She peeked inside and frowned.

"Papers?" There were a dozen or more pamphlets inside the bag.

"Keep digging."

She set the pamphlets, brochures, and postcards on the table and gave them a quick glance.

They were all dealing with headaches and migraines. She shuffled through them and looked at David searchingly.

"For Claire. I've been doing some research and found some alternatives to the pills she's probably trying to avoid." He leaned forward and reached in the bag, pulling out a box.

"I've got a friend who sent me this for Claire to try out. It's a device that's supposed to treat and prevent migraines. It's a band she wears on her forehead. There's a nerve close to our eye sockets that this triggers through electrodes. It is safe for the baby, and I've read some really good things about it.

"There's also some other teas in here. I know the skullcap tea I gave you before is probably not to her liking, so I found some others for her to try. They'll help with the nausea from the headaches as well."

Millie grabbed his hand and held on tight.

"Is she okay?" David asked.

Millie stared up at the ceiling, blinking her eyes rapidly. No crying allowed, she told herself.

"Millie? What's wrong?"

She shook her head. She couldn't tell him. Claire would be so angry.

"This is just very sweet of you, thank you." She breathed in deep. "Her headaches are getting worse, so I'm sure this will help." She picked up the box with the band in order to distract herself. She wasn't sure about this, it all depended on where the tumors were located, but Abby would know.

The look on David's face when she finally looked up told her he didn't believe her. But it didn't matter.

Years ago, Claire had accused her of never putting her first, of placing herself and her marriage ahead of everything else. Millie understood Claire spoke out of anger, but the words had hurt, nonetheless. It hadn't been true. Not then and not now.

Claire was all that mattered right now.

"So why did it look like you were about to cry?"

Millie held her tea between her hands and looked out the window, needing to get a hold of herself. After a few moments, she was able to look at David and smile.

"It's a woman's prerogative to cry and not explain herself. Didn't you know that, David Jefferies?"

"When it comes to you, Millie Jack, it's better to never assume anything. But if you need to cry, I'm okay with that. I've got big shoulders, just say the word, and they are all yours."

With those words, the walls around Millie's heart crumbled.

TWENTY-FIVE

JOSH

Present day

J osh pulled up to the curb outside of Abigail and Derek's house and
sat there, fingers clenched on the steering wheel.

He should be at home right now with Claire, but he'd almost
exploded at her earlier, and he'd stormed out, too afraid of what he
might say or do if he'd stayed.

A loud rumble from the dark clouds above had him rolling up his
windows. The sky had darkened in a matter of minutes, and he knew
they were about to get hit with a major storm.

By the time he knocked on their door, the wind swirled around
him, strong enough to push him around, and the temperature dropped.
The sky would open up anytime.

"Dude, you should have called." Derek opened the door. "We're
just sitting down to . . . what's wrong?" He pulled Josh inside just as
the rain began.

"I knew we were in for a storm, but that came from nowhere."

"Sorry for dropping in like this, I just—"

"Josh, nice surprise." Abby joined them, a smile on her face. "Join
us for dinner? Derek made spaghetti and we have lots." She looked from

Derek to him and the smile disappeared. "What's wrong? Is it Claire? Everything okay?"

Josh snorted and almost apologized but stopped himself. "Claire is fine. If you were to call and ask her just that, she'll tell you the same thing. She's fine." He spat the words out, the anger that he'd been trying for so long to push down, rising to the surface.

"Come on, let's eat. Good to see you're finally breaking. Took you long enough." He led the way into the kitchen.

"Lay off, Derek," Abby said as she dished Josh out a plate of spaghetti with meat sauce.

"Why? Mr. Perfect is cracking, and he came to us." Derek slid a bottle of beer toward him. "That tells me not only that he can handle it but that he knows we're a safe place for him to let go of all the things he's been holding inside. If he wants to deck me, so be it. If he breaks my nose, I'm married to a doctor. I'll be fine."

Josh kept his mouth shut but took the plate of food and managed a small smile of thanks. Derek was right. This was a safe place for him, and he should have realized that a while ago.

"Eat up because I plan on grilling you about what you said about Claire being fine."

"I'm not breaking anyone's nose," Josh muttered as he sat down and toyed with his food. The first few bites tasted like sawdust in his mouth, but eventually hunger replaced anger, and in no time, his plate was empty. He enjoyed being able to sit there and just eat, not worry about being polite or making dinner conversation or having to watch over Claire to make sure she ate enough.

For the first time in a long time, he could just relax, and that's exactly what he did.

By the time the kitchen was cleared and the dishwasher full, Josh had settled in their living room with a beer and was finally ready to talk.

Abigail sat across from Josh, her elbows resting on her knees as she stared at him. "According to her notebook, her headaches seem to be leveling out, which is great news considering how far along she is," she said. "Has she been lying to me?"

Derek sat beside her, his arm slung over the back of the couch, his leg crossed over his knee.

"I think so," Josh admitted. "Before we found out about the tumors, if you'd asked her, she would have said the headache was around a six. She was tired, loud noises hurt, and more often than not, you'd find her with a cool gel pack over her eyes. Nothing has changed. She's getting more headaches, and I'm finding her in our room, curtains closed. She doesn't draw for too long anymore either."

"And yet, she more often than not gives her headaches a four or a five." Abby leaned back, her brow knitted to match the frown on her face.

"I call bullshit," Derek said.

"I would say she's more at seven or eight." Josh pinched his lips together.

Abby looked at him in alarm. "Are you serious?" She leaned forward again. "Josh, I know you're worried, and you want her to get treated. I know that. But it's still not safe for the baby, and that's probably why"— she paused and shook her head, looking at Derek for a moment before she continued—"why she's lying to us. I told her if she got to a seven or eight that I would need to step in."

"I don't want our child at risk, either. I don't." Josh needed them to believe him because he had a feeling Claire didn't, no matter how many times he said it to her. "But I'm not okay with Claire putting her life at risk either. There has to be something, Abby, something that you can do." He buried his head in his hands.

"Has she been moody?" Abby asked.

Josh snorted.

"Okay, abnormally moody? More than what you'd expect from being pregnant? Excessive mood swings, like from being angry to isolating herself?"

Josh just looked at Abby. He really didn't need to answer that.

"Okay." Abigail looked up at the ceiling. "Damn it," she said. "We can get her massages and chiropractic treatments adjusted so they're more often. That might help. I prescribed a pill, but she's never had it filled—I checked with the pharmacy."

Josh lifted his head. "You did? When? What kind of pill? What will it do?" Why hadn't Claire mentioned it to him? He would have gotten it filled for her if that was the case.

"Last month, to help with the headaches. She's antidrug though, in case you haven't noticed. She'll take the over-the-counter medicines, but not anything I prescribe. Your wife is a tad stubborn."

"A tad?" Derek laughed. "We're talking about Claire here. For as long as I can remember, it's been her dream to have a baby again. Are you honestly surprised that she's doing everything she can to make sure nothing happens to the baby? Lay off a bit, guys."

Josh pushed himself to his feet. "That dream won't matter if she kills herself in the process, and it's not just her child, it's ours. She seems to forget that I should have a say in this too." A whole assortment of emotions rolled through him. Anger. Frustration. Grief.

"I won't let that happen, Josh. I made you that promise, and I intend to keep it." Abby sat up straighter and glared at Derek.

"Don't be upset with him. He's just saying what we all know." Josh grabbed the beer he'd set down. "I have an idea," he said after finishing half the bottle. "Why don't you try to talk some sense into my wife? God knows she might actually listen to you." He pointed at Derek.

"That's actually not a bad idea," Abby agreed.

"What exactly am I supposed to say? Claire, you need to start listening to my wife or you're going to die?"

Josh sunk back down on the couch.

"What about me? Do I matter at all in this? I'm just supposed to sit here and be okay with the fact that my wife is dying right before my eyes? That I'm going to be a single father? That I'm going to lose the love of my life? Don't I matter?" His body shook with the swell of emotions coursing through him.

"I sound like a baby," he said quietly as Abby and Derek just sat there, staring at him. What was he doing? He should be focused on Claire, finding a way to save both her and their baby rather than whining like a child.

"Forget it," he said. "I'm just . . . exhausted. I'm going to miss my deadline, and Claire won't let me explain what's going on in order to get an extension."

"Nah," Derek finally said. "You sound like a man who's finally realized he can't get through this alone." Derek leaned forward. "But you've got us, and you can bet we won't stop fighting—for you or Claire."

"I should get home. Claire is probably wondering where I am."

Abby laughed. "You're not going anywhere. I sent Claire a text saying you'd stopped by, and that we fed you. She said if you drink more than one beer, you're to stay, and she'll come pick you up. You've had two by my count, so guess you're stuck here."

"Claire is going to come here? You're sure?" That would mean she'd actually have to leave the house on her own.

"Want to make a party out of it? We could invite a few people over for drinks, have a bonfire, and eat s'mores." There was a glint in Derek's eyes that grew even after Abigail smacked him on the arm.

"Seriously, sometimes I swear you're a child in a man's body."

"We all are, sweetie. The sooner you realize that, the more fun we'll have." Derek pretended to duck her next blow. "But, I'm serious about the bonfire and s'mores. Text Claire and ask her to pick up marshmallows. I ate all ours last night."

When Abby pulled out her phone, Josh wanted to laugh but couldn't. "You're not seriously asking her, are you?"

"Doesn't hurt to try." She shrugged.

Josh sighed and headed into the kitchen where he grabbed another beer.

"Liquid courage?" Derek followed him and leaned against the counter, taking the beer Josh held out.

"Pardon?"

"Liquid courage." Derek nodded to the beer in Josh's hand. "You know, so you can tell Claire how you're feeling with us backing you up."

Josh hadn't thought of that, but his friend was probably right.

"I don't need to drink to tell my wife how I feel."

"Sure. I believe you. But, you might want to stop after that one, if you don't want things escalating. Trust me on that, bro."

From the tone in Derek's voice, Josh wondered what was going on, and whether he'd interrupted something when he dropped by.

"Things okay?" He said quietly after checking the doorway to make sure Abby wasn't standing there, listening in.

"Nope. We're not talking about me or my marriage. This is about you." Derek pointed his beer toward him and frowned. "It's okay to admit you're not perfect. You know that, right? Things don't always have to be awesome in your little world," he muttered.

"I know that." What was going on here? It almost sounded like Derek was gloating over the fact things were rough between him and Claire. "Is there something you want to say to me, Derek? Now's the time. Spit it out."

"Nah, man. We're good." Derek shook his head and walked out, leaving Josh alone.

Claire coming here wasn't what he wanted. He should have thought this through better. He'd left the house to grapple with his thoughts, and he was nowhere close to the peace he needed before seeing his wife. Nor was it fair to ambush her with his feelings when she was trying hard to shelter herself from stress.

"I can't do it, guys." Decision made, Josh pushed himself from the wall and headed into the living room. "Claire doesn't need . . ."

His wife stood there, bag in hand. "Claire doesn't need what?"

"That was fast." That's all Josh could say. He didn't expect her here so soon.

"What was fast?" Claire handed Abby the bag she'd brought with her. "Marshmallows as requested."

Abby grabbed the bag. "You stopped at the gas station for these? You know they mark these up by at least four dollars. The grocery store would have been cheaper."

"There were too many cars there. I didn't want to run into anyone." Abby crossed her arms, and when she refocused her attention on Josh, he winced. "What don't I need, Josh? You drunk? S'mores? To come and get you? What?" She counted off the list of ideas on her fingers and looked at him expectantly.

Josh was at a loss. "All of the above?" He chickened out. And from the look on Abby's and Derek's faces, they knew it too.

Claire must have noticed as well. "Should I take a seat, or is this something we'll talk about when we're alone?" Her tone held a hint of frost, and Josh knew he was in trouble. "Or do you need Abby and Derek here as backup."

"It's not like that, Claire. Josh—"

"Can speak for himself." Claire interrupted Abby who was kind enough to come to his defense. But he didn't need it.

"Claire's right." He went and gently squeezed Abby's shoulder in thanks and then went to stand in front of his wife. "I can speak for myself, but you don't always hear me. Not lately at least."

Claire's shoulder's dropped. "Josh, do we have to do this here?"

"No." He shook his head. "We don't."

"Well, you might not. But I do." Abby stepped forward, arms folded over her chest, and tapped her foot. "You wouldn't be lying to me about how severe your headaches are getting, are you?"

Claire looked from Josh to Abby and back to Josh before she shook her head. "Why?"

"Claire," Josh said quietly in rebuke.

Claire's lips thinned. "You're kidding me, right?"

"You tell me," Abby said. "Josh seems to think they're getting worse. Yet you tell me they're around a four or a five on the pain scale."

The moment Claire closed her eyes, Josh knew. It was like a sucker punch to his gut. They were worse. He'd been right.

"Why, Claire?" He breathed. "Don't you realize what you're doing?"

"Protecting our child. That's what I'm doing. Can't you see that?" There was both anger and heartache in her voice.

"I see it, hon. I see it." Josh stepped toward her and grabbed her hands, holding them tight in his own. "But I also see you giving up on yourself, and I can't accept that. I won't. You might be okay with your dying, but I'm not."

"You can't look at it that way, Josh," Claire said.

Josh attempted to disagree, to explain more of how he saw it, but the words wouldn't come.

"Want to know what I see?" Derek said, standing beside Abby. "I see a woman being selfish, and it surprises me more than anything, because you're normally anything but selfish."

A flash of pain appeared in Claire's eyes before she closed them and stared down at the ground. Her hands instinctively wrapped around her growing belly, and it angered Josh. He turned, ready to tell his friend off for hurting his wife. Then he stopped.

"Derek's right," Abby said. "You made me a promise, Claire, and you're basically forcing me to break my word to you and your husband. I promised that I would keep both you and your baby safe, but when you lie to me, when you try to hide the truth, you're tying my hands. What if it's too late? I'm going to carry that guilt forever."

Claire shook her head, and all Josh wanted to do was hold her in his arms and protect her from this. He could see they were hurting her, that it was all too much. But at the same time, he was glad they were finally being honest.

"I just want to give our baby more time, that's all."

"So you're a doctor now?" Abby's voice was terse.

"No."

"Have you stopped trusting me?" Abby demanded.

Claire shook her head.

"Then tomorrow morning I'm requesting a new MRI and I expect you to show up. You're also going to bring me your journal and you're going to fix all the entries where you attempted to hide the truth from me, got it?"

"Abby, I—"

"No." Abby interrupted her, her hand held up high. "I won't allow you to sacrifice yourself, not like this. Enough is enough, Claire. If I have to, I'll admit you into the hospital for twenty-four hour observation. Do you want that?"

By now Claire's eyes had grown wide, and Josh could tell from the way she clenched her fists that the message had gotten through.

"No. I'm sorry, Abby." Claire's shoulders sank as a heavy weight settled upon her.

Josh gathered his wife into his arms. "I love you," he whispered into her ear.

"I came here tonight needing friends to listen and tell me the truth, but it turns out, we both needed to hear it." He looked up and smiled at Derek and Abby. "Thank you."

"I've said it from the very beginning. You're not in this alone, and it's time you both stop acting like you are." Derek stepped forward and shook Josh's offered hand. "I've got your back, dude. Don't forget it."

"Claire?" Abby called out.

Claire half turned in his arms to look at her friend.

"I love you," Abby said, her eyes bright red from withheld tears.

Things were quiet on the way home. He tried to apologize a few times, but Claire would have none of it.

It wasn't until they were home and he offered to run her a bath that she finally said what she was feeling.

"I get it. You didn't feel you could be honest with me, and I get that. I do. But I'm not going to apologize either. Sometimes I feel like I'm the only one who sees the big picture here." She stood on the steps, her hand clenching the railing.

Josh crossed his arms. "The big picture is us raising our child together, Claire."

"I know."

"No, I don't think you do. You think you need to do everything you can to protect our baby even if it means protecting it from me. What do you think I want? For our baby to die? What kind of man do you think I am?" The words hurt as he spoke them. They tore at his soul, and yet, saying how he truly felt was like being cleansed.

"That's exactly the type of man you've been ever since you found out about the tumors."

In that one moment, everything that had held them together, disintegrated. Josh could see it clear as day. The trust they once had destroyed. The honesty between them, the safety in that honesty, withered.

Josh stepped back while Claire ran up their stairs. The sound of the bathroom door slamming vibrated along the walls, the glass in the hung picture frames ringing from the impact.

TWENTY-SIX

CLAIRE

A memory from Rome, Italy
End of April

Claire relaxed at the rooftop terrace of their hotel. She couldn't get over the size of the lemons on the potted trees that surrounded her. She sipped her white wine, savoring its crispness, and was thankful to have escaped the craziness of the mob below.

They were staying in Rome only a few days, but she was so ready to leave. They'd filled their days with tours and booked a room directly across from the Spanish Steps—both rookie mistakes she wished they could take back. Rome was meant to be enjoyed slowly, to let the history and power soak one's soul, but she'd insisted on cramming as much as possible in their few short days, despite Josh's hesitation.

She should have listened to him.

"Okay." Josh sank down in a plump chair beside her and put his feet up on the footrest. "We've got an hour before we have to meet the group in the square. Why don't we head down to our room for a quick power nap and give our feet a break? I'm exhausted from the Vatican tour." He yawned and leaned his head back.

"I won't be able to sleep." Claire yawned as well. "The noise from the steps is almost deafening."

"You were the one who insisted staying here." Josh yawned again and Claire smacked him playfully.

"Stop that," she said, stifling her own yawn. "We can relax after dinner tonight." Which meant they had another, oh, six or seven hours to go. She dug her finger into a painful point on the side of her face, close to her hairline. The pressure helped stave off the headache that was only just beginning.

"I need to find a local pharmacy or something," she said. "I used up my last Tylenol this morning, and I've got another headache."

Josh partially opened one eye and looked at her. "Again?"

She nodded. "I really hate headaches." Until recently, she could count on one hand the number of headaches she'd had over the past few years.

"Maybe your body is trying to tell you something?" Josh suggested.

"Like what?"

"Oh, I don't know. Maybe you're exhausted, trying to do too much, not dealing with things the way you need to . . ." His voice trailed off, and for a moment, Claire wondered if he'd actually fallen asleep.

"I'm dealing just fine, thank-you-very-much," she muttered.

"Sure you are." Josh's lips quirked in what she assumed was a grin.

The pounding of feet up the stairs shattered whatever illusion of peace and quiet Claire had hoped for. A family of four joined them on the terrace.

"It's so beautiful up here. Are those real lemons? I'm starving."

Claire smiled at the mother of two as she passed by.

"If you were hoping for some peace and quiet, sadly my children don't know the concept," the mother apologized, shooting deadly glances toward her son and daughter. "Ethan, Olivia, what do you say?"

"Sorry, Mom. Ma'am." The boy apologized before he turned away to fill a plate with finger food.

"Oops, sorry." The girl grinned. "Mom, they have your favorite—that tomato and mozzarella dish."

"We won't be here long," the mother said. "We have to meet our tour guide within the hour, so we're stocking up on food. Who knew boys could eat so much," she mock whispered.

"I heard that," her son groaned, his face a red so bright that Claire could see it from a distance.

Claire smiled. "No worries. We have a tour as well, so we're just resting our feet. I think at this point, even walking on cotton balls would hurt, let alone the cobblestones of the streets."

"Oh, what tour are you headed to? We've been on so many since we arrived, we might have done it." She leaned over, extending her hand. "I'm Sylvia by the way, and that giant of a man over there is my husband, Justin."

"Claire." She introduced herself. "And this is my husband, Josh." She gave a small wave to Justin who had sat down at a table with a plate loaded with fresh food.

"We're going to the Colosseum this afternoon," Claire glanced at her watch. "Which we should probably get ready for." She nudged Josh with her foot to wake him up.

"Oh, we're headed there as well. Wouldn't it be funny"—Sylvia glanced behind her at her husband—"if we were on the same tour together. This and the Capuchin Crypt were the top two things our son had on his list."

Claire finished off her wine and stood. "The Capuchin Crypt was amazing. I could have stayed in there for hours. It was so hard for me to not sit down against the wall and draw everything. The artistic display of the bones . . . mesmerizing."

"You draw? Are you an artist or . . . ?"

"A children's book illustrator," Claire answered. "Have you been to the crypt yet?"

Sylvia shook her head. "We'll head there tomorrow before our flight home. Olivia got to pick what our first adventure here in Rome would be, and Ethan picked the last."

Claire glanced over at the two teenagers who had joined their father at the table.

"Let me guess. Olivia wanted to go shopping."

Sylvia laughed. "I believe her exact words were *Shop till Ethan drops*. The two love to challenge one another." She shook her head. "They keep life interesting, that's for sure."

"I can only imagine." When Josh stood beside her, she entwined her fingers with his. "Enjoy your lunch. Who knows? We might see each other soon." She waved good-bye to the family and made her way down the stairs, Josh following behind.

"Looked like a nice enough family," Josh said as he wiped his eyes.

"I wonder what it's like to view the history of this city through the eyes of a teenager," Claire said as she grabbed her purse, their tour tickets, and her camera.

"Well, I've been trying to see it through Jack's eyes, and honestly, teenage boys are probably no different. We tend to mature at a snail's pace when it comes to stuff like that. The boy is probably imagining all the gladiator fights and wishing he could step back in time to be there himself."

"Oh really?" Claire stood on tiptoes to give her husband a kiss. "So is that what you'll be imagining while we're there?"

"You can bet on it. I'll be looking through Jack's eyes while you take a copious number of photos. Hmmm . . . Now I wonder if we should have just gone by ourselves, so we could have found a place to sit awhile. You could draw, and I could plot out Jack's scene."

"Well, we are coming back to Rome for a few days after our cruise, so if we need to, we can come back." She winced a little as she bent over to tie her shoes.

"You okay?" Josh asked.

She slowly straightened back up. "I'll be fine as long as we can grab some water and something for this headache." It was only a dull throb right now, but a headache was a headache.

"Do you think it would be too morbid if we included a scene with Jack at the Capuchin Crypt? You'd have to include all the skeletons, though," Josh said.

Claire considered for a moment. "I could. The hanging lanterns made out of arm bones might be more fascinating than morbid. Or, we could do one of those 'Where is Jack?' pictures at the back of the book, and I can add some pictures of monks and a few skeletons. Or, we could do a whole Halloween book and have Jack trying to get his mom to decorate the house like the crypt," she thought out loud. There was a lot they could do.

"I also think we should have Jack climb the Spanish Steps, don't you?" Claire said. "I can see him making his way through the crowds, his mom losing sight of him until he's at the top, waving at her. I drew a few sketches early this morning and took a lot of photos."

Josh nodded his head, continuing to brainstorm as they exited their room and took the stairs down to the main floor.

"I see Jack leaning far out the window trying to catch a glimpse of the steps, and then his mother pulling him back in. Kind of like what you did on our first day. I can't believe those windows open up like that with no screens," Josh said, while Claire couldn't help but giggle.

That had been hilarious yesterday. She'd leaned out quite far to snap some photos, only to have Josh haul her back in, his face almost white. Apparently, she'd leaned so far out she'd been standing on tiptoes, and it scared him.

She shouldn't laugh, but she couldn't help it.

"If we hurry, we might have time for more gelato before the tour begins." She tugged his arm. They weaved through the crowd as they made their way up the Via dei Condotti and turned right. She spotted a little pharmacy just down the street, close to a gelato storefront where crowds were lined up. "Or, you could stand in line, and I'll be right back?"

Josh looked at the line and shrugged. "Don't take long. I'm not liable if I pick the wrong flavor for you."

She'd better hurry. Knowing her husband, he'd get her pistachio or something equally horrendous just so he could eat it. "Coconut or vanilla, please." She blew him a kiss as she walked away.

She pushed her way through the throng and was so glad they had booked a small boutique hotel for their return trip. She'd had enough of this mob. Tomorrow, they would head to Positano, where they could relax on the beach and enjoy the quaint little town before going to Civitavecchia to begin their cruise. They were on the tail end of their European adventure, but Claire wasn't ready to head home. Home meant returning to life, accepting reality, and planning a way to move forward.

TWENTY-SEVEN

CLAIRE

Present day

The hospital waiting room was both sterile and cold, and Claire refused to sit in those uncomfortable seats any longer.

"I want to go home." She stared at her husband, challenging him to disagree with her.

He leaned back in his chair and crossed his ankles.

"We're not going anywhere. Abigail will be back with the results after she speaks to the radiologist. She said she'd meet us in the cafeteria."

"It's too crowded."

He cocked an eyebrow. "So then we sit here." He patted the chair beside him, but Claire turned her back. She pulled out her phone and sent Abby a text.

I'm going home.

She waited for a response. If she said fine, then regardless of what Josh said, she was out of there.

Sit. Almost done.

"Abby's almost done." She gritted her teeth.

"*Almost* means we have time for coffee. Tell her we'll be in the cafeteria." He stood up, smoothing his jeans as he did so.

She shook her head.

"I'm not going alone, Claire." He held out his hand. She stepped back, away from him.

"Why not? It's just a coffee, Josh. I'll let her know we're here." She sat down and started her reply to Abby. When she looked up, Josh hadn't moved.

"The cafeteria won't be crowded, for Pete's sake, Claire. You need to get over this." He shook his head in exasperation and stepped toward her, his hand still outstretched.

Claire breathed in deep and slowly let it out through her nose. He was right. It was only a coffee, and it was a small hospital. How crowded would the cafeteria be? She placed her hand in his and followed as he led her out of the room, down the hallway, and into the main lobby, where the door to the cafeteria was.

As they turned the corner, Claire froze. Every time she came into the hospital, she entered and exited through the rear entrance, the staff door just off from the kitchen. Since she used to volunteer here, any time she ran into hospital staff, they'd just nod in greeting as they rushed past.

But this wasn't the back hallways, and it was more crowded than she expected it to be.

"A couple more steps, Claire. Come on, you can do this."

Josh led her into the cafeteria, where only a few tables were occupied. She didn't recognize anyone she knew personally, just doctors, nurses and others who kept their gaze on their coffee cups, not wanting to exchange pleasantries.

She let out the breath she'd been holding. This wasn't so bad.

Josh grabbed a tray, grabbed a few disposable coffee cups, and pushed the tray along the silver rollers. He stopped at the see-through cooler. He plunked a container of chocolate pudding with whipped cream and a small container of fresh fruit onto their tray.

"You need to eat something," he told her before continuing toward the cash register.

Claire grabbed a few cracker packets as well.

"Well, hello stranger."

Claire turned to find Gerry Stam behind her, coffee in hand.

"Gerry." She swallowed past the lump in her throat. "Fancy seeing you here."

The older man shrugged. "I need something to do with my time, so after the summer season, I volunteer here to keep me busy. Besides, Georgia is here, and it keeps me close."

"How is your wife?" Claire placed her arm on his hand in sympathy. Georgia broke her hip years ago and now spent a lot of time at the hospital.

"Her dementia is getting worse by the day, but my girl is still in there. Can't walk worth beans anymore, though. Her bone mass keeps deteriorating from the cancer."

"I'm sorry," Claire said. She couldn't imagine what his life must be like right now.

"No apologies needed. How's the little one doing?" He nodded toward her swelling belly.

Claire smiled. "Doing fine. Thank you for asking."

He nodded, his lips twisting into that half smile of his. "Haven't seen you much but figured you were drawing." It wasn't so much a question, but still, Claire knew an answer was expected.

"Blame it on Josh. If he would slow down the writing a little, I'd have more time to breathe," she quietly teased. Josh's hand rested in the curve of her back, and she appreciated the support.

Talking to Gerry wasn't as bad as she thought it would be. She sucked in a long breath and slowly let it out.

"Just trying to free up our time when the baby comes, that's all."

Gerry nodded. "Smart man." He put some money down on the counter and shuffled out of the cafeteria.

"That wasn't so bad, was it?" Josh said after paying for their items. "You okay to wait here?"

Claire looked about the room and nodded. She sent Abby a text, letting her know where they were.

Thirty minutes later, Abby poked her head through the cafeteria door and waved. Her expression gave nothing away, but considering she walked over to grab a coffee first, Claire was able to feel a little bit of relief. If things were bad, Abby would be hauling Claire to her office for a talk. If she had time for coffee, then all was well.

She headed to their table but didn't sit down. Instead, she took a long drink of her hot coffee and shuddered.

"Sorry I took so long." She held the cup between her hands. "I spoke to the specialist, and he gave me his office for us to chat in. I've also slotted you in to sit with him later, but for now we can go over the results together, okay?" She didn't leave them time to respond, just turned and walked out.

Claire noticed how straight Abby's back was, how measured her footsteps seemed to be, and the way she flexed her fingers as she walked. Claire glanced at Josh and knew he'd noticed too. He threaded his fingers through hers and held on tight.

Once at the office, Abby waited for them to sit down before she closed the door. She didn't sit behind the desk, rather she sat on the corner of it, coffee held tight so that her knuckles looked white.

"It's not good, is it?" Josh was the one to break the silence in the room.

For a moment, it looked like Abigail was going to tear up.

"It's not. Claire, the tumors are growing, which is why the headaches are increasing and may explain some of the other things happening to you." Abigail looked her straight in the eye, and Claire flushed.

"Things happening . . . what do you mean?" asked Josh.

"The larger the tumors grow, the more pressure on her brain, which can cause any number of things. Fainting, mood swings, even panic attacks. The specialist you're meeting with later today will go over this is more detail," Abigail explained.

"So." Claire struggled to process the news. "My constant panic attacks are expected?"

Abby nodded and set her cup down.

"But the tumors are growing. What does that mean?" Josh asked, his voice sounding pinched.

"What it means is that it's time to act."

Claire jumped to her feet. "I'm not putting my child in danger. It's not time."

"Of course not. Settle down." Abigail gripped the edge of the desk with both hands and leaned slightly forward.

"You're far enough along that we can now discuss bumping up your delivery date, which is where I come in. We're obviously not going to hit the projected late January time frame. The earliest I would consider delivering your baby is twenty-eight weeks. There's a 96 percent success rate if we wait till then." She held up her hand as Claire was about to interrupt her. "We'll have a team in place, and everything will be fine. Trust me. I'm not just pulling a number out of the air, Claire. I've been consulting with colleagues for weeks about this."

"You have?" Claire was at a loss for words.

"I asked you to trust me, right? I made you a promise, and I intend to keep it. I will not allow you to argue with me, Claire. Do you understand me? I will save your life and this baby. I will hold my godchild in my arms and help plan birthday parties with you. This will work."

Josh's hold of her hand tightened. "You promise?" When Abby nodded, he reached over and held Claire tight.

"We're going to be okay," Josh whispered.

"We're going to be okay," Claire whispered back.

She looked to Abigail and mouthed *thank you*. She knew there was more, that more needed to be said. But for now, this was enough.

"So what's the next step then?" Josh asked. "Surgery? Radiation?"

Before Abigail could respond, a cold tingling coursed through Claire's body, from the tip of her head down to her toes. She didn't want Abby to respond. She wanted to live in the blissful ignorance that once her baby was born, all would be okay.

"As long as the tumors haven't grown more in the next month, we can still do surgery."

"And if they have?" Claire found the strength to ask.

Abigail remained silent.

"How much time do we have?" Claire held on to Josh's hand as she asked.

"One month," was the response. "We have four weeks until you are twenty-eight weeks along."

Four weeks. Four weeks for her body to behave itself. Four weeks for her baby to grow and her tumors to . . . no, she wasn't going to go there. She had four weeks for her baby to grow. That is what she would focus on.

"Well then," she said with false cheer. "We've got four weeks to meet all our deadlines and get ready for our baby. Guess we'd better get to work."

THINGS TO EXPERIENCE WITH OUR CHILD

1. Watch a balloon take flight and fly away.
2. Watch a parade. *(Claire: I want to take a photo of our boy/girl on daddy's shoulders while eating ice cream. Josh: I'd prefer the ice cream to be eaten first. Otherwise, Mommy can be the one holding you while I take the photo.)*
3. See Mickey and Minnie Mouse for the first time.
4. Teach you to ride a bike.
5. Teach you to drive. *(That is a Daddy job, just FYI.)*
6. Christmas. *(Claire: We'll need to make new traditions and go on a lot of trips. Josh: Are we actually going to take one of these holiday trips or just keep talking about them? Claire: Let's go to Germany and see Father Christmas in person as well as the Christkind angel in Nuremberg. Oh, let's not forget the markets— all those Christmas markets with gingerbread. That's been on my list forever. Josh: Sure, Claire. Whatever you say. Note to child: Mommy always makes these plans and never follows through. She loves to spend Christmas at home.*

TWENTY-EIGHT

JOSH

Present day

The soft cadence of Claire's voice as she read a story to the children surrounding her on the floor was almost too much for Josh. While he videotaped her, all he could think about was that they had three weeks left of *this*.

This meaning just the two of them, pretending all was well, that their lives were not about to change irrevocably. In three weeks, Josh would hold his son or daughter in his arms. In three weeks, his wife would know if she were to live or die.

He was going to throw up just thinking about it.

"She's a natural, isn't she?" Alice whispered into his ear.

He nodded. She was indeed a natural—both as a storyteller and as a woman who loved children.

A mother.

The past week had been a whirlwind. It was as though a switch had flipped on in his wife's brain, and everything she'd been worried about for the past few months had disappeared. She still had headaches and took a lot of naps, but there seemed to be a drive, a determination to make this time count.

Including being here at the Hospital for Sick Kids in Toronto. Josh had begged to reschedule it for a later date, but Claire wouldn't hear of it. He knew, even now, that she suffered from a headache. He could see it in her eyes, the way she carefully moved her head while reading the story.

"And that was how Jack decided he wanted to be a lion tamer." Claire closed the book and laid it in her lap.

"No!" said the kids at her feet.

"No?" Claire asked. She glanced up at Josh, her eyes sparkling. "He didn't want to be a lion tamer? But . . ."

"He wants to set the lions free," one little boy, bouncing on his knees, yelled out.

"Ah! So that's why Jack picked up the flute—to lead the lions back into the jungle." A huge smile appeared, and Josh fell in love with her all over again. Her eyes sparkled, her cheeks bloomed a soft red, and Josh was struck by her beauty.

Please God, don't take that beauty away from me, he prayed.

"No!" This time a little girl shouted.

"Well, I'm confused. What did Jack do then?" She had purposely closed the book before she read the last page. She once told him this was her favorite part of the storytelling, listening to the children get excited about the book.

"Jack picked up the mouse and tucked it in his pocket. He wanted to keep it, but his mom wouldn't let him." Sami said proudly as she stood beside Claire, her hand on her shoulder.

The moment Claire saw Sami, it was like a weight lifted from her shoulders. He knew Claire kept in touch with Sami, but he hadn't really realized just how close they'd become.

"Now the lions weren't afraid," another voice said.

"Silly lions for being afraid of a mouse," Claire teased. She reached behind her for a large gift bag they'd brought with them. They had just enough stuffed little lion cubs to give away to the kids, and while Claire read the story, one of the nurses had left more gifts in each bed—a stack of signed books.

"Is everything okay?" Alice asked after Josh stopped the recording.

"Everything is fine, why?" They'd discussed sharing with Alice what was going on, but Claire decided against it. The fewer who knew, the better.

"Just making sure. You know I'm here if you need anything." Alice smiled at Marlene, Sami's mother, as she joined them.

"Sami was so stoked to have you guys come today," Marlene said.

"I'm glad. What's this I hear about her getting discharged? You've got to be excited about that." Josh couldn't have been happier to hear the news.

"You have no idea."

"No idea about what?" Sami bounded over and grabbed her mother's arm. "Wasn't that just awesome, Mom? I want to be a writer when I grow up." She looked at Josh and beamed a huge smile at him. "I'm going to write your son or daughter a story. Is that okay?"

Claire joined them and heard Sami's words. She wrapped her arms around the young girl and kissed the top of her head. "You write all the stories you want, and I'll draw pictures for them. But you've got to come visit, so you can read the stories personally. Deal?"

Sami's intake of air could be heard by almost everyone, along with the squeal that followed. "Oh my goodness, yes. Yes, yes, *YES!*"

Claire winced slightly and leaned into Josh, who literally held her up. He could see her weakening the longer they stood there. He noticed most of the kids were headed back to their rooms, which gave him an out to leave, otherwise he knew Claire would want to stay.

"Claire, honey, if we want to get home before it gets too dark, we need to leave now," he said quietly.

Claire nodded and focused on Sami.

"I hear you're heading home. Does that mean you get to dress up and go out for Halloween?"

Sami looked up at her mom before she leaned forward and whispered in Claire's ear.

"You are? That is going to be so cool!" Claire mock whispered back. "Take pictures and send them to me, okay?" She wrapped her arms around Sami and held her tight.

Josh saw her struggle to hold back the tears.

Was Claire imagining this would be the last time she saw the young girl? Was this how the next three weeks would be—her trying to say good-bye to those she loved, just in case?

Screw that.

"You know what, Sami? We want to have a big Christmas party, and we'll go on sleigh rides and toboggan down a huge hill. We could even make a rink in our backyard. Do you think you could come join us? We've got enough room for you and your family."

"I think that would be fantastic," Marlene said. "A sleigh ride through the snow would be so much fun."

Claire gave him a worried look, but he ignored it.

"It's a date then."

Sami jumped up and down with excitement. "Will your baby be born by then?" she asked.

Josh smiled. "You never know. It's our miracle baby so keep your fingers crossed," he said. He caught the concerned looks from both Marlene and Alice, while Claire wouldn't even look him in the eye.

"I love you, Sami girl." Claire knelt down and looked Sami straight in the eyes. "You are amazing and so full of life. Don't ever stop smiling, okay?" She gave her another squeeze before she clung to Josh's arm and almost pushed him to move.

Alice joined them as they walked toward the elevators. "What's going on?" she asked. "And don't you dare tell me nothing, because that back there sounded a hell of a lot like a good-bye, and I know that little girl isn't going anywhere."

When Claire looked up at him with pain in her eyes, he came to a decision. It wasn't fair of her to keep asking him to lie for her, nor was it fair to keep their friends in the dark.

"Claire has—" He stopped as Claire squeezed his arm.

"I have to go for surgery as soon as the baby is born. I have a brain tumor. Well, technically two."

Alice remained calm. She folded her hands together and looked Claire over.

"Oh Claire. I'm so sorry. I bet your head is hurting right now, isn't it? You refused treatment until the baby is born, didn't you? Which explains why the little one might be here before Christmas." She nodded deeply.

Josh was impressed.

"I've been around enough to read between the lines. Just tell me you haven't given up, please," she said to Claire.

Claire's chin rose, and Josh waited to hear what she'd say.

"I'm not giving up," she said quietly.

Josh actually believed her.

Dear child of my heart,

I love you.

    If you are reading this, then it means I'm not in your life, and for that, I can never apologize enough.

    There are so many things I wish I could have experienced with you. Your first words, your first smile, your first . . . everything as you grow. Walking with you as we head to your first day of school, helping you with homework, making your first costume for a school play from scratch. I already miss snuggling with you before bed as we read a story together, and I wish I could have seen you first discover the joy of words as you read a story all by yourself for the first time.

    I regret not being there to see you fall in love for the first time, to be there to give you advice as you go through life, to give you those motherly talks, where you roll your eyes but all the while take my words to heart.

    I hope you travel. Go on trips with your father to see new places, take photos of the world as you fly overhead, try new foods, listen to people's stories of their life, and never be satisfied with being stagnant. There's so much more to life than what you are living right now . . . Embrace it with everything inside you. See where your adventures take you.

When you're lonely or afraid, think of me beside you, supporting you in every decision you make. I'd be there to give you a hug when you need it, a shoulder to cry on, and a hand to hold.

I wish I could be there to give you hugs. All the time. Even when you think you don't need them anymore. I will miss telling you just how much I love you and how proud I am of you—because I am—so very proud of you. I know you will be amazing. Of that, I have no doubt.

I'm going to miss doing everything with you, and I'm not sure I can handle that.

All I ever wanted was for you to live and live life as fully as you can. Even if it means I won't be around to experience that life with you. I love you, the child of my heart, and I will do everything and anything that I can to protect you—even if that means giving up my life for you.

There has never been a choice for me. Never once have I regretted putting off my own treatment to ensure you are born healthy. Never. If I'm not here with you as you read this, it's because my own wish for you has come true—that you are alive.

I love you. I always will.

TWENTY-NINE

CLAIRE

Present day

A ll her life she'd created lists. List of things she wanted to accomplish in life, lists of attributes she wanted in a husband, lists of
what she planned to do with her career.

She never thought she'd be planning a list for the things she needed
to do before she died. It wasn't as if she knew for sure her life was going
to end, but she wanted to be prepared. The last thing she wanted was
to leave Josh with things unfinished, or to die with regrets. Did that
mean she wanted to die?

She never had more reasons to live than she did now.

It wasn't like planning a three-week vacation. There were no snorkel
trips, no massages, no must-see sights to check off her list.

How could she pick with only three weeks left?

Reading at children's hospital. Check.

Finish her secret story and send it off to Julia. Almost done.

See Sami's beautiful smile one more time. Check, except, she
could never see enough of her smiles, so really, should that be
unchecked then?

Buy all the necessary baby clothes Josh would need for the next year or so.

Buy the ultimate dad's guide to raising a baby by himself.

Smile as much as possible because people should be remembered as joyful and fun loving, right?

She didn't want to spend her last possible days preparing to die rather than enjoying life. And yet, the controlling part of her wanted to be prepared.

Whether her tumors grew or not, that was out of her control.

Whether she could have surgery and survive, that was also out of her control.

Whether Josh would be left raising their child alone, there was nothing she could do about that.

But what she could do was live these few weeks with her life full of love and pray that everything would be fine.

"That looks serious."

Startled, she found her hand clutching her chest before she laughed along with her husband, who stood there with a grin on his face.

"I haven't seen you jump like that in a while," he said.

She set her notebook down and stood, crossing the room to snuggle into her husband's warm chest for a hug.

"What are you working on?" Josh glanced at her notebook, and Claire wished she'd closed it.

"Just making a list of everything that needs to be done before baby arrives."

Josh placed his hands on her belly and leaned down.

"Hear that, monkey? Your mama is making a list. That means she's probably putting me to work." He looked up and winked. "The first thing on the list had better be to pick a name."

"Maybe we'll let the baby pick?"

Josh's eyebrows rose. "Really? I'm not willing to spend years calling our baby *Baby*. Just saying."

Claire lightly punched his arm. "You know what I mean. Maybe once we hold our son or daughter in our arms, the right name will come to us."

"Maybe. You don't mind if I bring my own list of names to the delivery room though, right? As back up?"

"You bring your list, and I'll bring mine." She gave him a smile and rested her head on his shoulder.

She already had an idea of what she wanted to name their child if it were a girl.

"I'm serious," he said. "What can I do to help? Any baby things I need to build? Help organize? Take you shopping? Rub your feet? What do you need?"

"A warm bath?" Her fingers and toes were frozen, and even though the heat was on, there was a cool draft coming in through the windows. "I thought we were supposed to have a warm fall this year. It feels like it could snow any day."

"Well, it is almost the end of October, so I wouldn't be surprised. A warm bath? That's all? Are you hungry? I need to run into town a little later. Did you want to come with me?"

Claire gave him a hug. "Just a bath. It's hard to bend down to turn on the taps, so that would be a great help. As for going into town . . . what if we head to Last Call for dinner? I could go for wings and potato skins and . . ." She stopped at the look on her husband's face. "Shocker, right?" she said.

He slowly nodded.

She didn't want a big deal made out of it, but yes, this was the first time since she found out about the tumors that she'd suggested going out. "Well, it's time to stop hiding, isn't it?"

"Are you sure? Do you want me to invite anyone? Abby and Derek?"

Claire didn't know how to answer. On the one hand, yes. She'd love for their friends to be there to be a buffer, but on the other hand, she wanted this time with Josh all to herself.

"I'll leave that up to you," she said instead. She shivered and rubbed her hands together.

"One warm bath coming up." Josh gave her a small kiss on the forehead and left.

Claire waited until she heard the water running before she went to her notebook and picked it up.

> *Go out in public. Check.*
> *Write letters to Abby, Derek, her mother, Dr. Will, and*
> *   Sami to say good-bye.*
> *Write more letters to her child.*
> *Take some videos.*
> *Create a keepsake box for her baby, for sentimental and*
> *   important things for the future.*
> *Go on dates with Josh.*
> *Plan a girls' night with Abby and the others.*
> *Pick a name for the baby.*
> *Live each day as if it were . . .*

The worry and fear of what could happen would always be there, but she didn't have to let fear take hold of her. She'd been frozen long enough.

Claire couldn't get over how packed the main street was.

"Is there a game or something happening?" she said as they drove down, turned around, and parked on a side street.

"I don't think so, but you never know. Maybe Fran has a special on wings and everyone is there."

Claire stumbled on the sidewalk, and Josh grabbed her hand. "I'm teasing," he said.

"Why don't I just wait in the car while you do whatever it is you need to do?" Maybe this wasn't a good idea.

"Claire, it's okay. Just take a deep breath. Why don't you stop in at the bakery and chat with Kat or Kim. I won't be long."

She breathed in and let it out just as they turned the corner. The bakery was just down the way.

"How about you pick dessert tonight," Josh said. He listed the different things he'd like her to get, everything from apple pie to a chocolate cake to some of Kim's famous shortbread cookies.

She knew he did that to distract her, and it worked. Before she had a chance to reply, they were in front of the store and Josh was reaching for the door.

She reached out to stop him.

"I think it's closed. It looks like the lights are off and the blinds are down." She looked around them. Why would it be closed? It was still early.

He only shrugged and pulled the handle. The door opened, and he stepped to the side.

"After you," he said with a smile on his face.

Things were still dark inside, but Claire could hear whisperings.

"What's going on?" she said to Josh, but his smile only grew as he gently pushed her inside.

"SURPRISE!"

The lights flicked, revealing a room full of everyone she knew and loved. A banner strung from the ceiling had the word *Congratulations!* Helium balloons in all sorts of pastel colors added to the chaos.

"What . . ." She turned toward Josh for support.

"Smile," he whispered.

She forced a smile onto her face, while she gathered her hands together, clasped them hard, and struggled to remain calm.

One by one, people came up to her, giving her hugs, touching her belly, and telling her how much they missed her and were so happy for them both.

One by one, friends surrounded her letting her know she wasn't alone.

"People were missing you, love." Millie stood to one side and rested her head on Claire's shoulder for a moment.

"You look good." Liz kissed her cheek. "My Abby had better be taking good care of you."

Claire squeezed her hand tight in reply.

"We know you've been under some tight deadlines, but we figured it was time for you to come out and have a little fun." Gloria came over and handed her a cup of water. "But I'm not too happy you haven't been in for dinner in a while. I expect you at least three times a week until this baby is born, do you hear me? I'll make all your favorite things."

Claire's stomach grumbled at that exact moment. "Let me get you a plate of things to eat," Gloria said. "Your table is set up right in the corner."

The table Gloria mentioned was not only set up but was surrounded by mounds of gift bags and wrapped boxes.

That's when she got it.

"This is a baby shower?" She looked to Abby, who only laughed.

"What was your first clue, honey?" Abby rolled her eyes.

"But . . ." She was at a loss for words.

"But nothing. You are going to smile, give everyone hugs, and let them spoil you. There's more love in this room than you give these people credit for. Enjoy it." Abby wrapped her in a hug. "Please."

Claire nodded.

"Now, if you don't mind, there's a little too much estrogen in this room, so I'm just—" Josh began.

Claire reached out and grabbed hold of his sleeve. He was not going to leave her. She needed him.

"Claire, honey, it's going to be okay. I'm here," Abby said softly. "Besides, Derek has something planned for him over there, and it's quite hilarious. They'll pop back over in a little bit."

Josh frowned at Abby's words. "No one said anything about that."

"Surprise." Abby giggled and then hooking her arm through Claire's, dragged her across the room.

Claire knew what Abby was doing, focusing her attention on something other than herself.

"Can you give me a minute? Just a minute." she said. She headed to the bathroom at the back of the bakery without giving Abby a chance to respond. She ran in to Kat, who gathered her in for a hug before she had a chance to say hello.

"You're probably hugged out, aren't you?" Kat, wearing her Sweet Bites apron, grinned broadly. "Everyone is just so excited. Gloria provided all the finger food, Kim and I made the desserts, and your mother . . ." She stopped. "Hey, Millie."

"Everything okay? Abby said you needed a moment," her mother asked.

"I was . . . I just . . ." Claire stumbled over her words. She needed to get a grip. This was fine. This was doable.

This was on her checklist—being out in public.

"I know it's a lot to take in, especially . . . but we all love you here." Millie stroked Claire's arm in what she assumed was meant to be a comforting gesture.

"Is everything okay?" Kat asked, catching the undertone.

"It's fine. I'm fine. I just . . ." She shook her head. "Nothing. It's all good. Please tell me you made some vanilla bean cupcakes?" She linked arms with Millie and Kat and forced herself to be in the moment.

By the time things began to wind down, Claire had a massive headache and was being watched closely by both her husband and her doctor.

"Why don't I drive you home, and we can let the boys pack up all the gifts and follow us?" Abby suggested.

Nauseated, Claire could barely nod. Josh picked her up and carried her to Abby's vehicle.

"Did you have a good time tonight with the boys?" Claire whispered. Everything spun around her, so she closed her eyes and focused on her breathing.

"It was fun. Derek arranged an open mic and had all the men come and give me advice on raising kids. I'm not sure who was more entertained, the guys or Fran, who laughed so hard she cried."

"I'm glad," she said.

She couldn't believe how much her head hurt. Even the slight pressure from Josh's kiss hurt. All she wanted to do was cry, but she knew even that would be agony.

On the drive back to her house, Claire kept her eyes closed and listened to Abby make small talk.

"All those outfits were adorable. I can't wait till we can play dress up with your baby. Did you notice the size of some of those stuffed bears? I loved Julie's idea of taking photos of the baby and bear together, so you can see how fast he or she grows. Oh, and that book of advice? It's awesome. There are some great stories in there."

Abby tried to help her out of the car, but Claire just didn't want to move, so they agreed to wait for the boys, who were only a few minutes behind them. Abby made a dash into the house to grab her some pills for the pain.

"You're an angel," Claire whispered moments before her body seized up. Her arms went rigid, and she fell into Abby's arms before things went black.

By the time she came to, she was lying on the ground, her husband crying as he called her name over and over. He lifted her into his arms and carried her into the house and up the stairs to their bed. The cold compress laid over her forehead felt like heaven as she gave in to the sleep that called her.

But not before she heard Abby and Josh whispering in the room.

"That's the first time that's ever happened," Josh said. "I knew it was possible she'd have a seizure, but I was hoping we'd be lucky."

"It's not good, Josh."

"What do you mean?" Josh asked. Claire struggled to remain awake long enough to hear Abby's response.

"I think you know what I mean."

Claire let out a small groan, not liking what she heard.

THIRTY

MILLIE

Present day

The fireplace blazed in Claire's front room, and Millie was sweating like a pig. She fanned herself furiously and wondered how her daughter could be curled up on the couch with a blanket covering her legs with a hot mug of tea in her hands and not be melting.

Getting old sucked.

She gulped back her cold glass of water, but it did little to cool her down.

"Aren't you warm, honey?" she asked for the umpteenth time in the past hour.

She'd come over to help sort through all the gifts, and they'd spent over thirty minutes so far oohing and aahing over the little sleepers and onesies. Her favorites were the little black sheep gifts. From stuffed animals, to books and outfits with little lambs on them . . . The fact that people went to great lengths to find things with black lambs, something everyone knew Claire collected, was special in its own way.

"Go ahead and shut the fire off, Mom. I'm not frozen anymore." Claire gave her a smile as she rested her head against the top of the couch and turned the page of the memory book from the surprise baby shower.

"Who thought of this idea?" Claire asked as she giggled over something she'd read.

"I did. I figured it would be something you'd always cherish. I had a memory book given to me at my own shower. Did I ever tell you that? Your grandmother and aunts wrote the most practical advice I'd ever received. Some silly," she said with a shrug. "But practical nonetheless."

"Like what?" Claire's interest was piqued, Millie could tell.

"Well, your grandmother would dip a soother in honey for teething babies."

"That's a lot of sugar."

"That's a hyped up baby who wouldn't sleep." Millie laughed, but only because she had to learn the hard way.

"Thanks for organizing the baby shower, Mom. I know it was your idea, wasn't it?" Claire set the book down and looked at her with sleepy eyes.

"I wasn't the only one involved. Abigail helped a lot, and Liz rounded everyone up. It was a community effort of love." She'd been pleased with how well it had all come together. Claire hadn't suspected anything, which is what she'd wanted.

Otherwise . . .

"Yeah, yeah. But you instigated it and decided to keep it a surprise—admit it," Claire accused.

"Would you have come if you'd known about it?"

Claire shrugged.

"Didn't think so." Millie leaned over and patted Claire on the leg. "Which is why we kept it a surprise. You didn't mind, right?"

"No, it was fine."

Millie knew from the tone that it had been anything but fine, but she was so proud of her daughter for not freaking out last night and leaving.

"I don't think there's anything you guys need to buy for your little one for the next year, other than diapers." Millie glanced over at the piles of bags, and her heart swelled with the amount of love her daughter was shown. "Do you want help putting everything away?"

"Josh and I can tackle that, but thank you." Claire yawned, compelling Millie to yawn with her.

"You know a good way to find out if someone isn't a sociopath is to see if they yawn after you."

"What?" Claire gave her a weird look.

"No, I'm serious. Something about how our brains are wired and yawns being contagious." Millie tried to explain.

"Mom, you say the weirdest things sometimes, you know that?"

"I know." She really didn't know where that came from other than she knew she needed to give her gift to Claire and she was hesitating.

Millie stood and paced around the room, tidying things up here and there.

"Quit stalling," Claire said.

Millie turned. "What do you mean?" Had she been that obvious?

"I love you, Mom, but you're the worst at hiding things from me," Claire said.

"Other than the baby shower," Millie muttered.

"Which explains why you were avoiding my calls the past few days." Claire frowned at her. "Spill."

Millie bit her lip and plopped down on the couch again. She reached for the bag she'd set on the ground and held it in her lap.

She had no idea how to give this to Claire. No idea what to say or how to explain it.

"I wasn't sure when to give this to you, but . . ." She rubbed the back of her neck. "With your delivery being bumped up and all, I figured I should do it now rather than . . ."

"I'm not going to die," Claire said quietly.

"Of course you're not," Millie snapped. "You'll be fine. I know that," she said, softer this time. "I just . . . you'll be so busy and preoccupied and not feeling your best after the baby is here and with Abby forcing you to start the treatments right away, so . . ." She rambled as she held out the bag.

"What is this?" Claire reached for it and looked inside.

"Mom?" Claire pulled out a photo and choked up as she stared at it.

Millie leaned forward, crossing her legs as she stared down at the carpet.

"I don't know how else to say this other than to just say it." Millie said.

Claire put the photo down and nudged her with her leg. "Don't you dare do this to me. I've had enough of people giving me bad news."

Millie turned, facing her daughter and looked her straight in the eyes.

"But it's not. I promise. It's not." She took the photo and looked at it. She couldn't help but smile at the quirky smile and messy hair on the boy. Her grandson.

"I have a story to tell you, but I'd like you to promise that you'll listen to me before you say anything. Please?" Millie begged.

Claire slowly nodded, her hands gripped together on her lap.

"I know sometimes you think I'm cold or indifferent about your first child, but that's further from the truth than you could ever imagine. I can't live in regrets, honey, I just can't, but I can't forget either. I know you needed to learn to walk away, to find a way to keep going after you gave your son up for adoption, but I couldn't." Millie saw the shock on her daughter's face, mixed in with pain and remorse. And she knew she was to blame.

"I know you decided to have no contact with the family, but I wrote the adoptive mother a letter, from one mother to another and asked her to cherish my grandson and that if he ever asked, to tell him a little about his mother. Then I told her stories of how much you loved him and what kind of girl you were . . . you know, just in case he ever wondered." Millie had to look away, the pain in her daughter's gaze was too much for her.

"The mother, Marie, wrote back. She sent me photos of Jackson as he grew, ones taken on his birthdays and when he took his first steps . . . Those things that she thought maybe you wished you could have been there for.

"I wanted to share these with you," Millie continued. "But every time I asked if you wanted to keep in touch, you said no. I worried that I would be opening up a wound you couldn't handle if it were open."

"I said no," Claire cried, "because it would hurt too much, because I needed to move on, because I was worried I would lose myself in the pain of giving my child away to a complete stranger." She wiped the tears off her face. "I said no because I knew his life would be better without me in it."

She looked at the image of her son, and Millie's heart crumbled at the love and fear on her daughter's face.

"He's happy and loved, and Marie has written so many letters sharing his life with us."

"Does he know of me?" Claire clutched his image to her chest.

"No."

The questions regarding that one small word hung between them.

"So why . . ."

Millie scooted closer to her daughter on the couch and gathered her in her arms.

"Because he wants to know you, or of you. But not until he's eighteen."

Claire slowly nodded.

"Does he know about you?"

"No. I promise. I wouldn't do that to you, or him. All communication was between myself and Marie, and only for a few years. That's it, and as you'll see in the letters, it's only once or twice a year. Birthday and Christmas."

"Birthdays." Claire leaned her head back on the couch and closed her eyes. "Every year when I remembered his birthday, every card, every gift I donated in his name . . . you had a photo. Something to look at, to see the changes as he grew up, while I only had the memory of holding him in my arms." She pulled the blanket off and tossed it to the side. "Every birthday when I would try to talk to you about him, and you'd brush it aside, you read about his life while keeping me in the dark."

Claire stood and stared down at Millie.

"I need some time to process this," she said.

Millie stood. "Of course. Honey." She reached only to have Claire step back. Millie's hand dropped to her side. "I . . . I did what I thought was best, and while I know I haven't always been the best mother to you, all I've ever done is loved you the best I know how."

When Claire didn't respond, Millie gathered her purse, shrugged on her coat and scarf, and slowly opened the door.

"Why now?" Claire called out.

"Because I wanted you to have another reason to fight, to live."

"I have lots of reasons." Claire's hand caressed her swollen belly.

"I know, honey. One more doesn't hurt though, right?" It was so hard for her not to run to her daughter and hold her close, to tell her how much she was loved and how sorry she was for not telling her sooner.

"Thank you."

What?

"I'm angry and hurt and very, very confused," Claire said. "I'm also happy, though. To know he's with a good family, that he's okay and loved." She tilted her head up and groaned. "But my heart hurts, Mom. You kept something from me for sixteen years. That's no different than what dad did."

"Oh honey, no." Millie dropped her purse and rushed forward, taking Claire's hands within her own. "Please don't think that. It's not what I wanted. I just—"

"Just wanted to make sure the chance was there, of getting to know him, right?"

Millie nodded and breathed a sigh of relief. Claire understood. She understood.

"It still hurts."

"I know. And I'm so sorry." Millie brushed the tears from her daughter's cheek and placed a kiss on her forehead. "I'd hoped there would be a day when you were ready for him to be in your life, and I wanted to do what I could to make that happen. I only ever thought of you. Maybe I did it wrong . . . but I did it with love."

A smile played with Claire's lips, and she gasped. She took Millie's hand and placed it on her belly.

Millie marveled at the tiny movements she felt beneath her palm.

"I love you, Mom."

"Oh honey, I love you too. There isn't anything I won't do for you and this little one. I want you to know that. Anything."

"Good." Claire leaned into her for a hug. "I'm going to hold you to that," she whispered.

THIRTY-ONE

CLAIRE

Present day

> *Walk daily.*
> *Reduce sugar intake.*
> *Sing songs to the baby every day.*
> *Record bedtime stories for the baby and place headphones*
>   *on my belly every night before bed.*
> *Sort through all the baby clothing and place them in*
>   *containers according to size.*
> *Learn to drink decaf coffee.*
> *Finish my story.*

While she didn't get everything checked off the list she'd created, she was close. She would never learn to enjoy decaf and some days her headaches stopped her from going for that walk, but she was close to being finished with her story.

Claire was antsy. She pushed her notebook away and paced the upstairs floor, walking from her bedroom to the baby's room and back to the office. She needed to do something to keep herself busy.

Abby would be calling any time now to give them the results of the MRI she had this morning. If it was good news, then it meant the tumors hadn't grown, and she could have surgery after spending time with her baby.

If it was not-so-good news, then the tumors had grown, and there would be no surgery.

She once thought she would be okay with that. She'd made the decision to forgo any sort of treatment in order to give her child a chance to live, even knowing it could mean her death . . . , and she'd been okay with that.

She wasn't sure anymore.

"I want to get to know you, watch you grow, and listen to your laugh. I want to hear you read me stories and witness how easy it is to wrap your daddy around your little finger. I want to dress you up for your first day of school and cry as you climb onto the bus. I want to bake you cookies and play hopscotch and maybe one day introduce you to your big brother." She rubbed her belly as she talked to her baby.

Despite telling Abby at her first ultrasound that they didn't want to know the sex of the baby, Claire really did.

From the very beginning, she'd wished for a girl.

Josh hoped for a boy. One to play baseball with and roughhouse on the grass.

Abby let it slip one night when it was just the two of them—that she couldn't wait to see her goddaughter in the cute little dresses she'd bought. She hadn't realized what she'd said at first, and then apologized profusely for spilling the beans.

Now Claire just wanted to meet and know her daughter.

"I can hear you pacing up there. Come on, come join me downstairs." Josh called up to her from the living room.

She leaned over the railing, as much as she could, and smiled down. "Sorry. I have just a few things left to take care of, and then I'll be down."

"Can't they wait?"

"I'll be down soon, I promise. Besides, Abby won't be calling for a few more hours."

Josh shuffled his feet. "I might go for a run then, do you mind?"

"It's not too cold?"

"Nah. I'll warm up quick enough anyways."

"Go. Burn off that energy. I'll just work on some more drawings."

She was glad he was getting out of the house, even if it was to run in the cold. She could use the time alone.

Over the past couple of weeks, Claire had been working on some special projects. Along with letters and audio recordings of her reading her favorite stories, she'd also recorded several mom talks to her child, the things she might not get to say if things didn't go as well as she hoped. She gave her advice about puberty and how important it was to have a girlfriend you could count on, she told her stories about Josh, and she gave her advice on dealing with Dad as she got older. Then there was the boy talk. But the one that was hardest for her was for when she was getting married. Claire had done a few retakes for that one.

The idea of not being there for her daughter's wedding, or seeing her grandchild—that gutted her.

She had one last project to record, and today was the only day she could do it.

Over the past few months, she'd been working with her editor on a secret project, and she'd e-mailed the final draft this morning.

Josh thought she'd been working on a project for a client, but instead it was for herself. For them. For their child.

There wasn't a title yet for the story. She wanted to wait until after their baby was born, because their child's name would be on the book. *The adventures of xxx and her little black lamb.*

Claire looked at the little black porcelain lamb that sat on her desk and smiled.

Claire pulled up the document on her computer and then started the recording.

"All right, love. Are you ready for your bedtime story? This is a special book, created just for you, and it's extra special because . . . Well, because it's all about an adventure I hope one day you'll be able to take. There are special clues hidden not only in the story but in the pictures too. See if you can find them. Ask your daddy for help if you need to . . . but see if you can find them first, okay?

"Now remember . . . I love you. You are the child of my heart, the love of my life, and no matter how old you get or what roads you take, my love will always be there to help you if you need it.

"Ready now? Try to read along with me if you can."

By the time Josh returned, Claire had completed her recording and cleaned up her office.

"No word?" Josh wiped the sweat off his forehead as he stood in the hallway.

"Not yet. How was the run?"

"Exactly what I needed. Want a hug?" He opened his arms and stepped forward while she backed away.

"You smell." She wrinkled her nose. "Go have a shower and—"

"And you join me? Help me dry off? Get me all sweaty again?" His eyes twinkled with laughter as she swatted his arm playfully.

"What's that?" He pointed to a box she'd set on the middle of her desk.

"That's for later, you know . . . just in case."

"In case what?" The teasing glint in his eyes disappeared. "In case what, Claire?"

She winced. She should have thought this out better, been more prepared. "In case something happens."

"What's in the box?" The iciness in Josh's tone had Claire hugging herself. She hated this even though she knew it was necessary.

"Some letters, to you, my mom, Abby, Sami, and our baby. I also made some recordings and saved them on a thumb drive. It's all explained in a note, just in case."

Her husband stared at her. It wasn't difficult to read his thoughts.

He was angry. Angry at her for needing a "just in case" plan, and no doubt, angry at himself for not doing enough to avoid this situation.

"Just in case, Josh. You know me, always needing to be prepared. You can tell me *I told you so* after we come home from the hospital, and I'll eat crow with grace, okay?" She needed him to understand.

"Nothing is going to happen. You know that, right?" Josh gripped her arms. "I need you to know it, Claire, to believe it deep inside. Because if you give up on me and our baby, I'll never forgive you."

"I am so confident that Abby is going to call us with good news that I called the bakery and asked them to make us a special cake that was half chocolate and half coconut. My mom is going to pick it up and bring it to the hospital, so we can celebrate after our baby is here." She rose on her tiptoes and kissed him with all the love she had within her.

"You'd better get her to add the image of a crow on the top of it," Josh mumbled, and he pulled her tight against him.

She pushed away, not enjoying his *eau de sweat*. "Already taken care of."

When Claire had called the bakery earlier this morning to place the order, Kat had answered.

"Not again," Kat said with a giggle. "Doesn't Josh realize he's not to fight with his pregnant wife?"

"This time I'm the one at fault," she said. "Hopefully," she added under her breath.

The first time Claire had ordered a crow cake was a few years after they were married. They'd fought over who would win the Stanley Cup, and she'd lost that one. The next time, Josh lost a bet that he could win a pie-eating contest during a local fair. For that one, Kat had made an apple pie with the cutout of a crow on the top crust. It had become a running joke, and either Josh or Claire ordered one at least once a year.

Claire curled up on their bed and waited for Josh to finish up with his shower. The phone rang just as he was getting out. They both froze.

After the third ring, Claire picked it up.

"Please tell me it's good news," she said after checking that it was Abby's cell number. She put it on speaker.

"I hope your bags are packed, because I've got a delivery room scheduled this afternoon with your name on it."

"What does that mean?" Josh asked. He wrapped a towel around his waist and dripped water on the carpet as he stood by the bed.

"It means, things look good. The tumors haven't grown since the last MRI, and I've got a team on standby not only for helping deliver and take care of your baby but for your surgery as well." Abby said, her voice swelling with happiness.

"I'm going to be okay?" Claire checked, her hand covering her mouth as the news set in.

"I promised you I'd take care of you, and that's exactly what I'm doing, girl. You're not out of the woods yet. There's the surgery and then the radiation, but you're going to be okay. You'll see your little one grow up, I promise you."

She was going to be okay. She still had the tumors, but she wasn't going to die. Not today. Not tomorrow . . . not anytime soon, not with Abby by her side.

"I'm going to be okay," she whispered to Josh who leaned down and kissed her.

"Grab your bags and stop in at the Wandering Table. Gloria wants to feed you before you come in, because once you're here, all you're going to get is ice chips and Jell-O. But don't eat too much . . . I don't want you getting sick, so just eat the soup she made along with one of her biscuits. And bring me some too, okay? Delivering a baby is a lot of work, let me tell you."

Claire leaned back in the bed and laughed, really laughed, as the fear of not knowing, of facing death directly, melted away.

"I love you, Abby," Claire said before she hung up.

"I love you, Claire Turner." Josh leaned down and captured her in his arms. "Now, shall we get ready to welcome our little girl into the world?"

"You knew?"

He nodded. "Derek kind of let it slip."

"Go figure." Claire chuckled.

"Go figure, indeed. Come on, let's go have this baby." Josh pulled her up off the bed and grabbed her bag.

Claire waited until he was about to walk out of their room before she stopped him.

"Um, Josh?"

She held his towel up by her fingers, laughing as he looked down at himself and then back at her. "I think Abby would appreciate it if you were dressed."

Josh set her bag down and leaned against the door in a somewhat seductive pose. "I don't know," he said, "I've always kind of thought Abby had the hots for me, you know? After all, I am Mr. Perfect."

THIRTY-TWO

CLAIRE

Present day

The small hospital room was crowded with well-wishers, who had shown up to welcome baby Turner into the world.

Gerry Stam brought an assortment of ice creams as a gift, which Josh promptly confiscated. Fran came by with a menu plan for the next month and borrowed a house key so she could stock their freezer.

Abby had poked her head in for a few minutes, requesting a little one-on-one time with Claire. Till this point, she'd been entirely in doctor mode, but a hint of a smile on her face caught Claire's attention.

"You look happy," she said.

"Of course I am. You're having your baby."

Claire shook her head. "No, that's not it. There's something else. 'Fess up."

Abby sat down in the chair and propped her feet up on the bed frame. "Derek and I had a really good talk last night, and while not everything has been figured out between us, we're in a little bit of a better place. Plus"—she leaned forward and looped her hands around her knees—"he talked me into a beach vacation. Jamaica maybe." Her eyes twinkled. "We haven't really gone away, just the two of us, for a very long time."

"I love that idea," Claire said. She was glad her friends were figuring things out, the last thing she wanted was to see their marriage fall apart.

"Don't worry, though, we won't leave until after your treatments are done. I'll be right here, by your side, through it all."

"No way," Claire disagreed. "Josh will be there to hold my hand. Making sure you're happy and less stressed is more important to me. Honestly."

"Well, I'm not going anywhere any time soon. I've got a little girl to hold and cuddle. Which reminds me, it's time to get this show on the road." Abby stood. "I'm going to go check in with your surgical and delivery teams, and I'll send your nurse in. She's amazing—one of the best we've got."

As soon as she left, Liz came in with homemade pie, and then Julie brought thermoses of both coffee and tea, along with a platter of treats from the bakery, which she left in the cafeteria for everyone to enjoy. Her room bustled with people, and Claire loved it.

"You're all too much, you know that, right?" Claire couldn't keep the grin off her face. She loved how much their community acted like a family, and it meant so much that they were there to support her and Josh today.

"I agree. Time to empty this room." A nurse walked into the room and began to shoo people out of it. "Who here is not related to our soon-to-be mother?" With hands on her hips, she stared down Liz, Millie, Derek, and Josh and tapped her foot.

Liz and Derek tentatively raised their hands.

"Then I need you out. Claire and I have things to discuss, and I don't imagine she needs you to know all the intimate details of what's about to happen." She all but pushed Liz and Derek out of the room and closed the door after them.

"Now, Dr. Abigail asked me to look you over, and that's what I'm going to do. I'm your go-to girl, got it? Any questions you have, any concerns, anything you need, you come to me or ask for me." She pointed to her name tag, which read "Kathryn." "I've been briefed by both Dr. Abigail and Dr. Will as well as the surgical team waiting in the wings to deal with the tumors."

"Thanks, Kathryn. This is my husband, Josh, and Millie, my mother." Claire liked Kathryn's no-nonsense style.

"Anyone here get woozy when it comes to blood or other fluids?" Kathryn's brow rose as she stared specifically at Josh, who blanched.

"Thought so." She nodded. "You'll want to stay up by Claire's head then, hold her hand if you're not in the way. Normally we let the dads cut the umbilical cord, but since this little one is a bit early, we're going to have a team there to whisk baby Turner away for a little bit."

"Why?" Claire asked.

Kathryn helped Claire get comfortable in the bed and wrapped the blood pressure cuff around her arm. She held up her index finger in reply, and then she went about her work. Claire tried to be patient.

Looking around the room, she realized she hated hospitals. Whether it was the smell or the sounds or just wearing the ridiculously short hospital gown, it didn't really matter.

"Honey, you're twenty-eight weeks pregnant, which makes this baby a preemie. Little Turner will need oxygen to help him or her breathe and will need help with feeding. Do you know if you're having a girl or a boy?" Kathryn asked.

"A girl." Claire rubbed her stomach and loved the feel of her daughter's hand or foot pushing against her hand.

"Okay then. Once your little girl—"

"Will Claire go into labor at all?" Millie interrupted. She stood at the foot of the bed, her fingers clenching and unclenching as she tried to smile.

Her mother was probably more nervous than she was.

"Absolutely not." Kathryn patted Claire's shoulder. "We don't want any pressure affecting those tumors and that includes contractions where Claire will feel the need to clench, push, or anything else that might be instinctive. In about a half hour, the anesthesiologist will be here to give you that epidural you're going to love. You'll be fully awake, and only your pelvic area will be numb."

"I've done labor before. I'm more than happy to skip that part." Claire cleared her throat. "Will I feel anything?"

"Is it safe?" Josh asked.

Kathryn smiled. "Dad, you've got nothing to worry about. Mom, what you'll feel is the pull of your baby from your womb, it's a . . . funny . . . sensation, and one I can't quite describe. There will be a screen, so you won't see anything—neither you nor your squeamish hubby. We've got the pink team here for you, which is the NICU or neonatal team, which also means"—she turned to Millie—"Grandma, there's no room in there for you. It's a pretty tight squeeze as it is."

"Oh, I'd hoped . . ." Millie's shoulders dropped at the news. "Okay."

Claire, too, had hoped to have her mother there to help Josh with his queasiness and be one of the first ones to welcome their baby girl into the world.

"Sorry, guys. I hate to be the bearer of bad news, but . . . you'll see the baby girl soon enough, Grandma. Besides, we need someone to be the herald of the good news once she's born, so keep an eye out for me. I'll be the one who comes to the window and gives you the thumbs up. That'll be your clue to tell the rest of the crowd waiting in the cafeteria."

"So I can watch, but from the other side of the window? That's okay then."

"You got it." Kathryn refocused on Claire. "Now, the team will whisk your girl off, clean her, weigh her, do some testing, and make sure she's warm enough. If all is well, meaning she can breathe on her own and her scores are good, I'll bring her back in so you get some cuddle time. But it won't be for long, because she'll need to be placed in her warming unit. All in all, it should take about an hour."

Claire's stomach flopped as the understanding of what would happen sank in.

"You've got questions. I can see it in your eyes. Let me see." Kathryn smiled gently, as if this was the most natural thing, and she completely understood. "Your baby will be fine, I've got a feeling about it, and in all my twelve years of being in the neonatal ward, I've only been tricked twice by my gut. Generally, we like to keep the little ones with us until they are full term, but since you're going to be here awhile anyways, things will work out fine. You'll be able to bond with her, and I'll make sure Dad here gets lots of skin time with her."

"Skin time?" Josh frowned. "What is that?"

"Once your baby is stable, we'll have you sit and hold her close to your chest, skin to skin. Trust me, it's something you won't want to miss. It helps to create a bond, and the body heat helps your baby as well, calms them and such. We call it kangaroo care."

Claire felt a measure of relief having Kathryn there. She knew what she was doing. That much was obvious.

"Now, I hear there is coffee and treats in the cafeteria. I'd better go snag some before they're all gone." Kathryn made some notes in Claire's chart. "Anyone else want anything? I'm all yours for the day, Claire, and that goes for your support team as well."

"Want to bring me back a plate full?" Claire already knew the answer, but she thought she'd ask anyway.

Kathryn shot her a look that had Millie chuckling. "I heard you already had a bowl of Gloria's cream of broccoli soup and not just one but two of her fresh butter biscuits. You'd better hope you don't react to the anesthesia and get sick."

"I told you, you should have had the chicken soup she made," Millie teased.

"If you think I'm going to pass up Gloria's cream of broccoli soup when I know I'll be eating hospital food for the next week, you're all crazy."

"I'm sure Gloria will sneak some real food in for you. Don't you worry." Millie squeezed Claire's foot.

"I'll pretend I didn't hear that," Kathryn said as she left the room.

No one said anything for a little bit. Claire shifted in the bed, trying to find a more comfortable position.

"Well, kids. Are you ready?" Millie said. "Liz is going to pick up the cake you ordered for celebrating while you're in recovery. Do we know yet when you'll go into surgery? Will you have some time afterward to be with the baby?"

Claire shrugged. "I assumed the surgery would be shortly after, but I hope not." She really didn't get a clear answer from Abby.

Josh jammed his hands in his pant pockets, then rubbed the back of his neck before crossing his arms over his chest.

"Josh, why don't you go grab a coffee? You're making me antsy." Claire knew he didn't like being cooped up any more than she did, but at least he could leave.

"What if Kathryn or Abby comes back? I don't want to miss anything." Josh tapped his fingers against his leg until Claire put a hand out to stop him.

"Go," she said. "If they come back before you do, I'll make them wait. Okay?"

She breathed a sigh of relief as he left the room.

"I've never seen him this nervous before," Millie said as he bolted from the room.

"I know. It's almost kind of funny." God, she loved that man. "Listen, while we're alone, I wanted to talk to you about . . . Jackson." She sat up straighter in the bed and pulled the blankets up to cover her belly. "Thank you for . . . for not forgetting about him."

"Did you read the letters?" Millie asked.

Claire shook her head. "I wanted to wait until later. I . . . I knew I'd cry if I started, and crying means headaches. But, I have the photo of us all in Rome in my purse."

It was hard not to read the letters. She ached to know more about him, to see him—to let her feelings about him flourish without having to rein them in.

"I always thought you didn't care, that every time you told me not to live in the past that you meant to ignore it. But that's not what you meant, was it? I'm so sorry for—"

"Stop." Millie came over and gave her a long hug. "You don't apologize for anything, okay? I'm the one who should apologize. I should have stood up to that father of yours years ago. If I had, then maybe things would have been different. It was wrong of him to push you to give your baby up, and it was wrong of me to be a pushover and go along with it. I should have known better. No." She pulled back. "I did know better, but I thought I was wrong. I was too afraid to stand up to him, and it's something I will forever regret."

"Mom, it's okay."

"No honey, it's not. But thank you for saying that anyway. Now," she said as she hopped up from the bed. "This day isn't about me or about the past. It's about you and that beautiful little girl you're about to have. I'm so proud of you for doing everything you could to protect her, but I've got to say, you scared me. I'm so glad you're okay, that you'll be okay, and that I won't have to figure out how to live without you." Millie took a tissue and wiped the tears that ran down her face.

"No talk of death, okay? Not in here. I'm going to be okay. My baby is going to be okay, and we're going to spend years arguing over how much you spoil her." She couldn't wait.

"Have you picked out a name yet?" Millie asked.

Claire nodded.

"Will you tell me? I promise not to tell Josh."

She laughed. As if her mother could keep a secret like that.

"No way," she said. "Josh doesn't even know the name I picked."

"Oh . . . that's so not fair," Millie said. "Oh and I wanted to tell you, I told David about the cancer. I was so relieved when we heard the news that the tumors stopped growing, I had to tell someone. I hope you don't mind?" The words rushed out of Millie's mouth.

"You told David?" Claire was a little surprised about this but not upset. In fact, she liked the idea of her mother sharing something so private with David. He was a good man, someone Claire always looked up to and enjoyed talking with.

"You don't mind, do you?"

"It's about time!" Claire teased.

Millie's face was awash with relief, which made Claire laugh. Her mother, the strong, independent, and somewhat crazy woman was finally letting someone in past the wall around her heart.

"I've been waiting years for you to find someone, you know?"

The door swung open with a whoosh, and Millie shushed her.

"Who found someone?" Josh asked as he came in carrying a tray of drinks and plates of food.

"My mother." Claire grinned.

"Claire!" Millie's face reddened.

"Please tell me it's David. He's outside, by the way. He was afraid to come in with Kathryn standing guard out there. She says we have five minutes before Abby comes in and fifteen minutes before the anesthesiologist."

Millie perked up at that. "He's outside? He came? What a sweetie. I should tell him to go home. He's not needed." Millie bit her lip as she contemplated leaving the room versus staying.

"Go. But don't you dare tell him to leave. He came here for you, to keep you company." Claire pointed to the door.

"I love you, Claire." Millie put her hands on Claire's cheeks. "I'm so proud of you, of the woman you are and the mother you'll be. I'll see you soon, okay?"

Claire mouthed *I love you* back to her mom. Suddenly overcome by emotion, she felt the words stick in her throat as Josh squeezed her hand.

It was almost time.

THIRTY-THREE

JOSH

Present day

From the moment they walked into the hospital, Josh's stomach was doing its woozy dance, and he was afraid that at any moment he might upchuck in front of not just Claire and all those who came to support them, but in front of Nurse Kathryn too.

She scared the bejesus out of him.

"I need to know you can handle this." She had pulled him aside before he stepped back into the hospital room. She surveyed the tray he'd brought and sighed. "I've seen bigger men than you faint in the delivery room, but your wife is going to need you. If you can't do it, we'll have her mother come in."

The way she said it, it sounded like a threat—man up or else.

He manned up.

"We've got this," Josh whispered to Claire as Millie left the room. The moment Claire squeezed his hand, he knew she was just as scared as he was.

"I brought you something to eat, but from the look Nurse Kathryn gave me on the way in, I'm not sure you should eat it." He eyed the goodies on the tray before pushing it away with his foot.

"I'm not really hungry," Claire admitted.

"Neither am I. We should discuss names. I like Pepper or Piper. They're still my top picks." He placed his hand on her belly and leaned forward. "What do you think, baby girl, do you like my suggestions?" He waited for the usual kick or flutter he'd get when he spoke to the baby, but there was nothing.

"Guess that's a no then?" He looked up at Claire wondering if he should be worried at the lack of movement, but then he felt that kick.

Claire laughed. "I think that's a no. Besides, you've already got your name picked out, don't you, baby girl?" Claire rubbed her belly with a mischievous smile on her face. There was a flurry of movement beneath their hands.

"I can see where this is going," he muttered. "You're already ganging up on me. Two against one. That's not fair."

A whoosh of air hit them as the door opened, and they both looked up. When Abby walked in with the nurse behind her, Josh swallowed the lump that suddenly appeared in his throat.

"Breathe, Josh," Claire reminded him.

He nodded as he pulled his chair closer to the bed.

"Are you ready?" The grin that stretched across Abby's face helped put Josh at ease, but not enough to take away the fear that gnawed in his gut.

"Are you sure everything is okay?" he asked.

"Absolutely. I just finished speaking to the surgical team. They're confident they'll be able to get the tumors. But right now, we're just going to focus on one thing at a time."

"But I thought—"

Abby gave him a warning as she interrupted him. He groaned under his breath.

"We're going to focus on getting this baby delivered first, okay guys? One thing at a time. Josh, Derek is waiting for you out in the hallway if you want to join him? We need to go through some things with Claire before we roll her into the delivery room."

She was kicking him out? That wasn't right.

"Things like what?"

"I heard there was a party going on earlier, and I feel left out. You can come back in, I promise." Abby sat down on the edge of the bed and leaned on one arm.

Josh glanced at Claire, unsure whether he really should leave.

"Go," Claire said. "You don't need to know all the girly details about the delivery and my body." She rolled her eyes in jest, but Josh knew she was anything but relaxed by the way she refused to let go of his hand.

"Tell Derek to calm down, will you? I swear he's more nervous than Millie, and she's pacing a mile a minute out there."

"What is it with men," Nurse Kathryn mumbled as she literally pushed him out of the room. She closed the door and stood in the hallway with her arms crossed.

"She's going to be okay, right?" Josh bent over and gripped his knees as the weight of everything hit him.

He slowly looked up and found Kathryn, Derek, and Millie staring at him in exasperation.

"Your wife is the one giving birth, man. All you have to do is hold her freakin' hand." Derek slapped him on the shoulder.

He wouldn't be okay until their baby was born and the tumors were out of his wife's head.

"I don't know what I'm supposed to do," he admitted.

"Just hold her hand," Millie said. "Tell her how beautiful she is, keep her laughing, and don't let her see your fear. Not until later. She'll need you to be strong."

"What's with everyone asking or reminding me to be strong? Since when have I not been strong for her? Give me some credit." He ignored the way his hand shook as he struggled to get the cap off the water bottle.

After what seemed like forever, the door to Claire's room opened, and Abby poked her head out. "We're ready, Kathryn." She looked Josh in the eye, and then she propped the door open. A few minutes later, they walked Claire out of the room, Kathryn bringing along all the monitors and instruments she'd hooked his wife up to earlier.

"Let's do this," Claire said to him. She held out her hand for him to hold as they walked down the hallway and into the delivery ward.

After that, things were a blur. He stood off to the side while Claire had the epidural administered and then listened as she answered questions from the doctors. So many things were beeping and a general busyness took over the room as they waited for the numbing to occur.

"Okay, Dad. We need you to stand here." Nurse Kathryn led Josh to Claire's side, and he stood at her shoulders. There was a curtain over her belly, separating them from her lower half and the team that stood by.

"What do I do?" he dared to ask.

"I have a secret to tell you," Claire said to him.

He looked over at the doctors and caught one of them smiling. It was Dr. Will.

Abby stood next to him.

"Josh, just focus on Claire for now, if you can," she said. "Don't look over here. There's no one to catch you if you faint," she warned him.

Josh focused all of his attention on his wife's beautiful face.

"I thought we agreed not to keep secrets," he said to her.

"This was a *just in case* secret." Claire smiled up at him. There was a calmness on her face, a peacefulness that soothed the panic inside of him. She was going to be okay. If she believed it, it must be true.

"Does it have to do with that box on the desk?" He hated that box from the moment he saw it. He'd known exactly what it was for, and the fact that Claire had put it together, that she thought she would need to, seared him.

"I wrote a story," she said.

Josh leaned down and kissed her forehead. "Of course you did." With all the deadlines with her illustrations, not to mention their own books, she'd had no time to write a story.

It must be the drugs talking.

"I'm serious," she insisted, and he almost believed her.

"What kind of story?"

"One that we'll read to our daughter every night before bed. It's about our trip to Europe. One day, I want us to take her and go find all the postcards and little black sheep we left in the places we stayed."

"We didn't leave any little black sheep," he said. Postcards, yes. When Claire had told him what she'd been doing, he loved the idea.

"Yes we did. Or, I did. Remember how I found those little figurines at the market in Venice? I left a few here and there along the way." She giggled at the memory, and he knew for sure that the drugs had taken effect.

"So it's like an adventure with a scavenger hunt?" Josh asked. "Did Jack go along, or was this only the little girl, the one you wanted to write about?"

Claire giggled again.

"She meets Jack, but it's not our Jack. It's my Jack." She teased him with her wordplay. "Oh, that feels funny," she said louder.

"We're almost there, Claire," Abby said from behind the screen.

"Pink team, get ready," Kathryn called out.

Mere minutes later, though Josh would swear it took hours, the sound of a small cry could be heard. Josh tried to see their daughter, but the pink team was quick. They whisked her off to the side and swaddled her in a blanket. Josh couldn't see what was happening.

"Is she okay? Did we wait long enough? Should we have waited longer?" Claire's voice rose with each question.

"Your daughter is beautiful, Claire." Abby came over to Claire's other side and pulled her mask down. "She has all her fingers and toes. Everything is okay. Trust me. She's beautiful and alive and healthy."

"Can we see her?" Josh asked.

Abby looked over at the team. "Let me go see how she's doing while you get stitched up, okay? I'll be right back."

"She's okay." Claire smiled up at Josh, relief pouring out of her as she looked into his eyes.

"I love you," Josh whispered. He leaned down and kissed her. Her lips felt a little cold, and when he stood up again, he noticed her skin was very pale. He looked over at the doctor, but he was too focused on the monitors to catch Josh's eye.

"Abigail." Dr. Will called Abby over.

Josh wouldn't have paid any attention had he not been struck by the faint edge in Dr. Will's voice.

Abby must have caught it too, because she rushed over, and then Josh couldn't see anything because of that blasted curtain.

What was going on?

"Josh? Can we see her? Please? I need to see her," Claire urged.

He turned to Nurse Kathryn, but she was focused on Abby and Dr. Will.

"Abby? Can we see the baby?" He spoke up.

Within moments, Kathryn left his side and headed over to the pink team. She came back with their little girl in her arms.

"Here she is." Kathryn swallowed.

She held their daughter down close to Claire's chest so she could see her.

She was perfect. From her little button nose to the dainty bow-shaped lips, his beautiful little girl was perfect.

She was a miracle.

"Hello, peanut," Claire whispered. "I'm so glad to finally meet you. You're everything I ever wanted and dreamed of." Tears gathered in his wife's eyes as she looked from their baby to him.

"What did you decide to call her?" Abby was suddenly at their side, her words a jumble as she struggled to maintain her own composure.

Claire smiled. Her gaze never left their daughter's face.

"She's our beautiful miracle baby. It's because of you that we made it this far. I want to call her Abby." Claire's lashes fluttered for a moment.

Josh's throat tightened. Abby. It was perfect.

"Abigail . . ." Dr. Will called out.

Abby leaned down and kissed Claire on the forehead. "You be strong, honey," Josh heard her whisper.

What did she mean?

There were frantic murmurs on the other side of the curtain.

"Abby, what's going on?" Josh called out.

"I'm sorry," Kathryn said. "I need to get her back."

Before Josh knew what was happening, his daughter, Abby, was back over with the pink team.

He glanced down at his wife, stroking her hair.

"She's our angel, Claire . . ."

Something was wrong. Her skin was a pasty white and her eyes closed as if she'd fallen asleep.

"Claire?" he called out. "Claire, speak to me."

"Josh, come with me, we need to give them room." The nurse was back at his side, trying to pull him from his wife.

He wasn't leaving her.

"Claire? Claire!"

THIRTY-FOUR

JOSH

Eighteen months later

All right, peanut." Josh scooped his daughter up in his arms and spun her around. "Time to get ready for bed."

He could listen to Abby laugh all day. He was in love with the vitality behind the sound, how it resonated all through her body until, sometimes, she would vibrate from the energy. She was very much like her mother in that regard.

He could listen to Claire laugh all day as well. As funny as that sounded, there was peace for him in that laughter, as if he'd found his home within her heart.

Abby handed him the stuffed animal and blanket she'd been carrying around the house and slowly climbed the stairs, her hands holding on to the posts as she struggled to lift each leg one stair at a time. Josh held on to her other hand and tried his best to make it easy.

This was new. Before, she just liked to clamber up the steps on all fours and slide down.

Halfway up, Josh picked Abby up in his arms and carried her like a football the rest of the way. Abby just giggled.

They went through the whole bedtime routine—washing her hands, brushing her teeth, wrestling to get her pajamas on—with Abby insisting on putting her little black sheep to bed in his own little cot, which Josh had made out of a box.

The idea was that if Sheepie could sleep in a bed all by himself, so could Abby.

Abby didn't agree with him.

Abby was too big for her crib now, so Josh recently changed the crib into a single bed. And so far, Abby had resisted sleeping in it. Maybe it looked too much like the bed she'd had at the hospital. She had been born with a weak heart and lungs, and the Hospital for Sick Kids in Toronto had practically become their second home.

Except for tonight. Tonight was their first night back at their real home after two weeks fighting pneumonia.

"Come on, sweetie. You're getting to be such a big girl now, remember? And big girls sleep in big beds."

The way her lips quivered made his heart skip a beat until he saw the crocodile teardrops in her eyes.

If there was one thing his daughter knew how to do, it was cry.

"No story until you're tucked in to your big girl bed," Josh warned. He hated giving her ultimatums, but sometimes it was the only thing that worked.

Especially when it came to story time.

He sat down on the edge of the bed and waited for her to realize he was serious.

It took a few minutes, but eventually she began her nightly routine of saying good night to all her stuffed animals—the tigers and lions Robyn had sent over from New Zealand, along with some beautiful framed prints of baby cubs, which hung in the hallway outside Abby's room. Every few months a small box would arrive with a gift from Robyn, and whenever Josh sent her an e-mail thanking her for spoiling

Abby once again, the offer she originally made back on the cruise ship, to come and stay in her guesthouse, was repeated.

As soon as Abby was a little older, they'd be there with bells on, he told her.

"Night, tiger." Abby held the stuffed animal tight in her arms before giving it a big kiss and setting it back down. Then she climbed into bed of her own accord.

"That wasn't so bad, now was it?" He tickled her gently as he pulled the blankets up.

She only frowned at him. She got that stubborn streak from her mother.

"Are you wanting a story tonight?" he asked.

She nodded.

"Do you want Mommy or Daddy to read it to you?" He touched the tip of her nose with his finger, and that smile he'd been hoping for finally appeared.

"Mommy!" she called out.

Josh leaned forward and placed a kiss on her forehead.

"Mommy it is then."

He got up and turned on the lamp beside her bed, then crossed the room to turn off the ceiling light.

Abby had grabbed the storybook from her bedside table and held it in her lap.

The soft black lamb on the cover of the book always made him smile. His wife had not only written it but also drawn the illustrations. And it was perfect. He couldn't believe she'd done it without him knowing about it.

"Are you sure you want Mommy to read it? You're old dad isn't good enough, huh?" he teased her.

"Mommy!" His little girl called out again.

Josh picked up the tablet from the small bedside table and turned it on. He pulled up a video and sat back, drawing his daughter close into his side.

"Say hi to Mommy, peanut," he said.

"Hi Mommy. It's Abby."

"All right, love," his wife's image on the screen said. *"Are you ready for your bedtime story?"*

"Ready," Abby said. She snuggled closer to Josh, and he opened up the book to its first page.

Almost every night he played the video of Claire reading the story she wrote for Abby. It was one of the many videos Josh would play throughout the day.

For months, Josh had dreaded the idea of the tumors killing his wife before their baby could be safely born. Instead, Claire passed away on the delivery table due to a pulmonary embolism causing cardiac arrest.

She may have died on the day Abby was born, but he was determined to keep her alive for their daughter. Even if that meant watching videos of Claire as she read her stories and listening to the recordings she'd created.

As Abby grew older, he would read the letters to her. Eventually.

"Daddy." Abby poked at the book. Josh refocused and realized he needed to turn the page.

"This is a special book, created just for you, and it's extra special because . . ."

ACKNOWLEDGMENTS

No story is written by an author all on her own, and this is so true in regards to this story. I have a fabulous group of friends who helped me when I needed the encouragement. Dara, Elena, and Trish: you literally are "my girls."

A special thank you to Marlene Roberts Engel. Little Sami was created with your own Samantha, who passed away from cancer at age thirteen, in mind. Thank you for sharing her spirit with me. It has been an honor to include a little bit of who she was within the character I was able to create.

Dr. Jaime Blackwood, thank you for all your help with my pediatric questions. I have no doubt you are a blessing to your patients and their families. Who would have thought when we were in public school years ago that you'd be helping me with my story?

Garrity Beales, your strength amazes me. Thank you for your courage in sharing your story of losing your son and for walking me through various scenarios.

Angela Jack, thank you for answering all my last-minute emergency medical questions—you're a fabulous cousin for helping me!

To those in my Steena's Secret Society, thank you for all your help with names and suggestions and for your belief in my storytelling. I hope you catch all the little things that only you would notice about me in this story. Special shout-outs to Amy Coates and Patricia Viviano for helping me create characters—without you, Kathryn and the sisters at the Sweet Bites Bakery wouldn't be the same.

Lastly, to my family, both near and far, for your love, support, and encouragement as I wrote Claire and Josh's story. All your help has not been lost on me, trust me!

ABOUT THE AUTHOR

After writing her first novel while working as a receptionist, Steena Holmes made her dream of being a full-time writer a reality. She won the National Indie Excellence Book Award in 2012 for her bestselling novel *Finding Emma*. Now both a *New York Times* and *USA Today* bestselling author, Steena continues to write stories that touch every parent's heart in one way or another. To find out more about her books and her love for traveling, you can visit her website at www.steenaholmes.com or follow her journeys over on Instagram @steenaholmes.